Daughter
of the
Great River

Khalil Rahman Ali

HANSIB

HANSIB
Celebrating
50 years of
publishing
1970–2020

First published in Great Britain by Hansib Publications in 2020

Hansib Publications Limited
P.O. Box 226, Hertford, SG14 3WY

info@hansibpublications.com
www.hansibpublications.com

ISBN 978-1-912662-18-0
ISBN 978-1-912662-27-2 (Kindle)
ISBN 978-1-912662-28-9 (ePub)

A CIP catalogue record for this book
is available from the British Library

Design & Production by Hansib Publications Ltd

Printed in Great Britain

*To my wonderful wife Manjeet, and our
marvellous daughter Sonya, for their constant
and tremendous love and support.*

*To all Indigenous Peoples across the world, for
their preservation of what is left of our
rainforests and environment.*

*To everyone else, as well as organisations and
countries, dedicated to saving our planet.*

ABOUT THE AUTHOR

Khalil Rahman Ali is a successful author who was born in Guyana, South America, and has lived, studied and worked in London, England, since 1970.

His first three historical fiction novels titled, *Sugar's Sweet Allure* (2013), *The Domino Masters of Demerara* (2015) and, *In Pursuit of Betterment* (2017), are based on the experiences of the Indians who were indentured to work on sugar plantations between 1835 and 1920, in several countries around the world, including Guyana, Trinidad, Jamaica, Mauritius, Fiji, Reunion, Surinam, and South Africa, and, their descendants who are part of the Indian Diaspora.

Khalil has a keen interest in the environment, climate change and the sustainability of the planet. He believes that the Indigenous Peoples of the world are best suited to helping to sustain and save the planet. This latest novel offers an insight into the problems and threats facing Indigenous People living in the rainforests.

He is a keen traveller, loves sports and is an accomplished Indian singer and musician. Khalil hopes that *Daughter of the Great River* will help to inspire individuals, communities and governments around the world to work harder to save the planet.

PREFACE

Within the world's current population of 7.8 billion people, there are an estimated 370 to 500 million of Indigenous origin. They live in all the geographic regions of the world, and are of thousands of cultures. They are defined as, "having a historical continuity with pre-invasion and pre-colonial societies that developed on their territories, consider themselves as distinct from other sectors of the societies now prevailing in those territories, or parts of them. They form at present non-dominant sectors of society, and are determined to preserve, develop, and transmit to future generations their ancestral territories, and their ethnic identity, as the basis of their continued existence as peoples, in accordance with their own cultural patterns, social institutions, and legal systems." (United Nations (UN) Working Group on Indigenous Populations, 1982).

They continue to "suffer from disproportionately high rates of poverty, health problems, crime, and human rights abuses." (The UN).

Daughter of the Great River is a fictional story based on the struggles of Indigenous Peoples in a country called Kayana, "Land of Many Waters". She emerged from over five hundred years after her ancestors were brutally suppressed by invading Europeans, and were forced to flee from their territories, to the safety of the rainforests of Kayana.

Her tribe of Kayanese is one of several Indigenous Peoples preferring to live in the hinterland of Kayana's vast rainforests. She is identified as Onida, the chosen one to lead her peoples out of their challenging situations where the natural resources of gold and timber were being exploited by local and foreign miners and loggers.

Onida is taught and mentored about her history, customs, values, language, and the vision that she is entrusted to achieve for her people. The odds are heavily stacked against her, her people, and the other Kayanese making up the multi-racial, multi-cultural, and multi-religious country. Will she succeed?

CONTENTS

GLOSSARY

Annatto	(*Bixa Orellana*): Sometimes called *roucou* or *achiote*. A red colouring used by Indigenous people as a body paint.
Benab	Indigenous language for the "meeting place of the people". It is normally a round shaped structure, constructed with local timber, and the branches and leaves of the ite palm. It is essentially built around a central pole made of the resilient purple heart timber.
Buck	*(or Buck Man, or Buck People)*: Term used to describe the Indigenous People. It is believed that the Dutch colonists who settled in the then Guianas in the 17th Century, likened the agility of the Indigenous people, who were extremely swift whilst running in the forests, to springboks. They leapt like the springboks of South Africa, and hence the term "bok" or "buck". The term is deemed to be derogatory and is outlawed as racist.
Cacique	A term for Chief or Leader of a tribe.
Calabash	The name given to a bowl made from the dried and hardened fruit of the Calabash tree (*Crescentia cujete*).
Cassava	(*Manihot Esculenta*): Also known as *manioc, yucca,* and *mandioca.* It is an edible starchy tuberous root. *Cassava* is a major staple food of the Indigenous People. The white flesh is used to make a flat bread, the *kasiri* alcoholic drink, and the *cassareep* sauce.
Cassareep	A brown cooking sauce made from continuously boiling the juice of the *cassava.* It is also used as a preservative.
Cree	One of the largest groups of Indigenous or First Nations people in North America, primarily in Canada.
Harpy Eagle	(*Harpia Harpyja*): One of the largest eagles in the world. It inhabits the vast area of rainforests from

Mexico to Brazil, including the Guyanas. It has been known to prey on sloths and monkeys.

Howler Monkey (*Alonatta Macconnelli*): One of the largest monkeys in the world. It inhabits the vast area of Central and northern South America.

Imaam A Muslim priest.

Inuit A distinctive group of Aboriginal or Indigenous Canadians. They also inhabit parts of Alaska, Greenland, and Denmark.

Janaaza A Muslim funeral.

Kassequa Chief or Chieftain.

Korinaka Macaw.

Macaw (*Psittacidae*): *Macaws* are long-tailed, and very colourful parrots normally found in the rainforests of Central and South America. There are a number of varieties including the blue and yellow, Hyacinth or dark blue, the scarlet, and the red and green *macaws*.

Moccasin A casual shoe made of soft leather, usually deerskin, and stitched together with sinew. Some designs include colourful beads.

Ourali (*Strychnos Toxifera*): Also called *curare*. A plant used to produce a paralytic poison, and applied to darts and arrows. Indigenous People use this to stun fish, and other game such as small monkeys.

Piwari A mildly alcoholic drink made by fermenting burnt *cassava* with grated sweet potatoes.

Piaiman Or *Semechi*, or *Shaman*: A knowledgeable Indigenous person reputed to have power over evil spirits, and also knows the cures for sickness and diseases.

Porknocker A small time miner who digs for gold or diamonds in the rainforests, rivers, and streams. "Knocking Pork" is the term used by the miners to refer to pork meals in the mining towns.

Toucan (*Ramaphastos Toco*): The *toucan* is a short bird with an extremely large and colourful beak. It normally inhabits the rainforests of Southern Mexico, Central America, and South America.

ONE

CHILD OF THE MILLENNIUM

The world stood still as the midnight hour of a new millennium approached. Preparations had been completed by billions of people in every corner of the planet as the first second of the new year of 2000 was awaited with bated breath. Elaborate and costly plans were in place to manage the uncertainty of computer and other systems moving from the end of the year 1999, to the beginning of 2000.

Deep in the rainforest that made up of most of the land of Kayana, in the North of South America, all the members of a small settlement of the *Kayanese* tribe of Indigenous Peoples also sat silently and patiently around the outside of the *benab*, or big house. They were awaiting the arrival of a special baby whom they believed to be the chosen one to save them, the rainforest, Kayana, and the world. This was far more important to the residents than the anxieties of a changeover of computer systems from 1999 to 2000.

The settlement, situated deep into the lush green rainforest of Kayana, known as "The Land of Many Waters", was not easily accessible to others, except for the members of the two hundred strong resilient, and resourceful tribe. The site was carefully chosen by their Chief or *Cacique* over five hundred years prior, just off the tributary of the longest river, known as the Great River of Kayana. He, along with a handful of men, women, and children, had escaped from further northwards of the country, due to brutal persecution by invading Europeans.

The life-giving tributary was about two hundred yards wide at its mouth, and cut through the vegetation on both banks, narrowing to only a few yards wide further and higher into the rainforest. This allowed ideal protection for the settlement. It also offered a variety of fish, shrimps, and crabs which had always been a main source of food for the families.

The dark brown water flowed steadily through with small ripples lapping against the grey muddied banks. The first inhabitants who found and set up the settlement, had cut a narrow path through the vegetation, into the large opening where their huts were built in a great circle around one central structure called the *benab*.

The benab was circular in design, and built upon strong timber legs which supported the roof made of leaves and vines. It served as a communal resting, and meeting place. A carefully cleared and maintained bare earth area in front of the benab, was specially set out for celebratory dances, games, and day to day gatherings.

The population of the settlement had managed to grow and survive over the centuries through the successive Chiefs' astute guidance, and avoidance of contact with strangers, including members of other Indigenous tribes. Skills for hunting and physical self-defence were taught, and handed down to the young over time. The older women taught young girls essential weaving skills, cooking, and general housekeeping, as well as strenuous lifting and carrying of baskets of the main ground provision called *cassava*.

The peoples' watchful and protective approach had provided them with security over the centuries, until a more recent contact with strangers caused the outbreak of a severe incidence of pneumonia which almost decimated the entire population. However, over the last thirty years, the community had managed to rebuild itself, and had tried to adapt to their new situation.

The entire community initially sat quietly on their haunches outside the benab, as the oldest female member who would become the baby's great grandmother, offered traditional prayers throughout the labour. No men were allowed in, or near the birthplace, and they joined the gathering outside in a separate group.

The expectant mother was only eighteen years old, and had endured a very difficult first pregnancy. However, upon advice from her grandmother, she was not taken from the settlement to receive more modern maternity care and support from the midwives and doctors stationed at the community hospital in a small town about thirty miles up the Great River. The old lady was particularly keen for the special baby to be born within the benab, in the presence of the tribe.

The sombre chanting continued in a mesmeric rhythm for several hours into the night, only pausing at the sound of agonising cries caused by the acute pain of the labour. A local band of *Howler* monkeys responded noisily upon hearing the cries of the mother-to-be, as if in empathy with her. Their calls took their messages higher up, and deeper into the surrounding forest. Their black coat of hair made them more difficult to spot high into the trees, until they leapt into action from branch to branch, with the aid of their strong arms, legs, and long tails.

Finally, at midnight, the young mother-to-be gave a sustained cry as the baby was born. A few moments of utter silence were then broken by the faint wail of the newborn. Then, as the weary onlookers began to stir, they were alarmed to hear the screams of the women attending the birth.

The great grandmother, who was just less than five feet tall, slowly stood up, and cradled the baby which was wrapped in a white cotton towel. The tears from her tired and reddened eyes trickled down her wrinkled cheeks as she tried to forge a smile. She stepped forward to the open entrance of the benab, and stood at the top of the short stairway. The entire audience looked up with great joy at the new child of the millennium. They spontaneously raised their arms as if in prayers, to welcome the promised chosen one, and new Chief.

The old lady raised the bundle above her head as the baby began to cry.

She said, "Hail to our future Chief! Rise up to welcome our Onida, the Daughter of the Great River! Long live our chosen one!"

Everyone shouted, "Long live our Onida! Long live our Chief Koko!"

The Howler monkeys screamed excitedly as their message rang out through the forest.

TWO

JOY AND SORROW

The proud Chief Koko, the new great grandmother, carefully stepped back into the benab, and placed Onida into the specially made hammock, beside her mother. The other women sat around the lifeless body of the new mother, and were cautioned by Chief Koko to keep their weeping as silent as possible.

The members of the settlement waited for a few minutes, speaking amongst themselves until Chief Koko reappeared at the top of the stairway.

She said solemnly, "Today, we welcome the start of a new millennium as we are told by the President of Kayana. We do not agree that this is the year 2000 as we know that our world is much older than this. But, we follow the laws of this country which was stolen from our peoples by others who have forced their ways upon us."

An elderly man, proudly wearing the tribe's red markings on his forehead and cheeks, along with a single feather of the magnificent *Harpy* eagle neatly placed and tied at the back of his head of straight, grey hair, slowly stood up.

He said, "You are right O Noble Chief Koko. Let us rejoice at the coming of our future Chief, the beautiful Onida of Kayana."

Chief Koko said, "This is the moment that our ancestors had told us about. Our Onida is the one who will save us from our present troubles. She must be looked after with care by all of us. She must be fed to grow stronger than our strongest warrior. She must be taught our ways, about our peoples from all over this, our land. She must also be taught the language and ways of our invaders, and she must be listened to, and obeyed."

The entire gathering raised their arms aloft in unison, and in full agreement.

14

She continued, "But today is also a very sad one for us all. Before we celebrate our Onida, we must now prepare to bury her young mother who gave all of her strength to her baby, and lost her own life. Our Onida does not have a father nor a mother, or grandparents, but I shall be her guardian with your support. Now, please go and rest until the early morning, and we will prepare to bless and honour the Great Spirit who has brought us our Onida of Kayana."

The members of the settlement looked at each other in silence, and quietly turned away towards their houses. Each of the oldest dwellings was made of neatly cut timber frames set out in a circular shape with a floor space enough to accommodate a sleeping area for a family of up to six. The roofs were made of thatch, and were shaped in a conical fashion, tightly secured to a central main post, at its apex. The timber rafters were also held tightly across from the middle of the cone, and were strong enough to support the hammocks used for resting and sleeping. All the newer houses were built with boarded walls, and in a square shape, on stilts, as the community made efforts to improve the structures over the last twenty years.

The next morning was lit up by the bright rays of a golden sun, piercing through gaps in the canopy of tall greenheart, purpleheart, and other trees, onto the site of the settlement. Cockerels announced the arrival of the new dawn, and the pet dogs barked their approval. The group of Howler monkeys gathered restlessly amongst the trees, grunting and calling as if in animated conversations. The red and blue *macaws* which were tamed by the young boys and girls of the tribe, and looked after as pets, stood on their perches near to each house occasionally squawking in anticipation of their early treats of cut fruits including bananas and oranges. Pigs and piglets kept by the residents mainly for trading and food when necessary, grunted as they entered the shallow, and muddied feeding place set away from the central square.

All members of the tribe decorated their faces and bodies with the red dye or *arnotto* in preparation for the day long ceremony of special prayers, chants, and dances. Although most of the residents had been converted to Christianity, and bore such names as Peter, John, and Mary, they insisted on practising their traditional customs and rituals especially at events such as births, marriages, and deaths.

A small group of men, accompanied by the settlement's Christian priest and the Indigenous *Semechi* or *Piaiman*, solemnly walked in a single file to a selected spot in the cemetery, preserved for members of Chief Koko's family of leaders. The area of the cemetery was marked out, and bordered by tall bamboo trees which swayed gently in the soft wind. Deeper into the cemetery was a high grassy mound where multiple burials had taken place for the victims of outbreaks such as smallpox. Normally, if and when such mass deaths occurred, an Indigenous tribe would quickly bury their dead, and move away to another site. But this settlement was of far more significance for the people who had promised their Chiefs to stay until their sacred Kayana was freed of all invaders.

The ritual of chanting and dancing continued as the body of Onida's mother was placed in a simple woven open coffin, and gently lowered into the grave. Final prayers by both priests signalled the end of the ceremony, and after the burial, some bamboo leaves and flowers were placed upon the grave.

The burial party returned to the square in front of the benab, and sat down in a circle to participate in a grand feast of roast pork, cassava bread, boiled carrots, potatoes, and ample quantities of the *piwari* drink used to soothe their grief, and to rejoice at the coming of Onida.

The people had been hardened by numerous incidents of great loss, and suffering in the past. But now, they had every reason to accept the passing of the young mother, and to celebrate the happiness brought by the birth of Onida.

Within only two hours of such great joy, their peace was shattered by the unmistakeable crackle of rapid gunfire.

THREE

GOLD

P andemonium broke out as the men ran for cover into the forest. The women grabbed their babies and younger children, and also briskly walked further into the bush away from the direction of the ambush. Chief Koko picked up Onida, held her tightly to her chest, and moved as quickly as she could, until she tripped and fell.

A young man saw Chief Koko's fall, and turned back to help. He stooped down, looked anxiously around towards the direction of the ongoing gunfire, and took the baby with one arm. He then grabbed Chief Koko's left arm, and eased her up on her feet. She had badly injured her left ankle, and was in great discomfort and pain.

She gasped, "Please take Onida away. Run as far as possible. I will wait here."

The young man said, "No Chief Koko. I cannot leave you here. You will be killed. Please come with me."

Chief Koko held her swollen ankle, and said, "No my son. You must go now. You and Onida are the most precious ones we now have here. Please go."

The young man took Chief Koko's advice, and darted off into the thickest bushes of the undergrowth. Chief Koko slowly dragged herself away from the pathway, and hid amongst the bushes.

She was still within hearing distance as more gunfire rang out at the settlement. She heard the screams of her people who had not managed to escape the attack in time. She sobbed as she was helpless to even try to protect them.

When the shouting and pleas for help stopped, Chief Koko could see the rising black smoke and deep red flames from some of the abandoned houses, and heard the sickening crackle of the raging fires on the dried thatches, and timber.

All the animals and birds at, and in close proximity of the settlement, cried out in sheer fear. The monkeys who were safest high into the surrounding trees, sprang from branch to branch, howling their disapproval. The pigs and piglets squealed as they scampered into the bushes. The dogs appeared to stand their ground barking menacingly at the intruders who began to shoot at them.

Chief Koko was still peering through the undergrowth to see what was happening, when suddenly, one of the gunmen crept up behind her, and shouted at her. She was startled by the stranger, and looked up wearily. The gunman wore a handkerchief to cover his nose and mouth, and his dark eyes shone with a reflection of the fires from the settlement.

He realised that Chief Koko could not get up, and then held her arms tightly. He pulled her up, allowing her to reach around his waist as she tried to walk forward with him.

When they reached the centre of the square in front of the benab, Chief Koko was made to sit down on a wooden bench.

The six invaders gathered around her, and whilst four of them faced the houses, the leader of the gang stepped forward to confront her with his automatic rifle pointing at her chest.

He asked, "Are you the Chief here?"

Chief Koko looked at the eyes of the leader, and did not respond.

He asked again, "Are you the Chief here?"

Chief Koko looked around at all of the gang members, and then fixed an angry gaze at the leader.

She said, "Yes I am. What do you want from us?"

The leader said, "Gold. Give us all of your gold."

Chief Koko asked, "If all you want is gold, why are you burning down our houses? Why are you killing our people?"

The leader said, "We looked into your stinking houses, and could not find gold. We know that you must have gold here. Give it to us now or else...."

Chief Koko looked up at the leader with contempt, and said, "Or else what? Or else you will kill me? You are nothing more than a dirty scum. Go ahead and shoot me you coward."

The gunman was taken aback by the bold stance of Chief Koko. He looked around at his companions, and then at one of the houses which was still on fire.

He stared at Chief Koko with greater intensity in his eyes, and raised the rifle, pointing it to her head. She fixed her angry gaze at the rifle.

She said, "If this is the way I must die for my people, and all our peoples of this land, then do what you have to do."

The gunman said more firmly, "Show me your gold, and we will leave you now!"

Chief Koko said, "We have no gold here. We do not keep gold. You can have our money."

He grabbed her right hand, and tugged at a bracelet she wore. Chief Koko winced as the jewellery was forcibly pulled from her wrist.

He looked at the bracelet, and said, "Now old woman, tell me where you have hidden your jewellery."

Chief Koko's eyes momentarily glanced at the benab as she nursed the bruise on her wrist.

The leader signalled his men to search the benab. After a short while, the five men returned to their boss clutching a variety of gold and silver chains, and other pieces of jewellery.

He looked at Chief Koko with menace, and said, "Old lady, I will spare your life this time. Make sure you tell your people to get more gold for us when we come back. If you refuse, we will kill all of you."

The gunmen turned, and headed back in the direction from which they had come. Chief Koko, deeply saddened and hurt by the encounter, looked wearily around at the destruction wrought by the invaders. Within minutes of the departure of the robbers, the tribe's men, women, and children slowly returned, and stood in shock around Chief Koko. The houses that were set ablaze during the attack quickly became burnt out shells with black smoke rising high into, and beyond the surrounding trees.

The once bright, and promising sun which had lit up the day that began with the sadness of the burial, and the joy of the feast for the arrival of Onida, cast a weary shadow upon the scene of despair.

Chief Koko asked all the survivors of the attack to stay for the night in the large space within the benab where they would feel safe.

She said, "Tomorrow, a new sun will rise up, and show us the way to a brighter future."

FOUR

THE GREAT SPIRIT

F ive men and two boys were killed in the attack on the settlement. The surprise of the rapid gunfire was too great for them to grab any weapon such as knives, axes, bows and arrows, and blowpipes, to use in self-defence.

The bodies of the victims were laid out on simple stretchers hurriedly made of two eight feet long bamboo stalks with about three feet wide straps tied firmly across them. Each of the men who were only about five and a half feet tall, was placed on his own separate stretcher, and the two boys were laid together side by side.

Chief Koko was lifted up, carried by two young men, and was gently seated on the bench in the middle of the square in front of the benab. The survivors gathered around, and formed a large circle facing Chief Koko and the deceased. The women who lost their loved ones wept silently as all the others began to chant in honour of the fallen spirits.

There was a strange and unusual silence amongst the animals and birds as the chanting continued. Chief Koko raised her arms aloft to signal the end of the prayers. She asked the young man who had rescued Onida, to step forward.

She said, "We thank our Great Spirit for saving the chosen one. Her birth is blessed with the sacrifice of her own mother, and our fallen brothers and sons. This must be the wish of our Great Spirit. Let us now rebuild our homes, and open our hearts to a new start. We must never leave this place, and we must stand with Onida who will guide us. Let us pray for the spirits of our lost ones as they will also stand by us along with all of our ancestors."

The Piaiman stepped forward to stand next to Chief Koko. He waited solemnly until she signalled for him to speak.

He raised his arms aloft, and looking up into the tall trees, said, "Oh Great Spirit, give us the strength to rebuild our homes and lives.

Give us the patience to await for Onida to lead us forwards, and upwards. Let our eyes stay open to see our enemies before they see us. Let our hearts be filled with love to heal our hurt. Let our limbs grow stronger to fight for ourselves, and our tribe."

The Christian priest from the community offered the Lord's Prayer for the departed, and then led the gathering into a final hymn, before fronting an orderly procession to the cemetery. A mass grave had been dug to accommodate all the victims who were gently laid to rest, side by side.

When the funeral was over, the people refrained from any further feasting or singing. They spent the remainder of the day quietly clearing up the mess made by the fires, and the disruption caused by the attackers. Those residents, whose homes were unaffected by the incident, helped to start the rebuilding and repairs of the badly damaged houses.

Two weeks later, three members of the Kayana army arrived at the settlement, and asked to meet with the Chief. They were escorted to the benab, and Chief Koko stood up to welcome them.

The leader of the soldiers, a sergeant, held his right hand out, and shook Chief Koko's right hand.

He said, "Chief Koko, I'm Sergeant John Brown of the Kayana army stationed about thirty miles up the Great River. We heard that this settlement was attacked by a gang of armed robbers. Is that true?"

Chief Koko gestured for the three soldiers to sit on a bench in front of hers.

She said, "Yes. Six men with big rifles attacked us. They killed five of our best warriors, and two boys. They also burnt down some of our houses, and stole most of our jewellery. They said that they will come back for more."

Sergeant Brown, a tall and dark African Kayanese, leaned forward, still clutching his rifle across his knees, and said, "Chief, those bandits will not be coming back here."

Chief Koko frowned, and asked, "How do you know this? Do you know those criminals?"

Sergeant Brown glanced at his two colleagues sitting on either side of him, and said, "Chief, these two brave men, Private Abdul Rasheed and Private Suresh Nanan, had accidentally met up with the men who were boasting about their raid on your settlement at a bar in the mining town up river. They were miners who were also dangerous criminals. My soldiers challenged them, and although the miners ran away, they were caught up, and cornered. After a brief shootout, the gangsters were all killed."

Chief Koko was delighted, and relieved to hear about the demise of the gang. Other members of the settlement had gathered around in front of the benab, and she stood up with much more vigour than usual.

She said, "My people, these men from the Kayana army have brought great news for us. They have caught and killed all the men who had attacked us. Please bring some food and drink for our three brothers, and let us celebrate this victory, and our Great Spirit."

Sergeant Brown and his two brave soldiers ate some food, but refrained from drinking the piwari on offer. They spoke to many of the members of the settlement, and took notes of the accounts of the attack by the gang. Sergeant Brown, with Chief Koko's permission, took some pictures of the settlement, and the burial site.

At the end of the celebration, Chief Koko asked for Onida to be brought to her. She cradled the baby in her arms, and asked Sergeant Brown and the other two soldiers to step forward, and to touch the baby's forehead.

Chief Koko said, "This is our new baby Onida. We all wish to thank you for protecting our people here. We will tell Onida about you, and what you have done for us, and for her as well. We are afraid of these attacks by the gangs. We know that you and the army cannot be here all the time. But please try to come here more often, and in this way, criminals will keep away. We just want to remain a peace-loving people."

Sergeant Brown reached forward, and embraced Chief Koko. Private Abdul Rasheed and Private Suresh Nanan took turns to do the same. The younger boys and girls ran forward to touch the soldiers with great pride as a gesture of heartfelt gratitude, and admiration.

Shortly afterwards, the soldiers left the settlement, and headed for their canoe which was moored at the edge of the tributary. Their Kayanese guide steadied the canoe as the men carefully boarded. The children then thronged the edge of the water, and waved their goodbyes excitedly.

FIVE

ONCA

The people of the settlement enjoyed the next ten years of peaceful coexistence with all around them. The Kayana army lived up to Sergeant Brown's promise of regular visits which did help to keep attackers at bay. The community slowly rebuilt all the damaged and burnt out houses into more robust wooden structures on four feet high timber stilts made of the strong greenheart tree. The thatched roofs were replaced by corrugated zinc sheets. Over the years, the population gradually increased to about two hundred and fifty people.

Chief Koko was delighted to see Onida grow into an impish, and pretty ten years old girl. She seemed to be blessed with an independent and brave spirit. She learned to paddle her own canoe, and would slip away to explore the river both upstream and downstream. Her ability to swim faster than her friends, was also remarkable.

Initially, Chief Koko was very worried about Onida setting off on her adventures, and she asked others to follow her to see what she was up to. Onida, who was also very cunning, bribed the watchers to stop them from following her. They were made to wait for a while, and then follow her only upon her return to the settlement. Chief Koko was pleased to see that her instructions were being followed.

Whilst out on one of her investigative missions, Onida saw a baby otter struggling for survival near the water's edge. The young animal was clearly orphaned, and abandoned by poachers who had killed, and taken away the adults from their den. Onida pulled her canoe up the muddy bank, and carefully approached the otter. She knelt down beside it, and realised that she must save it. She then carefully lifted it, and gently placed it within the canoe. The otter continued to call out for its mother all the way back to the settlement.

The adult giant otter was under threat of extinction in Kayana. It grew to as much as six feet long, and weighed about seventy-five pounds. It lived in dens made by burrowing into the river banks, or under fallen logs. The babies normally stayed in the dens for about one month from birth, and grew quickly to the size of adults in about nine months. In an attempt to save the species, the killing of adults for their pelts, was prohibited. However, they continued to face demise through loss of their natural habitat, and increasingly, through pollution caused mainly by gold mining activity. Their most important sources of food were freshwater fish and crabs.

Onida fearlessly lifted the baby otter, and as she took it to the benab, a crowd of curious children followed her.

Chief Koko asked, "Where did you find this baby?"

Onida, still cradling the docile animal like a human baby, said, "I found him crying out for his parents who were killed by poachers."

Chief Koko said, "Well, you do know that we cannot keep him here in the open. He needs his own home near the water. How are you going to feed him?"

Onida gently kissed the nose of the otter, and said, "I am going to build him a den near to our waterway, and feed him with fish every day."

She then strode to the water's edge, and chose a safe spot up the muddy bank, and along with a group of children, they dug out a neat den. The young men of the tribe built a wooden fence along both sides of the path from the den, to the shallows of the tributary. This was intended to help keep predators away from the otter.

True to her promise, Onida woke up at about the same time at dawn every day, and with a few of her friends, she walked down to the river bank to catch small fish for the baby otter. The animal began to look forward to the meal time visits, and looked out at the front of the den with great excitement.

One morning, Chief Koko decided to join Onida and her party to observe what they were up to.

She said, "I can see how your young otter is growing so well. But you have to stop feeding him like this, and must allow him to fend for himself. Otherwise he will become too tame, and dependent upon you too much."

Onida and her friends listened to Chief Koko's advice, and they led the otter to the water's edge. They were delighted to see him take naturally to the water, and instinctively diving under an area of overhanging mangrove. He emerged within one minute, and had caught a small fish. The onlookers cheered the otter, and shouted encouragement for him to hunt for more fish.

Chief Koko smiled, and said, "You see, this is the best way for the noble otter to learn how to survive. You have given him a new home with new companions, and he knows what to do. This is how we as humans learnt to survive."

Onida hugged Chief Koko, and said, "Thank you Chief Koko. I know that I saved his life. But he also needs to look after himself, and learn the ways of his otter tribe."

Chief Koko said, "That is true. We humans have also learnt to survive here by listening to our elders, and practising what we learn. When we all do this we become stronger just like the otter. Soon, when he is more confident, you will have to let him go off with the others."

Onida frowned, and said, "Oh no. I love him so much. I do not want to see him go away. Can we keep him here?"

Chief Koko saw the disappointment in the children's faces, and said, "OK. You can keep him here until he has grown into an adult, and then we will decide what to do with him."

Onida and her friends shouted, "Hooray!" and the otter looked up as if it understood the joy of his friends. He squeaked with great pleasure.

Onida imitated the squeak, and said, "I will call you Onca."

Chief Koko looked on approvingly, and said, "Yes, he is like a jaguar of the water."

Onida's natural love for the animals and birds in and around the settlement became more obvious as she and her friends continued to show greater interest in them. Each household kept one or more pet dogs, at least one macaw whose wings were clipped to stop them from flying away, and, a tame monkey which was orphaned.

The settlement had not obtained its own primary school, and Onida and her friends shared canoes to travel up to about two miles to the nearest one. The school was staffed by Kayanese teachers, and the curriculum followed the national requirements of english and mathematics alongside other subjects. The languages of the Indigenous Peoples were not spoken or taught even as second languages. Chief Koko and the elders tried to encourage the young people to speak their traditional Kayana language, and she continued to campaign for this to be formally used in the schools throughout the Kayana hinterland.

As Onca grew over the ensuing months of special care, he was given more exercise by Onida who encouraged him to swim beside her canoe during her exploration trips. Sometimes, when Onca felt the need, he would clamber into the canoe, and lie next to Onida. She spoke in her Kayana dialect, and he seemed to respond to her. When she spotted a small cluster of fish, she asked Onca to go into the water and catch some, not only for himself, but also for the settlement.

Everyone in the settlement was fascinated by the new approach to fishing that was introduced by Onida and Onca. It even saved some of the young men the trouble of having to use their bows and arrows on their fishing trips. However, Chief Koko realised that the new habit could result in the loss of yet another tradition and skill, and advised Onida to use Onca only sparingly to fish.

SIX

POISONS TO FISH

O nida decided to join a few young men on one of their regular fishing trips further up the tributary, upon Chief Koko's advice. The Chief knew that learning the tribe's customs and skills were as important to Onida as the formal Kayana state education. The day began with a practical demonstration by the twenty-eight years old young man who had helped to rescue the baby Onida when the settlement was attacked.

He was Peter Thomas, the most experienced and accomplished hunter of the tribe. He had already shown Onida how a canoe was built using the purpleheart wood. This was followed by demonstrating the art of paddling with the most economical, and efficient ease. Although the making of arrows, bows, and blowpipes were exclusive to young men and boys, Onida was given special lessons as a future leader who needed to know everything about her people.

Peter chose the straightest piece of wood of about six feet long, and showed Onida how to drill a hole through to create a consistent hollow of the blowpipe. The poison called *ourali* was boiled into a sticky paste, and carefully painted onto the tips of darts carved to fit, and to be blown through the hollow of the blowpipe. The poison was so deadly, that even if it scratched the surface of the skin, it caused paralysis. Peter chose a much smaller piece of wood for the blowpipe to be used by Onida to practise with. She quickly learnt the art of breathing in sufficiently to power the dart through the mouthpiece of her blowpipe. Then, she trained long and hard to acquire the right power of blowing the fine arrow at targets higher up into the trees.

Peter also taught Onida how to make a strong bow, and several arrows which were intended to be used for hunting fish. She soon became very proficient at using her bow and arrows, along with her blowpipe and poison darts.

The tribe also relied on the use of daggers which they acquired through trading with Kayanese retailers who ventured up and down the Great River. Peter had made a special leather strap for an eight inches long steel knife, and Onida proudly wore this on her right hip, with a leather strap across her waist, as part of her normal costume.

One morning, after attending to Onca, Onida, Peter, and a group of young men went up the tributary on a fishing trip, armed with their collection of daggers, bows, arrows, and blowpipes. They soon encountered a shoal of fish jumping around in some foamy water ahead. As the three canoes drew closer, many of the fish were floating belly up as others around them struggled to survive. Peter quickly realised that the water was poisoned, and warned the fishing party not to touch it or the floating fish. He had experienced a similar event of much greater magnitude several years prior, and he turned around to face the others.

He said, "Do not touch the water. This looks like cyanide poison from the big gold mine ahead. Do not touch the fish. Let us turn around, and tell Chief Koko and the others."

Onida, although disappointed about the lack of a good fishing adventure, calmly turned her canoe around, and led the others back to the settlement.

She asked Peter, who was sitting behind her, "Why are those people still poisoning our waters and fish with their greedy search for our gold?"

Peter said, "The big company that caused a major disaster when cyanide escaped into the river, was warned by the Kayana government. Many of our people up and down the Great River and the tributaries became very ill from using the water. It killed thousands of fish and animals which were in contact with the deadly pollution."

Onida asked, "Did any of our people die from this?"

Peter nodded, and said, "Yes, we lost a few children who were swimming and playing in the water. They must have swallowed the poison."

Onida frowned, and asked, "Did anyone get punished for this?"

Peter said, "No, our lives do not matter to the people who own, and run the mining company. Not even our government could take action against such rich, and powerful foreign companies. Our politicians say that Kayana needs the money for the people."

Onida said, "But our own peoples do not seem to get much of that money from our gold. This cannot be right. We must tell the government. We must fight for what is ours."

Peter smiled, and said, "Yes Onida, you are right. The time is coming for one such as you to stand up and fight for what we already have. Let us speak with Chief Koko."

Chief Koko became visibly angry when she heard about the poison in the tributary. She summoned everyone to assemble in front of the benab. Onida stood beside her at the top of the steps.

One of the elders asked, "Chief Koko, what is the matter?"

Chief Koko scanned around the gathering, and said, "Yet again, and despite warnings by our Kayana government, the large mining company has let poison flow into our waters. Please do not use this water for the next few days. Also, do not use any fish or crab or anything else from the river water."

The old man looked at Chief Koko and Onida, and asked, "So what are we going to do about the poisoning this time? I am ready to fight anyone who is responsible for this."

Most of the men raised their clenched right fists in the air in anger, and defiance.

Chief Koko said, "Firstly, we must stay calm, and find out what has happened. Peter, Onida, and I will go up to the gold mine, and talk to the people there. Everyone else must stay here, and keep watch. Try to keep Onca and all the animals away from the water."

The old man asked, "What are we going to do about our food for today, and the next few days? We like to use only fresh fish."

Chief Koko said, "Do as we have done in the past. Let us share what we have, and if we need more we can use our pigs and chickens. We also have a lot of cassava bread. Use only the fresh water from the creek, but do check to make sure that it is clean."

The old man turned around to face everyone, and said, "We the people of this land of Kayana know how to care for it. We worship this land, the trees, the birds, the animals, and everything in our waters. Let us pray to our ancestors to guide us through this problem. But let us also be ready to fight for all of this around us. This land belongs to our children, and all those to come in the future. They have only lent all of this to us."

Chief Koko smiled at the wisdom of the elder, and said, "Yes, we must stay here, and not leave this sacred place where our ancestors have chosen to be. So, listen to our elders, and do as they say until we return."

It was early in the afternoon, and the sun was blistering hot as it cast its rays through the trees and shrubs near the water's edge. Chief Koko sat at the back of Peter's canoe, and Onida proudly took her place ahead of them. The foamy water had not yet reached their mooring, but they soon rowed into it further up towards the mining area. Peter and Onida carefully steered the canoe through the brownish red foam, and the hundreds of dead fish.

Officials from the mining company were inspecting the source of the breach through which the poisoned liquid entered the tributary. They signalled to Onida and Peter where they could moor the canoe, and walked over to speak with them.

A six feet tall white man stooped down to help Chief Koko to climb out of the canoe, and onto the wooden mooring. Peter helped Onida onto the walkway.

The host said, "Hello, I am John Jennings from the Canadian Mining Company. I am the Chief Engineer and Manager here. Please come with me to my office."

Chief Koko took her seat in front of John Jennings's desk, over which a large ceiling fan whirred.

She asked, "Mr Jennings, why has this poison been let into the tributary? When is it going to stop?"

John Jennings still presented an imposing figure as he sat behind his desk which was handmade from the local purpleheart tree.

He leaned forward, and looked at Onida and Peter who preferred to stand beside Chief Koko. Onida rested her left hand on Chief Koko's right shoulder.

John Jennings said, "Please drink some water. It is clean, and comes from the water container."

Chief Koko declined the offer, and repeated her questions.

John Jennings said, "I do apologise for this accident. The leak has stopped, and no more damage will occur. The water will go away in about a day or so, into the Great River, and then into the sea. I can assure you that we have taken greater care to avoid anything like this from ever happening again."

Chief Koko, although relieved to hear this, asked, "And why did you and your people not come to our settlement to warn us about this spill? Do we not matter to you? Can you not see why we think that you just want to drive us away from our land?"

John Jennings took a sip from his glass of water, and said, "Once again, I am very sorry. I can tell you that as a company that has been in this country for the last twenty years, we do care about you, and the environment. Is there anything I can do to help you and your people?"

Onida looked straight into John Jennings's eyes, and said, "Our people do not want your money. We have all that we need to live our lives here. Just clean up our waters, and tell us when you have done so."

Peter said, "Also, stop telling us lies. If you do not want us here, we will resist you until we all die. You will never understand us, and our ways. We do not need to learn anything from you, and your people. We just want to see you go away from our land. Just stop killing our rivers, our trees, our animals, and our peoples."

Chief Koko sensed Peter's growing outrage, and said, "Mr Jennings, please tell your masters what you have heard from us today, and promise that you will treat us with more respect for as long as you are here in our Kayana. You cannot pretend to protect these forests by the things you promise."

John Jennings sighed, and said, "I fully understand how you feel. I am here to do a job, and I do promise to do everything that is necessary to protect you and this environment. Once again, I am truly sorry for this accident."

SEVEN

PEACE

S everal days later, after Chief Koko received the news that the contamination of the tributary and the Great River was cleared, and that it was safe to use the water, John Jennings, along with three of his workers, arrived at the settlement.

Everyone was very surprised at the visit, and they gathered around him and his party in front of the benab. Chief Koko, Onida, and Peter Thomas stood together to greet the visitors.

Chief Koko said, "Mr Jennings, I never thought that someone as big and important as you will take the time to come here. If I knew that you would do this, I would have invited you."

John Jennings stepped forward, and shook hands with the Chief, Onida, and Peter.

He said, "I decided to come here personally to tell you that we have made the mine much safer, and that the tributary and the Great River are clear of the spillage. I also want you to see for yourself that I do care for you, the people here, and the environment."

Chief Koko said, "This is the first time that anyone senior from your mine has come here to show us that you care. Please come into our benab, and let us talk. I hope that you and your men will stay for a meal with us."

John Jennings and his three workers then followed Chief Koko, Onida, and Peter, and were shown four small wooden benches to sit on. An elder from the settlement, the Christian Priest, and the Piaiman, also joined the meeting. Some piwari was served in small *calabash* bowls to the visitors, and then to the hosts, except Onida. John Jennings looked at his drink with some curiosity, and smiled nervously.

The Piaiman held his bowl in both hands, raised it above his head, and pronounced, "Oh Great Spirit, bless us all with the wisdom to make this meeting good for everyone."

The Priest said, "Amen. Let us drink to that."

John Jennings took a sip from his bowl, and although clearly disliking the taste, said, "Yes. I hope that we can become friends, and live together in peace."

The elder said, "We respect you Mr Jennings, for coming to see us. Ten years ago, some men came from your mine, and attacked us with their guns, and set fire to many of our houses. They also stole all of our jewels. But, they were caught boasting about their terrible crimes at a bar in the mining town. The Kayana army chased them, and killed them. Your people from the company never came to see what was done to us."

John Jennings said, "Again, I am very sorry about what happened in the past. I was not here at the time, but I heard about the incident. In fact, I have warned all of our miners not to interfere with your peoples up and down the rivers."

Peter said, "Mr Jennings, I have seen miners in the forest, but they run away when they see me and our warriors."

John Jennings said, "I shall warn all of our workers to stop hunting in your areas, and to stay away from the settlement and villages. They should not be leaving the mine and the town as long as they work for us. Maybe those you saw are illegal miners who wander about looking for gold."

Chief Koko said, "I think that they are *porknockers* of Kayana, and they do not interfere with us."

John Jennings said, "One of the reasons for coming here is to offer you some help. What do you need most of all to make your lives better here?"

Chief Koko said, "We do not need your money. All we ask for is to be left in peace to get on with our lives. In fact, I really want to see your company leave this area, but you will not be able to promise this."

John Jennings said, "Well, if I could make that decision, I would do so. I see that many of the houses need better roofing. Will you allow me to get some people to repair or replace them? You can also save some of the rain water in special tanks. Will you accept my offer?"

Chief Koko was taken aback, and after noticing nods of approval around her, she said, "This is the best thing I have heard from a miner all my life. When can you start the work? Our men and boys will help your men, and at the same time learn how to build better roofs."

John Jennings and his men stood up, and he said, "I will get some more men here first thing tomorrow morning."

Chief Koko, Onida, Peter, and the others who had overheard the promise, smiled, and applauded the visitors as they walked towards their motorised canoe.

John Jennings suddenly stopped, and turned around to face Chief Koko and the other residents who also paused at the top of the river bank.

He said, "Chief Koko, I hope that you do not refuse this offer. I would also like to offer for my company to pay for all of Onida's education needs through secondary school, and to higher studies if she wishes to go on to the University of Kayana, or even at a College in Canada. I know that this will come as a great surprise to you. If you wish to think about it, please do so, and let me know when you are ready."

Chief Koko looked at Onida, and when she saw that there was no response, she said, "Mr Jennings, let us think about your offer, and we will tell you our decision."

Chief Koko and the people waved goodbye to John Jennings and his men, and stared at the motorised canoe as it sped off into the distance creating a wake which soon spanned the width of the tributary.

She asked Onida, Peter, and the elder, to follow her back to the benab. Over a meal of roasted pork, boiled potatoes, cassava bread, and some fruits, the group discussed John Jennings' offer.

Chief Koko asked, "Why do you think that Mr Jennings has made such kind offers to us for the new roofs, and to pay for Onida's education?"

The elder, a slim man of over sixty years, and with frail limbs, leaned forward to face the Chief and Onida.

He said, "I do not trust Mr Jennings and his people. I know that we have accepted his new roofs. But, to pay for Onida's education is not something I can accept. Onida must continue to learn about our ways, and not to be fooled by the white man's."

Peter said, "I agree. Our Onida must not leave this settlement without a good reason. All those who have gone away to higher schools have either not returned, or have come back here to do nothing."

Chief Koko said, "But how else will Onida learn of the ways of the foreigners who have come, and taken away our lands and our gold? She knows that her future is to lead us, and to preserve our customs. She will not need to go off and find a job in the city. Her job and future life are here."

Peter said, "Yes Chief Koko. I have taught Onida most of the things that I know, and I think that she is ready to take on the outside world. It will be good for her to take on higher education. She needs to know more about the whole of Kayana, the other peoples who run this country, and Mr Jennings' people from abroad."

Chief Koko said, "I think that you are right Peter. If Onida does not like being away from us, she can always stop attending the higher school, and return here. How do you feel about this dear Onida?"

Onida nodded, and said, "I do not wish to leave you Chief Koko. But, if you all think that I should accept Mr Jennings' offer, then I will do so. This may also help to bring us more peace and happiness here."

EIGHT

ONE OF US

True to his word, on the very next morning, John Jennings sent two motorised boats with workers of African and East Indian Kayanese descent. They contained many corrugated zinc sheets for the roofs, plastic guttering, metal downpipes, and steel barrels. In tow, was another boat laden with wooden planks for the rafters.

The workers appeared nervous as they walked up from the mooring to the front of the benab to meet Chief Koko. The children of the settlement who were always curious about visitors, gathered around the workers, and observed them in silence.

Peter, who was often one of the first to get up in the mornings, walked from his house whilst still pulling on a bright yellow cotton tee shirt over his head, and onto his bare bronzed chest. He hastily tugged the end of the tee shirt over his khaki shorts. He never liked to wear shoes or boots.

The leader of the visiting workers, a young African Kayanese, introduced himself and his colleagues to Chief Koko and Peter.

He and the others were wearing similar khaki overalls, and tough working boots.

He greeted Chief Koko, and said, "Madam Chief, I am James, and these four men are Joseph, Alfred, Inshan, and Kumar. We are all Kayanese people who work for Mr Jennings at the mine. He sent us to repair some roofs. Can you tell us which one to do first? We were told to show one of your men how to do this kind of work, and then he can teach the others."

Peter enthusiastically raised his right hand, and stepped forward.

Chief Koko said, "Please ask Mr Jennings to come back when you have finished Peter's roof. We would like to thank him face to face. You and your men must eat some lunch with us."

James said, "Thank you Madam Chief. I will ask Mr Jennings. But, we cannot have lunch with you as we brought our own food. Thank you for being so kind. Peter, let us go and make a start. It is a lot of hard work, and you need to wear some shoes. Or boots. We brought a spare pair of boots, and hope they fit you."

Peter followed the men down to the mooring, and tried to put on his new pair of boots. He managed to slide each foot into the correct boot, but struggled to tie up the laces. James stooped down to show him how it was done.

Peter eased himself upright, and began to take cautious steps with his new footwear. They were slightly too tight for him, and as he planted one foot down, he winced in pain. The children, who had followed the men, began laughing at Peter as he gingerly took each uncomfortable step forward. James stopped him, and loosened the laces to allow him some more comfort.

This worked very well, and Peter began to walk around more confidently, arching his back and chest straighter, and taking bigger strides. The children followed him, and applauded him as he continued to pace up and down by the water's edge. They began to copy his style of walking as they giggled amongst themselves. Peter stopped, and ordered them away.

The work to remove the dried thatch from Peter's roof took much longer than James and his team had anticipated. He then recruited a few of the more able-bodied young men of the settlement to help speed up the operation. The large bundles of the thatch were then placed in a huge pile in the centre of the wide open meeting place, and set alight.

Peter put a few of the young men in charge of the fire, and with clear instructions to prevent it from getting out of control. The young men lined up several buckets of water from the tributary, and used this to dowse any of the thatch which moved away from the main bonfire.

James then showed Peter and the other helpers, a plan for the construction of the new roof. It was based on a system of strong rafters made out of the tough greenheart wood which was well weathered for such use. Both teams of workers finally managed to assemble the rafters, and retired for the day at about four o'clock. James and his men headed for their boats, and instructed Peter and the young men to be ready for the next day's work at dawn.

Peter was very concerned about his open and unfinished roof, and Chief Koko advised him to sleep in the benab that evening. He said a prayer for no rain to fall, and after having a hearty meal with the young helpers, he slumped into a hammock, and fell asleep like a log.

He was awakened by the usual dawn chorus of squawking macaws, clucking chickens, howling monkeys, and barking dogs. He tried to stretch his arms, and felt great muscular pain through his entire body, and his feet throbbed from the effects of the discomfort of his new boots. He would have loved to lie in his hammock for much longer, but Chief Koko, Onida, and the arrival of James and his men hastened his getting up.

James and both teams of workers launched themselves into the task of nailing the new corrugated zinc sheets onto the rafters, fix the guttering, and a downpipe into a large water tank placed securely onto a timber based platform to allow water to be stored, and drained through a small tap. Peter soon forgot his muscular pains, and when the project was completed, he stood back to admire his house with its new roof. He smiled with great pleasure, and hugged James as teardrops fell from his tired eyes.

Chief Koko, Onida, and all the workers then sat down on stools in the open square to enjoy a celebratory meal of roast pork, boiled cassava and potatoes, roasted corn, and cassava bread. They shared the bottled water brought by James and his men.

Peter wearily stood up, and said, "Thank you James and your friends. Thank you all who helped us to do such a great job. My house looks more beautiful now, and I look forward to working on all the others that need to be repaired or replaced."

Everyone, including the children, applauded, and then turned towards the lone figure approaching on the path from the mooring. It was John Jennings. He looked up at the new roof, and smiled.

Chief Koko stood up, and asked him to join the gathering.

She said, "Mr Jennings, James, and everyone who helped to build Peter's roof, I wish to thank you all for such good work. I know that Peter and the young helpers have learnt how to do this work, and we look forward to more help to do the other houses."

John Jennings sat on his low stool, and said, "I am very happy that you like the new roof. I promise to supply you with whatever you need to make sure that you are all better protected, and more comfortable here."

Onida stepped forward, and said, "Sir, I love people who keep their word. Our people also love the truth. You and your men have done so, and I can trust you."

Chief Koko asked, "Mr Jennings, why have you done all of this for us? We have never had such kindness from any other white foreigner. You are so different. You behave just like one of us."

The entire gathering cheered as John Jennings stood up to accept Chief Koko's gesture.

He said, "Well, as I said, I come from Canada. I may look like a white man. But I am very different. I have Canadian Indian blood in me. I am half white and half *Inuit* Indian. I am your brother. I am one of you."

The Piaiman said, "All praise to the Great Spirit."

John Jennings said, "Yes, may the Great Spirit bless us all."

NINE

CONNECTING WITH THE OUTSIDE WORLD

O ver the next few weeks, Peter, along with James' guidance, led the work to repair and rebuild all the roofs in the settlement except for that of the benab. He and the other young warriors made sure that they learnt all the skills required to plan, and build the structures.

The unusually long dry spell meant that the new roofs were not fully tested as to whether or not they could withstand heavy rainfall and high winds. The water tanks fitted to the downpipes were virtually empty, but everyone was pleased with their repaired, and fortified houses.

John Jennings and James returned from time to time to check on progress, and to ensure that the quality of the work done was of a high standard. They were very impressed with Peter's management and guidance for each of the tasks, and how he was able to pass on his knowledge to others, especially the young warriors of the settlement. The elders looked on with great pride.

During one of the visits, Chief Koko, who was keen to learn more about John Jennings' ancestry, invited him to share a meal with her in the benab.

She asked, as John Jennings eased his six feet frame onto his low level bench, "Mr Jennings, have you got a family of your own?"

John Jennings stretched out his long legs, and said, "Yes Chief. I have a wife and three children. My wife is a full Inuit Indian."

Chief Koko smiled, and asked, "Are they here in Kayana with you?"

John Jennings said, "No Chief. The children are in school, and my wife has stayed back in Canada to look after them."

Chief Koko asked, "How do you cope with being so far away from them? You must miss each other greatly."

John Jennings took a sip of bottled water, and said, "Yes Chief. At times I do miss them quite a lot. But I get to speak with them through the phone or through the computer."

Chief Koko said, "That is very nice. Well, you can tell them that you are our friend, and you are most welcome here. I understand why you want to know about our people. Is this also why you have helped us?"

John Jennings said, "Yes Chief. When I got the job to come to Kayana, I was not told about your peoples. Only when I arrived here I realised that so many Indigenous tribes still exist, and your settlement is so close to the gold mine. I therefore wanted to find out more about you and your peoples. In fact, some of my Indigenous Kayanese miners told me about this place, and how you are all so peaceful."

Chief Koko leaned forward, and said, "Yes, we are peaceful people. All we want to do is to live a good life here. We do not like your gold mining, and we would like to see you all leave this place. But, we cannot force you out."

John Jennings nodded, and said, "Chief, I fully understand this. As I said before, it is not up to me to decide upon closing down this mine. But, as long as I am here, you and your community will be respected, and helped. Anytime you want for anything, please let me know. I am still awaiting your decision as to whether or not you will accept my offer to fund the schooling of Onida."

Onida joined Chief Koko and John Jennings, and took a seat beside the Chief.

She said, "Good afternoon Mr Jennings. Thank you for all the help you have given to us. I feel that we can all trust you and your workers. I have come to say that if Chief Koko and Peter agree, I am happy to go to the High School up the Great River. But I have never lived away from here, and I am very worried about that."

Peter arrived, and sat down on a stool next to John Jennings.

John Jennings smiled, and said, "I am also away from my family and my Inuit tribe in Canada. But I have learnt how to cope, and you and your people have also helped me to do this."

Chief Koko nodded, and said, "I think that the time is right for Onida to go to the High School, and she can stay with others who will look after her. Peter, what do you say?"

Peter stood up, and held Onida's hands. He said, "My Onida, I have taught you most of the things that I know. I cannot teach you

41

about the bigger things outside of our world. But, you must now go away to learn those things, and you can always come back to visit us. Also, if you do not wish to continue to stay there, we will always be here for you."

Onida, with tears welling up in her beautiful almond eyes, stood up and grabbed Peter's waist to hug him tightly. Chief Koko wiped away some teardrops running down her wrinkled cheeks.

She looked at John Jennings, and said, "Mr Jennings, I think that Onida has agreed to take up your offer to pay for her schooling, and her expenses at the boarding house there."

John Jennings stood up, and bent down slightly as he towered over everyone else. He said, "Well Chief, I am very happy to hear your decision. I shall ensure that Onida is very well looked after, and that she gets the time to return for visits here. I can also help you and Peter to speak to, and see her through a computer screen. This will not cost you anything."

Chief Koko asked, "Mr Jennings, how can we see Onida on your computer screen? This is like magic. We are not ready for such things."

John Jennings said, "Chief, I shall not force you to accept anything that you and your people do not want to have. But please come over to my office, and you can see how I am able to see, and speak with my family all the way from Canada."

Peter said, "I have heard about all these computer things. Our government even wants us to have solar panels on our roofs to give us electricity. We live well enough here, and can do without electric power. Nature gives us all that we need. We do not wish to hurt nature anymore than we are already doing. You people have taken away too much too quickly. You do not turn back to see the damage you have done. You may be helping your people now, but you may not have anything left for your grandchildren and their children."

John Jennings was quite taken aback by Peter's honest remarks, and said, "Peter, Chief, and Onida, you are all right. No one should try to tell you how to live here when you and your ancestors have survived here for hundreds of years in this very environment. You have also managed to preserve most of this natural resource, and its beauty. As soon as you are ready, I shall send over a boatman to take Onida to her new school. Here is a list of the things she will need."

Chief Koko took the slip of paper from John Jennings, looked at it briefly, and then handed it to Onida.

Onida hugged Chief Koko, and said, "I promise to study hard, and make you and our peoples very proud. Thank you Mr Jennings, for all that you and your company have done for us. This is a very important day for us all."

Chief Koko said, "I ask our Great Spirit to continue to guide Onida to success. Let her learn well, and bring light to our communities here and all over Kayana. Let the darkness of our peoples' past be washed away with the light of new knowledge."

Suddenly, dark clouds swept across the blue sky, and after flashes of bright lightening, followed by booming thunder, a massive downpour of heavy rain swept over the settlement. Everyone ran to the safety of their homes, and after about fifteen minutes, the storm subsided, and calm was restored.

TEN

LEAVING FRIENDS BEHIND

The Indigenous Peoples of the rainforests of Kayana had always lived in close harmony with everything within their environment. Every plant or tree, insect, bird, animal, and fish had a special purpose linked to, or attached to all the elements of life, including the water, the air, the sun, the moon, the hills, and the mountains. The Great Spirit was the master of all that existed. So, blowing up, digging, and excavating the land above and below the surface, was tantamount to a great, and unforgivable sin.

Peter's schooling of Onida created in her, a deep sense of personal attachment to the environment, and the need to save it from further destruction. She knew why she had to do something to protect what was left, to rebuild her community, to reinstate the close respect for their heritage, and to regain what was lost to the loggers, miners, and hunters.

Onida also instinctively knew why she had to save and protect Onca the otter, her pet macaw and toucan, her baby Howler monkey, and the orphaned tapir which was rescued by her friends. She did not blame the mysterious jaguar which had attacked the tapir's family, as such an act was the order of nature. However, she and her peoples held the jaguar with great respect as the most dangerous, and watchful guardian of the forests of Kayana.

Onida, whilst preparing to leave the settlement, met Chief Koko at the benab. She and her friends were accompanied by their pet birds and animals. The collective noise of the assembly caused Chief Koko to appear before them at the top of the stairs of the benab.

Chief Koko asked, "Onida, why have you and your friends come here?"

Onida, with her toucan on her right shoulder, and macaw perched on her left arm, said, "I have asked my friends and their pets to come here to tell you that we are worried as to who will look after them after I leave. I know that Onca is very sad, and wants to go with me to my school. I also want to take my toucan and macaw with me. They will always remind me of this place. Will this be allowed?"

Chief Koko smiled, and said, "I don't think that the schoolmasters will allow you to do this. I will have to ask Mr Jennings."

Onida frowned, and said, "I am happy to go to learn about the other world. But I also want to show them, and to teach them about our world. How we live, and how our birds and animals live with us."

Peter, who had heard the commotion, hurried along to join Chief Koko.

He said, "Onida, you are right about teaching others about our way of life. But you cannot do so by taking your pets there. Those people will think that we only capture these birds and animals for our own use. They will say that our pets should be set free into the wild."

Onida said, "I want to show people that we are not cruel. We have saved these pets from harm, and when they feel that they want to leave, then we let them go."

Chief Koko nodded, and said, "Yes Onida, I understand what you are saying. I do not mind if you take your toucan and macaw with you. But Onca will have to stay here until he wishes to leave, and to live his own life. Peter and your friends will look after him."

Onida then asked, "And what about my monkey? He will never leave me."

Peter said, "Whilst toucans and macaws are used to being away from their homes, I think that your monkey will suffer from being away from here."

Groups of Howler monkeys gathered around the trees nearest to the edge of the settlement, curious to find out what the commotion was about. A jaguar kept his distance, and peered through the undergrowth, ensuring that he could not be easily seen by anyone. Onca squeaked as if he wanted to be part of the conversation. The resident pigs and piglets just carried on with their ritual bathing in their muddy pond.

The Piaiman stepped forward, and placed his right hand onto Onida's head, and said, "May the Great Spirit always be with you. May your ancestors always walk by your side, and shield you from any evil actions on your body and mind. And may all our thoughts and blessings be your guide to help you learn your lessons, and impart what you wish to tell the outside world."

He then placed a beaded necklace over Onida's head and around her neck, whilst chanting prayers in Kayanese. He was then joined by Chief Koko, Peter, and five elders, as they began a special smoke ceremony invoking the Great Spirit to bless Onida, everyone in the settlement, and all around them.

As soon as the smoke ceremony ended, the watching jaguar emerged briefly from his hiding place, looked towards the gathering, snarled, and then turned and disappeared into the forest. An elder picked up the carcass of a slaughtered hen, took it to the place where the jaguar had hidden, and placed it as an offering to the king of the jungle.

Onida, and all those in the gathering waved in the direction of the jaguar's observation point.

She said, "Oh great jaguar of Kayana, please guard our settlement from strangers. Please avoid attacking our people and our animals, especially when they stray into your place."

Onca could not bear missing out on all the ceremony, and fond farewells to Onida. He clambered up the bank of the tributary, and onto the dusty pathway leading to the benab. Onida saw him, and ran towards her best friend. When she reached him, she stooped down, and kissed him on his forehead.

She said, "Onca, you will have to stay here, and help to look out for Chief Koko and everyone else. If you see any stranger approaching the waterfront, just get here, and let Chief Koko and Peter know."

Onca arched up, and Onida put her arms gently around his neck.

She said, "I will miss you too. One day we all have to leave our friends behind, but I will come back to see you, and everyone else."

Tears began to well up in Onida's eyes, and she noticed the same in Onca's. She kissed his forehead, and then hugged him more tightly.

Chief Koko and Peter stepped forward, and placed their hands on Onida's shoulders.

Chief Koko said, "Onida, your boat and boatman are here. Let us go to the waterfront."

Peter held Onida's right hand, and led her to one of the new water tanks. He opened the tap, and she was able to wash her hands using the rainwater collected from the storm.

ELEVEN

LOOSE LOGS

T he boatman held out a helping hand for Onida as she stepped
onto the motor powered vessel. She sat down on one of the two
seats near the middle, and in front of that used by the boatman. Her
case of clothing and other essentials was loaded onto the bow section
of the boat, by Peter, and secured firmly with a leather strap.

The boatman took his seat, held the steering handle of the outboard
engine, and pressed the starter button. The engine responded with a
roar as the propeller cut through the dark brown water. Everyone from
the settlement had lined the grassy mound by the edge of the waterway.
Chief Koko, the Piaiman, the Priest, and the elders stood together,
and joined the others in waving their goodbyes to Onida. She waved
back with her right hand, as the boat began to ease out of the mooring,
and moved further out into the tributary.

Everyone began to point and cheer more loudly as the boat picked
up speed. The boatman and Onida looked back, and they spotted Onca
swimming rapidly towards the vessel.

Onida leaned over the side where Onca was, and shouted above
the noise of the motor, "Go back Onca! Stay away from the boat! I
love you Onca!"

The boatman increased the speed, and Onca could no longer keep
up with the boat. He was left almost stranded in the water. Onida,
with tears streaming down her face, waved at Onca as the boat moved
further away. Her toucan and macaw became more agitated, and she
gently stroked their heads.

She said, "Never mind my friends. We will come back to visit
Onca, and everyone else."

The boat powered up the normally gentle water of the tributary,
making its own wavy wake as the bow lifted off the water from time
to time. Other users in their canoes and paddle boats kept closer to the

banks of the tributary, and allowed the motorboat a clear run in the middle. When the boat passed by any housing or other building by the edge of the banks, the residents waved at it. Onida waved back almost in the manner of royalty.

The boat finally reached the point where the tributary joined the Great River. The boatman slowed down as he steered the craft carefully into the much more turbulent water heading northwards. When the boat reached about two hundred yards from the left bank of the Great River, the boatman gently increased the speed.

The breeze created by the forward thrust of the powerful motor, ruffled the hair of Onida, and, the feathers of the toucan and the macaw. Onida loved the cool, and refreshing feeling of the breeze on her face. She allowed her long, and beautiful black hair to flutter wildly, and uncontrollably.

Further up the Great River the waves became much bigger, and lashed against the bow causing it to be partly lifted up, and then fall back onto the water. The boatman shouted to Onida to hold tight, and stay calm as he spotted a smaller motorised canoe trying to cut across in front of his vessel. He started to shout, and gesture to the other boatman to get out of the way.

Onida's boatman tried to swerve away from the other boat, and a combination of the rough waves as well as the speed caused their boat to rise up almost entirely off the water. He lost control as his hands slipped off the steering, and he was thrown into the river. The other boat just managed to get past, and avoid a collision.

Onida, who had fallen forward from her seat, quickly scrambled over to grab the steering, and managed to press the stop button. The boat settled silently on the water. Her toucan and macaw were very agitated, but soon stood onto the other passenger seat beside Onida's.

Onida looked back into the water, and spotted her boatman struggling to keep afloat. She immediately plunged into the river, and swam towards the stricken boatman. The driver of the other boat saw the rescue attempt, and turned back to attach his boat to Onida's.

Onida swam hard, against the three feet high waves, and finally reached the badly struggling boatman. She grabbed onto his right arm as he was about to be submerged. The other boatman who had also dived into the water, soon reached Onida, and he helped her to pull the injured man above the surface of the water. They both held onto him tightly, and slowly managed to pull him alongside his boat.

They spotted a loose log floating near to the two boats, and the second boatman reached out to grab it. Onida then helped him to ease the injured boatman across the log. After great effort, they managed to haul him onto his boat, and he slipped into unconsciousness.

Onida said, "Quick. We have to get him to the nearest hospital or clinic."

The boatman said, "I'm very sorry for causing the accident. I was trying to avoid hitting that loose log in the water."

Onida said, "I understand. Now, please drive us as quickly as you can."

The boatman, who was Indigenous Kayanese, started up the boat, and began to drive it forward, adjusting his steering to ensure that his boat remained securely attached.

He said, "My name is Michael. There is a clinic further up the river. It is near to the High School. We will get there soon."

Onida, still shaken by the episode, was very concerned about her boatman who was lying still on his back. She turned around, and looked at Michael.

She asked, "Do you know how to revive him? Let me drive whilst you tend to him."

Michael handed over the steering to Onida, and then tried to resuscitate her boatman. She held firmly to the steering, and managed to keep the boat at a steady speed. The stricken boatman finally emerged into consciousness, and Michael gave him some water to drink from a bottle.

Michael took back control of the steering, and Onida sat beside her boatman trying to comfort him. Her toucan and macaw looked on as if with concern.

Michael said, "It's only a few more miles to the clinic."

Onida said, "Thank you for helping us. It could have been much worse if we had hit that loose log."

Michael gradually increased his speed as he became more used to handling the outboard motor. He kept close watch on his attached boat as they rode the bigger waves.

Onida said, "Those logging people should be more careful about the loose logs that float away into this river. They are very dangerous."

Michael said, "I agree. But sometimes such smaller logs are there because of our people. It is not always the fault of the loggers. I work for a logging company, and we do take care to secure all the cut timber that we move through the river."

Onida shrugged her shoulders, and said, "Maybe your company is cutting down too many trees, and you cannot control everything."

Michael said, "My company does plant new saplings to replace the trees we fell."

Onida said, "Those great trees that you cut down have taken hundreds of years to grow. Your saplings cannot replace what you are destroying, quickly enough. It will take many decades, and the damage will never be repaired. I think that you and your company should only be allowed a small amount of logging."

Michael said, "I agree with you. You seem to have very strong views for someone so young. You speak like my Chief."

Onida smiled, and said, "No, I am only a student who will be attending the High School. Please try your best to moor the boats at the one next to the clinic."

Michael said, "Yes. I will stay here until your boatman is treated, and then I will accompany him when he is fit enough to return to your settlement."

Onida said, "Thank you very much. When you get there, please tell my great grandmother Chief Koko, about what happened."

Michael said, "Yes. So you are related to your Chief. You must be Onida, a future Chief. I knew that you are someone very special. I will also talk to my boss about taking more care with loose logs."

TWELVE

RULES

M ichael ferried Onida to her new school after they both ensured that the injured boatman was diagnosed, treated, and placed into a bed at the Community Clinic. Onida was very relieved that the injuries suffered by the boatman were not serious enough to warrant a transfer for further treatment at the large Regional Hospital. He was ordered to rest at the Clinic for a few days before he was to be discharged.

Michael also promised to return the injured boatman's vessel to the mooring by the Clinic. He then eased it carefully beside the steep stairway which was part of a larger harbour. As soon as Onida disembarked onto the landing area, she was welcomed and greeted by Mr Jacob Holmes, the middle-aged African Kayanese Headteacher of the High School. He was a short stocky man with a small beard which he loved to touch and fix with his right fingers and thumb.

Mr Holmes looked at his large wristwatch, and asked, "Mr Boatman, why have you arrived so late?"

Michael shifted on his feet nervously, and said, "Sir, there was a serious accident, and Onida's boatman was injured. I do not know what time you were expecting us, but I only offered to help this young lady who was so brave. She tried to save her boatman from drowning."

Onida, still wearing her damp clothing, said, "Yes Sir. We could not get here any earlier. After our rescue, we had to take the boatman to be treated at the Community Clinic."

Her macaw and toucan scrambled up, and perched on her shoulders as she tried to lift her carrying case. Mr Holmes stepped forward, and offered to help.

He said, "Here, let me take that."

He was startled as the macaw and toucan squawked excitedly.

Mr Holmes said, "I must tell you that I do not allow pets at my school. But as you are our very important student, I am making an exception to this rule. If there is any trouble, you will have to let them go."

Onida nodded, and said, "Thank you Sir. My friends will always behave themselves."

The short walk from the harbour along a narrow dusty pathway leading up to the High School caused the residents to pause, and look at Mr Holmes and the new arrivals.

Although it was late on Saturday afternoon, a small group of curious students who were residents, gathered around Onida as she waited for Mr Holmes to catch up. He struggled with carrying the case up the slope, and had to pause several times to rest after only a few yards.

When he finally caught up with Onida and her crowd of curious onlookers, he put down the case, and reached for the padlock of his office door bearing his name and title on a copper plate.

Mr Holmes opened the door, and waved his tired hands at the students, saying, "Now you lot, go back to your rooms. This is Onida, the future Chief of her people. Please allow her to settle down. You will all get to meet her later on."

The students looked at Onida with surprise, and nodded with respect. They quietly obeyed Mr Holmes's instruction, and walked off towards the two-storey wooden structure which housed all the boarders of the school. They were children aged from ten to sixteen years of age, and from different Kayana backgrounds including, African, Portuguese, East Indian, Chinese, and mixed races. Onida was to become the only resident Indigenous Kayanese, as Mr Holmes pointed out to her.

He sat behind his neatly carved and polished mahogany desk, on a sturdy but well-worn chair made of the same wood. He asked Onida to sit down on one of the two smaller chairs placed in front of the desk. The large ceiling fan was whirring around to provide some respite from the very hot and humid afternoon. The office walls were mostly hidden by a variety of wooden bookcases and shelves filled with an array of books and folders. Onida cast her eyes around the room as she had never seen such a display before.

Mr Holmes said, "As you can see, we are surrounded by all kinds of books. They cover all sorts of subjects that we teach here. Don't worry, you will not have to read them all, but you will enjoy studying here."

Onida nodded, and said, "Sir, I am not yet a Chief. Onida is the name given to me by my great-grandmother. I do not have any other name."

Mr Holmes smiled, and said, "I think I understand why you say this. But I was told about what happened when you were born on the first of January over ten years ago. Also, Mr John Jennings who is paying for your studies and stay here, has told me that you are a specially chosen, and long-awaited leader of your people at the settlement. You have not been baptised as a Christian, and you will not carry any other name."

Onida said, "Sir, Kayana is a very big country, and please do not make me into someone I am not. I wish to be treated just like all the other students here."

Mr Holmes nodded, and reached across his desk. He picked up a neatly stacked set of school uniforms including a white short-sleeved cotton shirt, a grey pleated skirt, two pairs of white socks, and a pair of black leather shoes. He then placed the bundle before Onida.

She picked up the items, and said, "Sir, I have not worn such leather shoes before."

Mr Holmes said, "Don't worry. You will get used to them. Do try them on."

Onida put on her new shoes, and then nervously stood up. Mr Holmes asked her to walk around the room. He tried to restrain himself from laughing as Onida nearly stumbled over. She steadied herself, and soon began to walk with more ease, and confidence.

The macaw and toucan adjusted themselves as they perched onto each of Onida's shoulders. Mr Holmes looked at Onida and her companions with some sense of disbelief, and then ushered them out towards the boarding house. Michael who could be seen in the short distance to the harbour, waved goodbye as he turned the two boats around for the return journey down river.

A few of the boarders stood by the entrance of the main front door of the boarding house. An African Kayanese girl who was about the same stature and age of Onida, stepped forward and reached out to shake her hands. Onida stopped briefly, and smiled as she shook the girl's right hand.

She said, "Hi, I am called Onida. What is your name?"

The girl smiled, and said, "I am Ruby Smith. I will be sharing a room with you."

Ruby Smith made an attempt at curtsying before Onida, and the other children giggled.

Onida said, "No Ruby. Please do not do this. I am not a Chief. This is just my name like yours."

Jacob Holmes said, "Well, Onida is a very humble person. Let me tell you all that she is the future leader of her people at the settlement which is about twenty miles downriver. I am told that she has a strong connection to the Great River. I want everyone at this school to show her the kind of respect that Ruby has just done. Now, all of you please stop your sniggering, and do as I say."

Everyone responded with "Yes Sir".

Ruby Smith, wearing her hair in two neat plaits, a sleeveless multi-coloured cotton dress which ended just below her knees, and a pair of white sneakers, walked just ahead of Onida, and opened the door to their room.

Onida said, "Thank you Ruby. You do not have to bow every time in front of me."

Ruby smiled, and said, "I am very happy to be with you. What do you call your macaw and toucan?"

Onida said, "Actually, I do not have names for them. I just look at them, and they know what to do. Maybe we should now give them names. What do you think?"

Ruby sat on the edge of her single wooden bed opposite Onida's, and said, "Well, we all call parrots by names such as "Polly". Your macaw is so pretty we can call it "Pretty Polly". How about that?"

Onida smiled, and tickled her macaw just below its beak.

She said, "I think he would love to be called "Pretty Polly". What about our toucan friend?"

Ruby said, "Well, the toucan is also very beautiful, and it is our national bird."

Onida looked at the toucan, and said, "I never knew that one bird can be so important. I think that they are all important. We treat all of our birds with great respect. It's the same for our animals."

Ruby pointed to the Kayana national flag which was pinned onto the wall just above the headboard of her bed.

She said, "You see, the national flag which we all salute, and sing to, has a toucan right in the middle of it. It also has the bright yellow, red, and green colours around the toucan."

Onida said, "I like this flag, but I do not agree to have only one bird on it. We try to show our love and respect to all of our birds, and we show this by the many feathers on our Chief's headdress. I have one macaw, one toucan, and one Harpy eagle feather on mine."

Ruby said, "Maybe you are right. Our flag does not represent Kayana properly. But we cannot change it."

Onida said, "Since our toucan is so important, maybe we can call him *Kassequa*, which means Chief."

Ruby asked, "Kassi? Kassi what?"

Onida said, "Kassequa. But I like "Kassi". And, maybe we can call our macaw "Kori" after *Korinaka*, our word for this beautiful bird."

Ruby smiled, and looked more closely at the macaw and toucan who were now perched on the small desk beside Onida's bed.

She said, "Kori and Kassi are nice names."

She asked, "Onida, do we not have to keep them in cages?"

Onida said, "No Ruby. They are more free than us, and will stay with us in our room. They know that they must not mess our room, and will go outside when they wish."

Ruby said, "Wow! That is amazing! I do not know why our Kayanese people have to cage up these beautiful birds."

Onida said, "You see, we are kept in this room for our safety. But we can come and go as we wish. So, why can't we treat Kori and Kassi the same way?"

Ruby opened her eyes widely, and said, "Oh no Onida. We are not that free. We have set times when we can come and go. Also, when we can wake up, and when we must go to sleep. These things are called "School Rules", and we even have "House Rules" for our boarding house."

Onida smiled, and said, "Our peoples' rules are all in line with nature's."

THIRTEEN

GO AWAY FROM HERE

A t precisely six thirty in the morning on the first Monday of Onida's new school week, Kassi the toucan, and Kori the macaw, started to squawk. They caused Onida to wake up from her deep slumber. She quickly stood up, and quietly visited the communal shower room before all of the other residents. The first amount of water from the shower head was very cold, and made her shiver. She hastened her wash, and tiptoed back to her room.

Ruby Smith was still sleeping under her thin cotton blanket whilst Onida put on her new school uniform.

She nudged Ruby, and whispered, "Ruby get up. We will be late for our breakfast, and first assembly."

Ruby turned over lazily in her comfortable bed, yawned, and said, "Let me have a few more minutes. What time is it?"

Onida looked at the small round clock on the dressing table they shared. It was already seven o'clock.

She said, "Ruby, get up or else we will be in trouble."

Kassi and Kori also signalled their warning, and Onida opened a window to let them out for their early morning feeding, and exercise.

Finally, after more persuasion, Ruby was ready to accompany Onida to the house canteen. As they approached a table with benches shared by the students, the four others stood up, and bowed in a show of respect towards Onida.

She sat down, and the other students followed suit. Ruby walked over to the serving area, and took a tray of fruits, slices of toasts, and a pot of tea to be shared with Onida.

Onida said, "Thank you very much Ruby. Please do not treat me like an important royal. I wish to be like everyone else. I must insist on getting my own meals."

Ruby said, "Onida, we understand this. But, Mr Holmes expects us all to show you respect, and to treat you well. I have to show the others by example."

When the students finished their breakfast, Onida stood up, and took Ruby's tray along with hers, over to the kitchen area. Then they followed the others as they strode over to the main school hall.

Mr Holmes stood as upright as he could before the school assembly of about two hundred students. The youngest children from the lowest forms, including Onida and Ruby, took their places at the front of the assembly, and the older students occupied the middle and back rows. The ten other teachers of the school took their positions beside Mr Holmes, and the assembly fell silent after a few seconds.

He said, "Good morning everyone. Today, I am very proud to announce that we have a new student amongst us. She is Onida, a future Chief of her people, and I request that she is given due respect at all times. She is the only resident student of the First Peoples of our nation, and it is a great honour to have her here. Now, let us all join in singing the National Anthem of Kayana."

Onida surprised Ruby and the other students nearby, with her clear rendition of the anthem. Mr Holmes noticed her performance, and nodded in approval.

When the anthem was concluded, and the assembly was declared over, Mr Holmes approached Onida and Ruby.

He asked, "Onida, how has your stay been so far? Do you have everything you need? Is Ruby helping you?"

Onida said, "Yes Mr Holmes. I am fine. Ruby and all the others are very good towards me, and very helpful. But, I do not like the very cold water in the shower room."

Mr Holmes smiled, and said, "Oh, you must remember to let the water flow for a while, and then it will feel a lot more comfortable. By the way, where did you learn to sing the National Anthem so well?"

Onida, said, "At my school near to our settlement. All of my school friends there know it by heart. We love the words which say that the land must only be used for what we need, and the forests must be saved. My people believe these things."

Mr Holmes turned to Ruby, and asked, "And how are you getting on with Onida?"

Ruby said, "Sir, I like her very much. She knows so much, and I am already learning from her. And, as you can see, she speaks and sings English very well, and, she also knows her tribal Kayana language."

Mr Holmes smiled, and said, "Well, I hope that someday we will all learn at least one of our Indigenous Kayanese languages. Perhaps Onida can start to teach us."

Onida smiled, and said, "Sir, that is a very good idea. Who knows, maybe I will become a teacher here."

Mr Holmes began to walk away, and then turned around suddenly to ask, "By the way, how are your toucan and macaw friends?"

Ruby said, "Sir, they are called Kassi the toucan, and Kori the macaw. They are beautiful, and good. We let them come and go as they wish."

Over the ensuing days and weeks of the first term, Onida and Ruby, along with Kassi and Kori, were almost inseparable. They established a good routine of waking up on time each morning of the school week, get ready for school, have their breakfast and other meals together, take part in the early afternoon sports and games in the school's grounds, and retire for the evening as required by the school rules. Onida and Ruby were placed in the same classroom, and they helped each other with their homework.

However, each Saturday and Sunday, when the strict regime of the school week was more relaxed, Onida became increasingly saddened by the loss of contact with those she loved in the settlement.

One Saturday morning, she sat up in her bed, and began to sob.

Ruby stood up, and then walked over to sit beside Onida. Kassi and Kori looked on quietly, as if they sensed that all was not well with Onida.

Ruby hugged Onida, and asked, "What is the matter? Why are you crying?"

Onida tried to wipe the tears from her eyes and cheeks with the back of her hands, and said, "I am fine."

Ruby asked, "Are you missing your people? Are you missing Chief Koko, Peter, and Onca?"

Onida could not control her tears, and said, "Yes, I miss them badly. I want to go back to see them. I hate this place."

Ruby sat up in surprise, and asked, "Please tell me what has happened? Is it to do with me?"

Onida said, "No Ruby. You are my best friend here."

Ruby said, "So, why do you want to go away?"

Onida then composed herself, and said, "Yesterday, as I was in the toilet area, two girls came up to me, and pushed me against the wall. I was shocked, and did not know what to do. Then they started to shout at me."

Ruby asked, "What did they say?"

Onida sighed, and said, "They cursed me, and said things like, 'Hey you buck, go away from here!', and 'We hate you! You're nasty people!'."

FOURTEEN

THE NEW WORLD

At the next day's assembly, Mr Holmes appeared to be quite sombre, and was unsmiling as he stood before the students.

He said, "Today, I am asking Ruby Smith and Onida to come up here beside me, and to sing our National Anthem. Then, I wish to discuss a deeply troubling matter with you all."

Ruby held Onida's left hand, and they took up their position beside Mr Holmes and the teachers. They sang the anthem beautifully, and their voices complemented each other's. Unusually, at the end of their rendition, the entire assembly applauded the two lead singers. Mr Holmes shook the girls' hands, and asked them to remain in their position.

He then turned to the students in the assembly, and said, "I am glad that you have all shown your appreciation for Ruby and Onida. That is very important as you instinctively recognised, and appreciated the talents of these two young girls. But today I also want to remind you as to why we are a great school with an excellent reputation. Apart from our high academic achievements, we are also known for our care and consideration towards our fellow students, teachers, and all of the other people who work here to make this place what it is."

The entire audience stood still, and the silence was so profound, one could hear a pin drop.

Mr Holmes continued, "So, when I hear that one of our best students has been assaulted, and called a terrible, and unacceptable, racist name, I was completely shocked. It was made even worse for me when I learnt that the two perpetrators are from amongst you students. Before I call out the names of these two people, let me remind you that racism in any shape or form, will never be tolerated in this school. I am so disgusted by this most recent incident, that I have changed the form of punishment for such assaults to one of zero tolerance. In other words, from now onwards, any act of racism, harassment, or discrimination, will be punishable by instant expulsion in the case of a guilty student, or instant dismissal if the perpetrator is a teacher, or other member of staff here."

Many of the students and teachers who were shocked to hear Mr Holmes's increasingly forceful announcement, turned to look at each other, and a few moments of murmuring broke the silence in the hall.

Mr Holmes pointed towards the two young ladies who had accosted, and insulted Onida, and said, "You two, come over here."

The two worried looking students, one an East Indian girl of Onida's age, and the other, an African girl who was about a foot taller, stepped forward, and stood next to Ruby and Onida. They began to weep, and tried to wipe away their tears.

Mr Holmes said, "I want the two of you to face this audience, and say that you are both very sorry for calling Onida a "buck", and for assaulting her. Then, I want you to personally apologise to Onida."

The two girls were still weeping as they carried out Mr Holmes's instructions.

He said, "In this school, no one is allowed to use such disgusting words or terms to describe another person. Furthermore, no one is allowed to shove or fight with anyone. You can only earn respect by showing others that you care for them. You can all compete against each other, but only with fairness. You can win your race, but only if you allow your competitors to use their space in such competitions. Now, do you all understand me?"

The assembly responded with a resounding "Yes Sir!"

Mr Holmes continued, "Now that apologies have been given and accepted, I wish to propose that with the permission of your parents, and the Chief of Onida's settlement, I would like to take the two of you, and Ruby, along with Onida, to spend a day at her settlement, and to learn about her people's way of life there. If this trip goes ahead, I shall then make arrangements for each class to do likewise over the course of the school terms. But this will only happen if the Chief and the people, as well as your parents, agree to such visits."

The students responded positively to Mr Holmes's suggestions, and left the hall in a more orderly fashion than usual. He asked Onida, Ruby, and the other two girls, to accompany him to his office.

He sat behind his desk as the four students stood before him.

He said, "Dear Onida, I wish to personally apologise to you for any hurt that you may have felt because of this incident. I know that you will not want to see these two girls punished for what they did to you. So, not only will I try to arrange our visit to your home, I am asking these two to sit beside you and Ruby in your classroom. Hopefully, you will all become good friends, and push this incident behind you."

The girls then shook each other's hands, and walked off together to join their classmates.

The first lesson of that morning in Onida's class, was history. Their teacher was a short, plump, middle-aged Portuguese Kayanese woman, who wore her spectacles just above the tip of her small nose. Her name was Isabel Rodrigues.

When Miss Rodrigues walked into the classroom of twenty-five students sitting at their individual wooden desks and chairs, everyone stood up as quietly as they could, despite the noise made by the legs of their chairs rubbing against the wooden floor. There was a large blackboard which was screwed against the wall just behind Miss Rodrigues's desk and chair. Natural light poured into the room through three large glass windows on one side. The room also had two large ceiling fans which whirred quietly above the students.

Miss Rodrigues said, "Good morning class. You may all sit down."

The entire class replied before taking their seats, "Good morning Miss Rodrigues."

Miss Rodrigues said, "Today, we will learn about how the Europeans discovered this part of the world. How many of you have heard of Christopher Columbus?"

Most of the students put their right hands up, and shouted, "Me Miss!"

Miss Rodrigues pointed at Ruby, and asked, "Tell us Ruby Smith. What do you know about Christopher Columbus?"

Ruby eagerly stood up, and said, "Miss, he was the one who discovered America in 1492!"

Miss Rodrigues asked, "And where did he come from?"

Many students in the class shouted out, "Spain!"

Miss Rodrigues said, "Yes Ruby, Christopher Columbus was a great explorer who, along with other sailors, made four voyages across the Atlantic Ocean, to what we now call the Americas, and a number of islands in the Caribbean. The first was in 1492, and only eight years ago there were great celebrations to mark five hundred years from this historic moment. No, he did not come from Spain, but was born in 1451 in a place called Genoa, in Italy. His Italian name was Cristoforo Colombo. His voyages were sponsored by King Ferdinand and Queen Isabella of Spain."

She continued to describe the main events of the voyages, the places discovered, how they were colonised, and how the whole view of the world was changed at the time.

The students were enraptured by the story, and they took notes which were written up on the blackboard by Miss Rodrigues. Onida sat and listened to the lesson, but did not write down any notes. Miss Rodrigues noticed this, and paused from her lecture.

She asked Onida, "Dear Onida, I notice that you are not taking any notes like the others. Why is this?"

Onida stood up, and pushed back her chair to give her more room.

She said, "Miss, I am confused by what you are telling us. I was told different things about Columbus, by my great grandmother Chief Koko, and the elders of my settlement."

Miss Rodrigues was taken aback, and gestured to Onida to continue.

Onida said, "First of all, these lands were not discovered by anyone else but my ancestors. Our peoples were here for thousands of years before 1492. I cannot tell you who was the first human to arrive in America or the Caribbean, but we have been here long before Columbus and others from Europe."

Miss Rodrigues shuffled uneasily in her chair upon hearing Onida's version of the history, and her cheeks became reddened with embarrassment.

She took a deep breath, recovered her poise, and said, "Onida, you are right. I should have made it clear that your ancestors were here long before 1492, and I am very sorry for this. Class, we do need to find out more about the peoples who were here, what they were like, how they lived, why so many of them were killed by foreign invaders and by diseases that they brought. Also, what the future holds for Onida and her peoples."

Onida nodded in agreement, sat down, and as she turned towards her friend Ruby, she smiled contentedly.

Miss Rodrigues said, "I was going to ask you all to read up about Christopher Columbus for your homework, and a short test next week.

But, instead, please try to find out more about Onida and her people who are still with us here in Kayana. Please note that Kayana is regarded as "The land of many waters". Those of you who will be spending some time with Onida and her people at the settlement must return to tell us about what you learnt. Hopefully Mr Holmes will arrange for our entire class to go there for a couple of days. The world of Onida may be seen as "The Old World", but our so-called "New World" is nothing in comparison to hers."

As soon as Miss Rodrigues completed her lesson and left the classroom, the students gathered around Onida eager to make her acquaintance, and to ask her questions as suggested by the teacher. Ruby held her friend's left hand, gently ushered her away from the crowd, and they both headed off for their mid-morning break.

FIFTEEN

OUR WAY OF LIFE

M r Holmes managed to persuade Chief Koko and John Jennings, as well as the parents of Ruby and the two classmates who had insulted Onida, to grant permission for the visit to the settlement. The two new friends of Onida and Ruby, whose names were Indra Persaud of East Indian, and Mary Brown of African heritage, took up their seats quietly, but nervously, in the middle of the motorboat which was sent by John Jennings, especially for the trip.

Onida and Ruby sat on the seats at the front of the boat, and Mr Holmes took up his place behind Indra and Mary. The boatman was in his seat alongside the powerful outboard motor. He asked all of his passengers to wear their luminous orange coloured life jackets.

The boatman recognised Onida, and said, "Hello Miss. I am Alfred, the boatman you saved when I was taking you to your new school."

Onida smiled, and said, "Oh yes I do remember you. I am very glad to see you."

Alfred, an Indigenous Kayanese of about forty years old, put on his life jacket and looked at each of his passengers to make sure that their life jackets were properly secured. He noticed that Mr Holmes was having some difficulty in trying to wrap the safety strap around his portly midriff, and he stood up to help to secure it as the boat bobbled slightly on the water.

He then took his seat next to the motor, and asked, "Is everybody comfortable? Do hold onto each other especially when we hit some bigger waves."

The passengers mumbled a "Yes" as the engine growled, and powered the boat away from the mooring. Kassi and Kori sat next to Onida, and squawked excitedly.

Ruby held Onida's left hand tightly, and Indra and Mary put their arms around each other. Mr Holmes sat upright, and looked straight ahead as the boat entered its position in the middle of the Great River. The brown water was choppier than usual, and Alfred gradually picked up speed. Onida allowed the wind to caress her face and hair whilst the others battled with trying to stop their hair from being blown out of place. Mr Holmes held onto his straw hat with both hands.

After only fifteen minutes into the journey, Alfred asked, "Is everybody alright? Please tell me as I need to pick up more speed."

Onida giggled, and shouted, "Yes Alfred. We are fine!"

The bow of the boat lifted higher above the water as the speed was increased. Onida calmly showed Ruby places of interest along both river banks, but she was much more concerned about sitting tightly to avoid being unseated as the boat rode the waves. The trip was finally completed after about an hour, and to everyone's relief, Alfred turned down the speed as he skilfully steered the boat through the estuary, and up to the mooring at the settlement.

Alfred shut down the engine, and climbed out onto the wooden platform to secure the mooring rope tightly around one of the two posts nearest to the edge of the water. He then assisted each of his passengers onto the platform where they were all greeted by Chief Koko, Peter, and the Piaiman. Onida grabbed Chief Koko around her waist, and squeezed her as tightly as she could.

Chief Koko said, "Oh Onida, I feel so happy to see you. Tell me, who are our guests?"

Onida held Ruby's right arm up, and said, "This is Ruby Smith, my roommate and best friend. Over there is Indra Persaud and Mary Brown my two new friends. And there is Mr Holmes, our Headteacher. Oh look! Mr Jennings is also coming to join us. And there is Onca! He seems to be so happy to see me again!"

She then stepped over to embrace Peter, and said, "Oh Peter, I have missed you all so much!"

The Piaiman waited until John Jennings stepped onto the landing, and greeted everyone. He then raised his arms into the air, and looking at the bright sun in the clear blue sky, he said, "Oh Great Spirit, please welcome our visitors and friends on this day, and show them all how beautiful is our way of life. Let them see how nature protects us, and how we protect everything offered to us by you, and all of our ancestors."

The visiting party, including Alfred, then followed the Piaiman to the benab. An inquisitive group of children walked briskly beside Onida and her school friends. John Jennings and Mr Holmes chatted quietly with each other as they ambled at the rear of the group. When everyone reached the entrance to the benab, Chief Koko ushered them into the middle of the building where a special dining table was set out with large bowls of food and refreshments.

Chief Koko, Peter, the Piaiman, John Jennings, and Mr Holmes sat on one side of the table. Onida, her friends, Alfred, and two elders sat on the opposite side.

The meal was sumptuous, and everyone was in very good spirits. Only the adults were allowed to drink the specially brewed piwari.

At the end of the meal, Chief Koko stood up, and said, "Thank you all for joining us today, and I am sure that Peter and Onida will show you around our settlement. I hope that you students will be taking notes about what you see and learn today. We are people of this earth, and what you have shared in your meal today came from the earth and its waters. We do not waste anything, and we only use what we need. If we have food left over, we give it to the animals and birds in the forest. I will wait here until you are finished with your tour, and we will send you away with a lot of joy and happiness to share with others at your school."

Onida and Peter asked the visitors to assemble just outside the main entrance of the benab. They quietly asked the group of local children to stay away from the tour party.

Peter said, "Welcome to you all. We are standing in an open area which we normally use to celebrate our various events. You have just been into the main building of the settlement called the benab where we also entertain our guests, and have our formal meetings. Our Chief Koko lives there, and Onida also stays there when she is not away at your school. Around this great square, you can see some of our houses. I will take you to see my family's house, and then we will visit the bamboo cemetery. After that we will walk into the forest, and hopefully we will see many of our animals and birds as well as interesting plants. We have a large fresh water creek where we bathe, and some of the children love to play in."

The pet tapir and Howler monkey which were being looked after by Peter in Onida's absence, joined the party. Onida stooped down to embrace them.

She looked up, and said, "I love our birds and animals here, and as you can see, so do everyone else in the village. We do not prevent

67

them from going off into the forest, and they are free to share everything that we have. Mind you, my monkey loves to snatch things from strangers. So, do watch out!"

Mr Holmes asked, "Peter, how long have your people lived on this settlement?"

Peter said, "Sir, I do not know the exact date, but our elders and Chief Koko have said that our ancestors came here over five hundred years ago. They were being attacked by European invaders. You may know that millions of our ancestors were killed by such people, and by the diseases that they brought here. In the past, as soon as such things happen our people would just abandon their villages, and run away. But we are determined to stay here, and will never move from this place."

Onida said, "Sir, the history that we are being told in our school needs to be changed to include the truth about Kayana and the other lands of our peoples. How many of them were attacked, enslaved, killed, or driven away by the White invaders?"

Mr Holmes nodded, and said, "We do not know the facts. I agree with you, and I have spoken with Miss Rodrigues about this. It is also one of the reasons why I am arranging for our students and teachers to come here to see, and to experience this environment. It is so beautiful, calm, and peaceful. We must respect this, learn from you, and share this with everyone in Kayana."

John Jennings fended off a loose branch from one of the small trees beside the pathway, and said, "I cannot answer for what my fellow foreigners did in the past, but I am keen for my mining company to do more to protect this beautiful place, and to support these peaceful people."

Peter paused, and said, "Here we are. This is my house. It is small, but please come in, and see how me and my family live. We have one space where we all sleep, one small kitchen, and an area where we keep our belongings. Thanks to Mr Jennings, we have a strong roof which does not leak when the rains come."

Ruby asked, "How big is your family Mr Peter?"

Peter said, "Here is my wife who is Kayanese like me. We have two children who are outside the benab playing with their friends. Actually, we all see the whole village as one big family. We all help each other."

Mr Holmes said, "Students, please take note of what you just heard. That is such an important lesson. In Mr Peter's culture, it is always about "We". But in ours, it is so much more about "Me"."

Peter nodded, and said, "Yes sir. "We" is much bigger than "Me"."

The Piaiman then led the visitors to the village's cemetery which was situated out of sight from the living areas, and surrounded by tall bamboo trees. He stopped briefly at the site where the victims of the last armed attack on the settlement, were laid to rest. He recited a Kayanese prayer as the party stood silently behind him.

He said, "These graves hold the bones of our most recent martyrs who were killed by a gang of miners. Their spirits will continue to guide our Chief Koko, Onida, and even our friend Mr Jennings here, in making sure that we stay here, and grow our children into peaceful citizens of Kayana. We do not want your wealth as we already have a living that is worth much more than our Kayana, or foreign money, can give."

Peter said, "Thank you Piaiman. Now let us go to the fresh water creek, and our farm where we grow our cassava and other vegetables. I hope that you three young ladies will help our women to clean, chop and squeeze the cassava, and make some cassava bread."

Ruby rubbed her hands together, and said, "Oh, I am looking forward to that."

Peter said, "That's good. It is very hard work. Our women do most of the hard work whilst we men go off to hunt for the entire community. Our way of life can appear to be simple and gentle, but it can be very hard with this kind of work every day."

SIXTEEN

READY TO LEAD

F ive years later, during the very hot month of July 2015, Onida and her classmates had completed their most significant challenge of their High School years; their Junior High School Examinations, or JHSE.

Despite the many term tests leading up to the final JHSE, the two weeks of intensive examinations created great tension, and anxiety for most of the students. Onida, although not an outstanding scholar, worked very hard on each of the ten subjects, and showed great determination to succeed. She was very fond of english, english literature, history, and the sciences. However, her weakest subject was mathematics, and Ruby tried her best to help her.

Mr Holmes had ensured that the school engaged in two-day visits to Onida's settlement, and the students of each class thoroughly enjoyed the experience of the boat trip on the Great River, meeting Chief Koko and the people, going on guided fishing trips, encountering some of the animals in the wild, and befriending those living in the settlement as pets. The visits helped to instil a greater sense of respect for the resident Indigenous Kayanese people, their way of life, and their passion for the environment.

John Jennings of the mining company, also initiated school trips to the gold mine as an example of his commitment for more sensitive operations of the business. He and Mr Holmes agreed to have mining engineers visit the school to deliver talks on the subject of engineering with a view to encouraging students to consider this as a future career.

At the final graduation ceremony, Onida and her friends received their certificates for their outstanding successes at a special assembly in the school's main hall. Mr Holmes stood proudly beside his entire teaching and support staff, and they were given an impromptu standing ovation by the students.

He said, "Today, I stand before you who are the future of Kayana. Your results have been really amazing, and easily the best ever for our school. You, along with your teachers, have put in one hundred percent effort, and you have achieved one hundred percent success. I hope that you will return next year to do the Senior High School Examinations. Then, I want to see most, if not all of you going on to even higher studies here in Kayana, or abroad. Today, I also want to speak about one of our very special students, and I think that you can guess who that is."

Mr Holmes asked Onida to stand beside him, and he said, "First of all, I want to thank you all for helping Onida through the last five years here. She has worked hard, and has been awarded with some excellent results. I know that she is going to be the leader of her people, and I am very proud that we have played a part in helping her."

The students stood up to give Onida warm applause before resuming their seats. She smiled, and waved her right hand in appreciation.

Mr Holmes continued, "Not only has Onida achieved so much here, but she has also taught us so much more about herself, her people, her community, and how we must all respect our amazing rainforests and environment that we are so fortunate to have here in Kayana. This has been a very important lesson and examination for us all, and for everyone else here in Kayana, and the world. I also wish to thank her great grandmother, Chief Koko, and everyone at the settlement, for the education they have given to all of us. Our next test will now be how we pass on this knowledge, how we educate others about our First Peoples of Kayana, and how we ourselves treat the environment we happen to be a part of."

He then asked Onida to say a few words. She responded by asking her closest friends, Ruby, Indra, and Mary, to join her.

She said, "Well, thank you so much Mr Holmes and all the staff here. Thank you my fellow students for your love and support. I am really happy that you all visited my settlement, and experienced a very different way of life. You may not choose to live like me and my people, but at least you will use some of what you have seen, and learnt. I am really happy to note that my friends Indra and Mary wish to study Botany, and especially the plant species we have in our rainforests. My friend Ruby wants to study finance, and to work for the government. Well, I am really happy about that as I know who to go to

71

when my community needs any financial help. My other companions, Kassi and Kori, have become a bit older now, and if they can speak, they will also say that they love you all. I think that the real reason why they never flew away from here, is that you fed them too much!"

Everyone stood up to applaud Onida and her friends as they took their seats. Mr Holmes then wished everyone safe journeys back to their family homes, and an enjoyable holiday break until the start of the next school year in September.

Onida, clutching her neatly rolled up certificate, ran towards Chief Koko and Peter as soon as she arrived at the settlement. Chief Koko stood up in front of the entrance to the benab, and prepared to greet her with her arms wide open. She hugged Onida tightly, and tears of great joy streamed down her well-worn and wrinkled face.

Chief Koko said, "Congratulations my dear Onida. We are all so very proud of you. I have waited a very long time for this moment. Now I know that the Great Spirit, and those of all our ancestors are also smiling with great joy. This is such an important achievement for all of our peoples of Kayana."

Peter hugged Onida as soon as he was able to, and said, "I am so proud of you my child. You are now ready to lead us into the future."

Onida stooped down to embrace her tapir and Onca who was fully grown, and had set up his own family at the den that was created for him by Onida and her friends. Her Howler monkey stood up excitedly on his legs, and appeared to clap his hands in appreciation of Onida.

Onida said, "Oh I am looking forward to spending all of my holidays here with you my dear friends. I cannot bear to be away from you all."

Peter said, "Onida, we have planned a very big party for you, Kassi and Kori. We did not get the chance to celebrate your fifteenth birthday in January, and this time we will make up for that. Now, all you have to do is get some rest, and leave everything to me and all of my helpers. Mr Jennings is paying for everything we need. I also hope he will come and join us tomorrow."

Alfred, the boatman, finally arrived at the benab fetching Onida's suitcase, and other belongings. He breathed a huge sigh of relief as he placed everything on the ground in front of Onida.

He was still breathing heavily as he said, "Onida, please carry less things when you go back to school in September. Otherwise we will need two more people to carry your stuff!"

Onida laughed, and said, "Thank you Alfred. I look forward to some lessons from you in how to drive your boat!"

Alfred said, "Of course Onida. I will also show you how to repair the motor. But please don't leave me without a job!"

Later that evening, after a heavy meal, Onida lay in the hammock next to Chief Koko's. They spoke for some time until they both drifted off into deep sleep. Several hours into the night, Onida was awakened by a growl from the edge of the forest. She peered at the direction of the sound, and saw the jaguar's eyes which were lit up by the reflection of the low moonlight.

She whispered, "And now, what do you want?"

The jaguar looked at Onida, opened his mouth to expose his large white fangs as if to speak with her.

Onida said, "Please go in peace."

The jaguar snarled, shook his head, and slipped away as quietly as he had come.

SEVENTEEN

THE END OF AN ERA

O nida rushed back to Chief Koko's hammock, and shook her in an attempt to warn her about the presence of the jaguar. There was no response.

She placed her right palm against the left cheek of her great grandmother, and was shocked by how cold it was. She then made another attempt to rouse the Chief, but to no avail.

Onida hurried out of the benab, and across the square to Peter's house. She frantically knocked on the front door until a bleary-eyed Peter opened it.

He asked, "Onida, what's the matter?"

She was breathless, and panted, "I think Chief Koko is dead!"

They both dashed back to the benab, and Peter tried to wake Chief Koko. He held her right hand for a short time, and then turned to face Onida.

He said solemnly, "You are right. Our great Chief has left us to join the Spirit World."

They embraced each other as tears streamed down their faces. Onida then stepped back to Chief Koko's hammock, leaned across her, and put her arms around the peaceful looking Chief. Her small face seemed to be calm, and with a hint of a smile.

Peter said, "Onida, let me go out to tell everyone about this very sad news. Before the funeral, we will have to select our new Chief."

Onida, still in a state of disbelief, simply nodded in agreement, and waved Peter on to do as he suggested.

In a very short time, the whole community gathered, and stood silently in the square facing the benab. Most of the women and children were openly sobbing at the loss of their great, and long-lived Chief.

Peter and the Piaiman, along with five elders, and the Christian Priest, stood before the people, and he raised his hands aloft.

74

He said, "Today we pay homage to the will and wisdom of the Great Spirit who has asked for our Chief Koko to join him. We have no choice but to respect his wishes, and we pray for a new Chief to lead us. I feel great sadness and pain in my heart because Chief Koko was like a mother to me, and to us all. Today, we have to select our new Chief, and I think that we all know who that person is. But our elders here will have a meeting, and their choice will be announced later."

Onida appeared at the doorway of the benab with tears still running down her tired, and reddened cheeks. She made no attempt to wipe them away as she stood beside Peter and the elders.

A lone voice shouted out, "Long live Onida! Long live our new Chief!"

Peter tried to quieten the people, and pleaded, "Yes, I agree with you. But we must allow our elders to decide. I hope that they listen to our voices, and to those of our ancestors. As soon as they make their choice, we will have to bury our great Chief Koko in peace, and with love."

The Piaiman, the Priest, and the five elders stepped into the benab to discuss, and choose the new Chief.

The Piaiman said, "My brothers, we have a very easy decision to make, and we must do this quickly. The people expect this, and then we can prepare for Chief Koko's funeral."

The Priest said, "If we appoint Onida as our new Chief, we will have to consider how young she is at only fifteen years. We have to think about her future studies away from here, and whether she will want to take on this tough responsibility at this time."

The Piaiman nodded, and said, "You are right Father. No one can deny that Onida has been carefully groomed to become our Chief, and indeed, the leader of all our peoples of Kayana. So, we have to ask ourselves whether this is the right time for her to take on such a huge responsibility."

One elder said, "I agree with you. But who else can we choose until Onida becomes old enough to take over?"

The Priest said, "Well, there is Peter who has been coaching and mentoring Onida for many years with the blessings of Chief Koko, and all of us."

The Piaiman said, "That is a good idea as we can all support him until Onida is ready. The only problem is that our Chiefs are appointed for life. Besides, I do not think that our people will accept such a situation. You have already heard how passionate they are about Onida being our new Chief."

Another elder said, "I think that we must appoint Onida now, and give Peter a title to make him her official guardian. Of course we will all be here to support them both."

The Piaiman nodded, and said, "I think that your suggestion makes sense. So, let me announce Onida as our new Chief with Peter as her guardian, and we can allow her to continue with her education whilst we all help to manage the community under her instruction. She already has a wise head on her young shoulders, along with the love and respect of everyone here in the settlement, and in the outside world."

They all raised their right hands in agreement, and the Piaiman strode to the doorway of the benab. The community had waited patiently for the meeting to be concluded, and for the announcement to be made.

The Piaiman raised his arms aloft, and said, "Oh Great Spirit, thank you for guiding us to make our decision today. We have listened to the voices of our elders, and our people, and we have made our choice. I now say to all the people here, and across the whole of Kayana, that our new Chief is our dear Onida!"

The entire gathering raised their hands in the air to acknowledge their new leader.

The Piaiman said, "We also wish to tell you that we have appointed our brother Peter to continue to be her guide, teacher, and mentor. And we also expect that Onida will continue with her studies. Our elders, Peter, and myself will do our best to carry out whatever our new Chief asks us to do. Now, let us prepare to give our beloved Chief Koko her peace in our garden of rest. Then we will perform the ceremony to anoint our new Chief."

Everyone applauded the decision to appoint Onida as the new Chief of the settlement. However, this moment of real joy for the people was quickly turned into one of sorrow once again as their attention was directed to the arrangements for Chief Koko's funeral.

The Piaiman said, "We need to send our request for all the Chiefs of Kayana, Mr Jennings of the mining company, Mr Holmes of our new Chief's school, and other friends of our people, to assemble here to witness the funeral of our great Chief. Let us give her a send-off that is befitting one of our greatest leaders in our history."

The Piaiman then placed the headband which Chief Koko wore as Chief, onto Onida's head. It was made of fine cane, and adorned with three feathers placed at the front. One was of the Harpy eagle, placed in the middle, and flanked by one of a toucan, on the right, and a macaw, on the left. She bowed gracefully before the Piaiman, and he smiled.

He said, "All hail our new Chief Onida of Kayana!"

EIGHTEEN

THE CHOSEN ONE

C hief Koko's funeral ceremony was a quiet, and dignified event in keeping with her wishes. The Piaiman, who led the traditional Kayanese prayers, revealed that Chief Koko had left specific instructions to him. It was written in the Kayanese language, and sealed in a large brown envelope only to be opened on the day of her passing. She had also included a statement that she wanted to be read out, and to be passed on to her successor.

Most of the invitees had managed to arrive at the settlement in good time before the start of the ceremony. Some of the Chiefs of tribes which were more remote in the South and South West of Kayana, could not secure the right transportation to be on time for the funeral, but decided to stay on to witness the anointment of Onida as the new Chief, and to celebrate her fifteen years.

Chief Koko's body was wrapped in white cotton, and placed in a specially woven cane coffin. It was then taken by a group of young warriors who wore red and black markings on their faces and body. They carefully placed the coffin on a table in the middle of the square. The Piaiman and the Priest stood side by side in front of the coffin, and all the guests and the community formed a large unbroken circle facing it.

John Jennings and Mr Holmes stood directly opposite each other, and all the other Chiefs present completed an inner circle around Chief Koko. Chief Onida and Peter then walked slowly from the benab to take up their positions at the toe end of the coffin.

The Piaiman recited the prayers for the interment after welcoming everyone, and passing on the messages from those who could not attend. Members of the Kayana government and opposition leaders, then walked up to stand just behind Chief Onida and Peter.

The Piaiman opened Chief Koko's envelope, and began to read her statement.

"Oh Great Spirit, now that you have called for me, and I have done my work here on Mother Earth, I have this message for all the peoples of Kayana, and especially for our new Chief. We are all here to live a simple life of peace, service, and respect for our environment. We are all part of nature's grand plan and laws. Everything in this world has a spirit, and the spirit world is everything. Everything depends on the functioning of all that is around us. What the trees breathe out we as humans breathe in, and what we breathe out, the trees breathe in. If we change this law, we will all eventually die, and so will our planet. We as humans like to live in our communities. We have and love our families, and all families must work for each other. But our peoples also rely on the communities of our trees and plants. A tree does not grow tall on its own. It has many plants living at its base. These plants also provide us with food and medicine, as well as good protection for the tree's roots. When we cut down a large tree, we kill its community. When we say that we will plant a sapling to replace a tree to rebuild the forest, we do not build what nature requires. Please learn these lessons because we are not saving the environment in this way."

The Piaiman paused, took a sip of water, and continued, "I ask you to love our jaguars, our eagles, our monkeys, our macaws, our toucans, our otters, our fish, our snakes, and all other creatures. Use only what you need, and do not profit from them. I do not agree with blasting and hurting Mother Earth for gold and diamonds. They have been here long before mankind and money, and they will still be here long after the money is burnt to ashes. We have proved for thousands of years that we can live well without money and greed. My spirit will never rest until the mining and deforestation ends here in Kayana, and the rest of the world."

The Piaiman turned the paper over. He looked up at John Jennings and the politicians, and then at the statement. Chief Onida's gaze was firmly fixed at Chief Koko's face, as the Piaiman continued to read.

"My people, please continue to listen to your elders, the Piaiman, and your new Chief. They have all the wisdom and knowledge we need to continue to live our lives with contentment, and happiness. We Kayanese are very peaceful people. But we must also be prepared to stand up for what we believe in. Stay strong with your leaders, and

79

preserve this land of ours. Our new Chief must also stand firm, and unite all our peoples of Kayana. We must not move from this place, and let no one say that they are giving you your rights. This land has been here even before our ancestors arrived thousands of years ago. And finally, like the jaguar, my spirit will be with you all forever. I love you all."

Remarkably, as the Piaiman paused at that point, he looked around the circles of the hosts and their guests, and seemed to sense that something was not quite right. Chief Onida's macaw and toucan bobbed up and down on her shoulders. Then, in the corner of his eyes, he barely saw the jaguar lurking behind some bushes at the edge of the square.

The Piaiman said, "I can see that the time has arrived for the body of our beloved Chief Koko to be taken to the place of eternal rest."

Peter and the elders covered the coffin, and with the Piaiman's permission, they slowly lifted it and carried it to the grave next to that of Chief Onida's mother. The Priest stepped forward to say the final prayers, and Chief Koko was put to rest.

As soon as the burial was over, Chief Onida briskly walked away to the benab. She could not contain her sobbing as she sat in her hammock facing Chief Koko's.

Peter was very concerned about Chief Onida's sudden departure from the cemetery. He quickly joined her at the benab.

He asked, "Chief, how are you?"

She continued to sob, and tried to ignore him.

He said, "Chief, I know how painful Chief Koko's loss is to us all, and you in particular. But please try to compose yourself for the ceremony to crown you as Chief."

Chief Onida said, "Peter, I am just too young to be your Chief. I can never fulfil what Chief Koko has asked for. It is too much for me."

Peter said, "Chief Koko really meant that you and all of us can do everything to protect our people, our land, and our rights. She does not mean that it will be all down to you alone."

Chief Onida wiped away her tears, and said, "I need to complete my education first, and then I shall be able, and be more prepared to lead this community. But Chief Koko is also asking for the unity of all the Indigenous Peoples in Kayana. I cannot do this at my age."

Peter said, "Chief Koko was a very strong person who, despite her size and age, always stood up for all of us. Likewise, you are also strong, educated, and have the love of our people. Also, the Great Spirit and all of our ancestors' spirits are here to guide and support us."

Chief Onida said, "I hear what you say, but my heart is aching at the moment. My mind is all confused, and my body is not strong enough to carry this kind of responsibility."

Peter said, "Chief, we are all here for you. Please think again, and accept our wishes. Please accept also, the wishes of our Great Spirit, and those of Chief Koko."

Chief Onida asked, "And what will happen if I refuse to be your Chief?"

Peter said, "I am here for you whatever you decide to do. This is my duty towards you."

Chief Onida stood up from her hammock, and embraced Peter.

She said, "Peter, you have been like a father and big brother to me. You have also been my teacher, and my guide. If you say that I can do this, then I have to believe you. So, let's do the ceremony."

Peter smiled, and said, "Chief Onida, you are the chosen one!"

NINETEEN

THE TREK

When the community and special guests saw the new Chief and Peter emerge from the benab, they greeted them with sustained applause.

Peter said, "Today has been a very hard one for us all. Our dearest Chief Koko has been laid to rest, but I believe that her spirit is still here with us to witness the crowning of our new Chief Onida of Kayana!"

The Piaiman held the simple headdress of three feathers firmly attached at the front of the neatly woven cane base, and raised it above Chief Onida's head. He recited an ancient Kayanese prayer for long life, and strength for the new Chief, before he gently placed it on her head.

He then announced, "Praise be to our new Chief Onida Ana! I have chosen this name which has been handed down by our ancestors over five hundred years ago. Chief Onida Ana is our chosen one who is here to liberate us all in Kayana. She will lead our fight for our rights, for our land, and for our forests. May the Great Spirit and all of our ancestral spirits guide her every step of the way from this moment onwards."

The entire gathering, including all the other Chiefs who had finally arrived after Chief Koko's funeral, raised their arms in the air, and acknowledged the new Chief in their own way.

Chief Onida Ana stood between Peter and the Piaiman, and although only about five feet tall, she adopted an air of regal elegance, and authority. Her headdress on her head added about another foot to her height and stature, and thus made her stand out beside her taller companions.

She said, "My elders, my people, and honoured guests, thank you for your show of great warmth, and friendship. I am very happy to be made Chief, and to have my mentor, Peter, to help me. He has always been my guide for most of my life. I promise to serve all of our peoples in the way they wish me to. You have all heard what my great grandmother has set out for us all to try to achieve. I look to all of you to help me with this. Thank you all for coming, and I hope that you will enjoy the food and refreshments we have set out for you. Then, I wish all of you who have long journeys, to have the safest return to your people."

Everyone cheered the new Chief Onida Ana, and then settled down to a programme of entertainment with traditional songs and dances, followed by a wholesome meal.

Very early the next morning, Chief Onida Ana awoke, and tiptoed out of the benab taking care not to disturb her friends Ruby Smith, Indra Persaud, and Mary Brown who had been invited to stay over, and spend the next two weeks of their school vacation with her.

Chief Onida Ana, without wearing her Chief's headdress, walked the short distance to the creek, and dived into the cold, dark brown fresh water for a short swim. She made sure that no one was watching as she quickly left the creek, and rushed back to her benab, to change her sodden wet clothes.

Shortly afterwards, Ruby, Indra, and Mary awoke, and sat up in their hammocks.

Chief Onida Ana asked, "Did you all sleep well?"

Ruby said, "Yes thank you. At first I could not get used to the buzzing noises from the forest, but I eventually fell into a deep sleep."

Indra yawned, and said, "Well, I felt a bit scared of the darkness, and shut my eyes until I fell asleep."

Mary said, "I was just too tired to notice anything, and just fell asleep like a log, as soon as I lay down in this hammock."

Ruby asked, "Onida, from now on, what must we call you? Do we say Chief? Or, Onida? Or, Onida Ana? Or, Chief Onida Ana?"

Chief Onida Ana said, "To be honest, I do not know. But it feels strange to be called Chief Onida Ana. I guess you can call me Onida as you have always done. But I think that everyone here may address me as Chief Onida Ana."

She continued, "You can all go down to the creek for your wash, and I will come along with you. The water is a little cold, but it is clean, and you will soon get used to it. It is very refreshing. Do take your towels and soap with you. Afterwards we will eat some food, and then go for our first trek into the forest. Peter and a few of our young warriors will guide and protect us."

Ruby, Indra, and Mary enjoyed their early morning swim in the creek. Chief Onida Ana ensured that their privacy was maintained as she turned away all other intended users from the settlement. The four friends then hurried back to the benab where they changed into similar white cotton tee-shirts, dark brown khaki trousers, and white sneakers. Ruby, Indra and Mary opted for similar baseball caps whilst Chief Onida Ana combed her long black hair into two plaits at the back. They all carried their rucksacks packed with supplies for the trip.

Peter and five young warriors arrived in front of the benab, armed with hunting knives, arrows and bows, and blowpipes, as well as cutlasses. Peter also proudly held a rifle, and a waistband with reserve bullets. His uniform was a short-sleeved khaki shirt along with full length khaki trousers and his well-worn leather boots. The warriors wore khaki shorts and nothing above their waists. They were all barefooted.

Peter said, "Today we will go as far into the jungle as we can during daylight, have an exploration, take some rest with our lunch, and then return home before sunset. I have told the elders and the Piaiman where we are heading towards, and that we will leave markers along the way just in case we do not return as planned. Myself and two warriors will always be at the front of Chief Onida Ana and you three young ladies. And, the other three warriors will be behind us. Any questions?"

Ruby asked, "What do we do if we are attacked by jaguars?"

Peter smiled, and said, "Jaguars do not come out looking for people during the daylight hours. They may be nearby, and may be watching. Besides, our Howler monkeys will be on the lookout, and we will all be warned of any such dangers."

Indra asked, "And what about snakes and spiders, and big red ants?"

Peter said, "Keep your eyes open at all times, and be careful where you walk. We will try our best to keep on some well-known and well-used tracks, so we should not have such encounters. But if we do see snakes, we must leave them alone, and proceed out of their way. Ants and spiders will be using the long hanging vines or the tree trunks. So, look carefully before you place your hands there."

Mary held Ruby's and Indra's hands tightly, and asked, "And what about other tribes, and robbers?"

Peter said, "Please do not worry about this. There are no other tribes living in this area. But if we meet anyone, I will deal with the situation. Regarding robbers, we have not had any problems with such people for a very long time now. So I am not expecting to see any. Have you got any other questions?"

Chief Onida Ana and her three friends shook their heads.

Peter said, "Right, let's get going. Do keep close together at all times. Try to relax, and enjoy the peace and beauty of nature. If at any time you wish to have a rest just let me know."

The party set out as planned, and the first few hundred yards were simple, and uncomplicated along the well-used tracks. This allowed the girls to become more used to the terrain, and the environment around them. A small group of Howler monkeys seemed to be following the party as they swung from limb to limb high up into the canopy. Other Howler monkeys could be heard well into the distance. Kassi the toucan, and Kori the macaw, perched quietly onto Chief Onida Ana's shoulders, and at times jumped onto the shoulders of her three friends.

The mid-morning sun's rays began to be noticed through the canopy, and casted shimmering streams of light through to the forest floor. The temperature and humidity were still reasonably comfortable, and this helped the party to make good progress.

A sudden increase in frantic howling caused Peter to stop. He put his right index finger to his lips to ask for silence from the group.

He whispered, "Keep still. Do not move. Look carefully around you."

He then held his rifle higher up across his chest, and then crouched down to peer through the surrounding undergrowth. He could not see anyone, and then as the howling stopped, he stood up.

Peter said, "Right. I could not see anything. But be alert. I think that a jaguar must have been seen by the Howlers. Don't worry. No danger. Let's continue."

The girls looked at each other, smiled nervously, and continued to follow Peter. The five warriors kept quiet, and were always scanning the area around looking for any sign of danger.

Further into the forest, the track that was chosen by Peter began to fade away as it was overtaken by over-hanging limbs, vines, and bushes spread across the barely visible path. The warriors took out their well sharpened cutlasses, and began to hack away at any obstruction. The party's progress became much slower, and everyone began to perspire greatly through the extra effort to clear the path, and the increasing humidity.

When they reached a small clearing at the base of a giant greenheart tree, Peter called a halt.

He said, "Let's take a rest here. Have some water, and if you wish to go further, do let me know. Are you alright?"

Chief Onida Ana said, as she opened her bottle of water, "I am fine. Are you girls OK?"

The three friends nodded, and took long drinks from their water bottles. The warriors sat on their haunches, and accepted bottles of water from Peter.

He said, "We are sitting under one of the oldest trees in this forest. It is a greenheart, and is many centuries old. The large grooves at the base allow a kind of hollow sound which was used by our ancestors to send messages. So, if I hit this part of the base it can be heard from afar."

Peter used the butt of his rifle to hit the base, and the hollow sound caused the Howler monkeys to respond.

He continued, "This tree is one of the toughest, and most resilient in our forests. They are so sturdy that the houses and harbours made with greenheart wood will last for hundreds of years. But we must preserve them, as this strength is also the strength of the forest. Kill them, and we do not only kill the forest, but the world. The mahogany tree over there is a relative of the greenheart, and is normally used to make beautiful furniture, and small souvenir pieces. Again, we must try to save these beautiful trees, and look for other materials for our use."

The party rested for another half hour, ensuring that they did not drink too much of their supplies of bottled water.

Peter asked, "Are you alright? Can we continue? Or, would you like to turn back, and head towards home?"

Chief Onida Ana said, "We have come so far, and as it is still very early in the day, let us go ahead, and then see how we feel after another hour or so."

Only about fifteen minutes into their further trek into the jungle, one of the warriors walking beside Peter, stopped suddenly. Then, without warning, a trap opened up, and he fell into a dark pit. The three friends of Chief Onida Ana held their hands to their faces, and screamed.

TWENTY

FORBIDDEN

P eter asked Chief Onida Ana and her friends to step back into the path that they had just taken. Then he and the other four warriors checked the trap to find out whether there was any sign of life from the bottom of the pit. He called out for the young warrior. But the Howler monkeys were screaming so loudly that he could barely hear the faint sound from the entrapped victim.

Peter and the other warriors then carefully cleared away the debris which had hidden the trap, and checked for any other similar traps in the surrounding area. They found one more on the right side of the track, and then commenced their rescue attempt.

A long and very strong vine was cut from one of the tall trees which partially obscured a huge mound covered with bushes, and more trees entangled with even larger vines. Peter carefully knelt down by an edge of the pit, and lowered the vine towards the warrior.

After securing a strong grip onto the vine, Peter and the four warriors began to pull up the stricken young man. They held firm for a short while, and then Peter gave the instruction to "Pull!" After each pull, they paused, and when the entrapped warrior confirmed that he was making progress, Peter and his team hoisted with great effort. Eventually, they managed to pull him to safety over the edge of the pit. He was covered with black dirt, but was unharmed. One of the warriors used a small branch to brush the dust off the young man. Peter then gave him a bottle of water to drink.

Peter asked him, "How are you feeling now?"

The young warrior, still visibly shaken from his ordeal, said, "I am well. Lots of bones down there. We must get out of here."

Peter looked at Chief Onida Ana, and said, "This place is forbidden. No one should come here. We must not go any further beyond that mound. Let us go back to the settlement now. Soon it will get too dark."

Chief Onida Ana nodded, and said, "Let our warrior rest for a while, and then we can go back. It will be better for us all."

Ruby, shaking with fear, said, "Chief, I am not walking back. I want to run like mad!"

Mary, with her big round eyes fully open with terror, said, "I don't want to be here anymore. I am really scared."

Indra held Mary's hands, and said, "Me too! But let us keep calm, and we will be alright. Chief, please let us go back now."

The rescued warrior nodded, and said, "I'm OK. Let's go back. I need to wash this dirt off my body."

The group set off at a fast pace, and after they reached the clear open pathway leading directly to the settlement, they slowed down through sheer tiredness. Peter suggested that they should take a rest at the same greenheart tree they had used earlier on in the day.

He said, "I must tell you that I had never been so deep into the forest in all my years of exploring the area. Chief, do you know what that place is?"

Chief Onida Ana took a sip from her water bottle, and said, "Yes, Chief Koko had told me about it. I cannot say anymore at the moment as it is forbidden to talk about, and to explore. Please promise me that no one here will ever mention this place to anyone else, and, what happened on this trip. Peter, we must ask the Piaiman to say a prayer for our brave warrior to ward off any evil spirit from him."

The girls asked, "Evil spirit?"

Chief Onida Ana said, "There are no evil spirits here, but just as a precaution, the Piaiman will do a blessing for us all. We were guided there and back by good spirits. So please do not worry."

Kassi and Kori who had remained quiet through the trek, flapped their wings, and then settled down on Chief Onida Ana's shoulders. The Howler monkeys stopped following the group and disappeared high into the canopy, seemingly chattering amongst themselves.

The next day, Chief Onida Ana got up early, and whilst her three friends were fast asleep, she walked over to Peter's home. He was already up, and promptly answered the knock on his front door.

He asked, "Hello Chief. What can I do for you today?"

Chief Onida Ana entered the house, and took a seat on one of Peter's mahogany chairs in his small living room. He sat down on one opposite the Chief's.

She said, "I need to talk to you about yesterday's trek. In particular, about the site we got very near to."

Peter handed Chief Onida Ana a bottle of water, and said, "Yes. I never knew about that place. But you said that Chief Koko told you about it. Can you tell me what it is all about?"

Chief Onida Ana took a sip from the bottle, and said, "Well, as I said, it is forbidden for anyone to go there. But Chief Koko said that I will need to unlock its mysteries. It contains the future of Kayana, and of all our peoples."

Peter asked, "Do you mean all of our Indigenous Peoples, or all the citizens of Kayana?"

Chief Onida Ana leaned forward, and said, "All the peoples of all the tribes of Kayanese here in Kayana, all the Indigenous Peoples everywhere, and, also the other citizens of this country."

Peter sat back, and said, "Wow! That is truly amazing. How do you propose to do this? And, when?"

Chief Onida Ana said, "I am very worried that my friends have seen this place, and they may easily give the secret away. So we need to do this very soon."

Peter asked, "Do you mean that we must do more exploration of the site? Bear in mind that our five young warriors will also be intrigued, but frightened to go there."

Chief Onida Ana said, "Yes, I will speak to them, and you will also have to keep your eyes and ears open when I am away."

Peter said, "Even if we have to go there with a small team, we will need a lot of help including certain equipment. For example, the trees and other large overgrowths hiding whatever is behind them will require a lot of heavy duty cutters, and other machinery. We cannot clear much of that covering with our bare hands and cutlasses."

Chief Onida Ana nodded, and said, "Yes, we need to plan for this very carefully, work out what we need, and only take people we can trust."

Peter asked, "Are you going to tell the elders and the Piaiman?"

Chief Onida Ana said firmly, "Oh no! We have to keep this as our secret. If and when we do find a temple or a complete city, then we can tell the world."

Peter asked, "Do you think that it is a lost city?"

Chief Onida Ana said, "Chief Koko did not say that it was a lost city. But she said that our ancestors never wanted us to leave this settlement."

Peter drank from his water bottle, and said, "I understand what you are saying. This is what Chief Koko meant when we were under threat by others. She always insisted that no matter what the provocation, we must never abandon this place."

Chief Onida Ana said, "Well, let this vacation pass, and the girls and I return to school. I will draw up a plan, and let you see it when we return in between term time. You can also think about what we will need for our expedition. I am really excited about this!"

Peter said, "Please speak with your friends, and I will do the same with our warriors."

TWENTY-ONE

UNLOCKING DOORS

Three years later, in July 2018, Chief Onida Ana and her friends passed their senior high school examinations with flying colours. They had become inseparable as friends. Ruby excelled in mathematics, and won a place in Kayana's best Accountancy College. Indra and Mary continued to pursue their interests in botany, and enrolled to study the science at Kayana's only University in the Capital City of the Central Region.

Due to her status as Chief of her people, and her interest in history, Chief Onida Ana was advised by Miss Isobel Rodrigues to take up a place at the University of Kayana, to study Political Science.

Upon her return to her settlement, having bade her friends goodbye and good fortune, Chief Onida Ana decided to discuss her next step with Peter, the Piaiman, and a group of elders.

She welcomed her guests to the benab, and after a special lunch, she broached the subject.

She said, "Thank you all for coming to discuss my future plans."

Peter said, "Chief Onida Ana, we are all so proud of you. Your success has inspired many of our younger children and youths to take up studying much more seriously."

The Piaiman smiled, and said, "And like you, they are all so bright, and doing very well."

The first, and oldest of the elders frowned, and said, "It is good to see our children and grandchildren learn so much. But they are neglecting our language, and our customs. They are only learning about things from outside of our culture. Then, just like what is already happening in our other tribes in all the four regions of Kayana, the educated ones are leaving their villages, and going far away to find work. This is not what our ancestors wanted."

A second elder said, "I agree with you. Our Chief Onida Ana has learnt a lot about our culture, beliefs, language, and so on. She also knows about the outside world, and must now stay here to lead us forward. We must regain our country, and take back control from all the others who were brought here by the Spanish, Dutch, and English. But first, we Kayanese of all the tribes here, must unite, and that is what our Chief must work on."

Peter said, "Your words are wise. You speak from your hearts. I am sure that our Chief Onida Ana has listened carefully. You talk about the past, the present, and the future. This is very important."

The Piaiman said, "As we sit here, so far away from the people who govern Kayana, and the place they have their big council called parliament, we will never be heard, nor understood. So, I say that our Chief must go there to study the politics, and that will give her the keys to unlock the doors to real power in this land. I also agree that we need to unite all of our Indigenous Peoples."

The third elder said, "You are all correct in what you think, and what you say. How long will our Chief go away for at the great school in the city?"

Chief Onida Ana said, "Three years, and I will graduate with a Bachelor of Arts in Political Science."

Peter smiled, and asked, "Chief, how can you become a bachelor when you are an unmarried lady? And, how is Politics a Science?"

They all laughed. Chief Onida Ana then explained that her designation will not matter, but her knowledge will be great.

The fourth elder smiled, and said, "My dear Chief, three years will be a very long time to be away from your job of leading us. I know that Peter, our Piaiman, our Priest, and we the elders will always work together for our people."

Peter said, "Well, our Chief will not just be away for such a long time. She will be in close touch with us by using the computer system, and the telephone. She will also return to be with us from time to time, and for all of our special celebrations."

Chief Onida Ana said, "I also need to talk about what happens after we get all of our tribes together. We will all need to agree as to how we can then convince the other citizens of Kayana that we must unite as one nation or one country."

Peter asked, "And what will happen to this place?"

Chief Onida Ana said, "Peter and I, and a few others have kept a secret from you for the past three years. But I think that before I go away, we must quietly put our plan to explore the forbidden city of our ancestors. This is the reason why we must stay here."

Peter looked up with surprise, and asked, "Are you sure that we must do this now?"

The Piaiman asked, "What city are you talking about? What is this great secret?"

Peter said, "Our Chief and I had found a place which was abandoned by our ancestors, and which Chief Koko had told her about."

The first elder frowned, and said, "If this so called city is abandoned and forbidden, we must not go there. It can bring great harm to all of us."

The second elder said, "I understand you my brother, but we must do as Chief Koko and Chief Onida Ana wish. I do not want to see this place, and most of our people will agree that we do not go there."

The other elders nodded in agreement.

The Piaiman raised his right hand, and said, "Gentlemen, I understand your fears. But let us all agree to support our Chief in this quest. The Great Spirit and the spirits of our ancestors will guide and protect us."

Peter said, "Thank you. The Chief and I have been working on this plan to explore the site, and at last we can take a small group of warriors, and some equipment, and have a look. If it is too big for us to complete, then we will return to talk about what we must do next."

The Chief said, "Good. We must still keep this a secret. We will not involve the government or the mining company. This is our history, and we must protect it for now, and the future. Chief Koko told me that all of our Chiefs had kept this secret for over the last five hundred years. It is the main reason why we must never leave this settlement."

Very early the next morning, Chief Onida Ana and her group of explorers gathered just outside of the benab. The Piaiman and the five elders stood beside the Chief and Peter. The original five young warriors were joined by another five of the most able-bodied young men from the settlement.

The Piaiman recited a short prayer in Kayanese, and said, "I am not joining you on this great mission, but Reverend Henry Small has agreed to be with you. He is an experienced trekker, and explorer. Our elders will stay here with me, and await your return. This mission has been planned for a very long time by our Chief and Peter. Now, I hand over to them to tell you more about it. May our Great Spirit and the spirits of our ancestors always stay with you, protect you, and guide you to success."

Reverend Small clasped his hands, and said, "Amen."

Chief Onida Ana, wearing her special headdress, said, "We have been blessed today to be able to go on this very important mission. Peter and I, and our brave warriors know where we are heading to. When we get there we must be very careful as to where we walk, and what we touch. Hopefully, it will not take us too long to discover what that ancient city is about."

Peter, with his rifle in his right hand, said, "Have no fear as we are all trained warriors. But we must stay alongside each other at all times. Please listen to my instructions. I am your leader for this mission, and our Chief will advise as needed."

The party left the village with Chief Onida Ana and Peter at the head, and Reverend Small just in front of the ten warriors following in single file. Their progress in the first two hours was fast, and after a short rest at the giant greenheart tree, they ploughed on. Progress was slowed down by a fresh set of undergrowth which had crept over the clearing that was made during their last trek over three years earlier.

Finally, as the evening began to close in, the group found a small, and less overgrown area, and Peter gave his orders to pitch tent there. The group took great care not to cause any commotion amongst the Howler monkeys, other animals such as sloths, and, birds in the vicinity.

The group enjoyed a meal of fried catfish and cassava bread. Chief Onida Ana advised them to try to conserve their bottled water, and not to throw away any empty containers.

After a much needed extended rest through a trouble-free evening, the party woke up to the familiar sounds of the forest. A short burst of thunder and lightning was followed by about fifteen minutes of heavy rainfall. Those with empty water bottles were able to refill them with the clean, and fresh rainwater.

Two of the warriors, along with Reverend Small, discovered a small creek only a few hundred yards from the camp, and everyone in the group enjoyed a refreshing dip in the dark brown, and cool water.

The group then set out on their trek after a light breakfast, and within a few minutes, Peter suddenly stopped near to the two traps which were covered over by dried leaves. He carefully led everyone through, by clearing a new path towards the wall ahead which was covered with vines, and numerous other plants.

He marked out the area directly ahead of the path, and after vigorously chopping the growth away, the outline of a great wooden gate could be seen. He carefully stepped through a slight opening, and stood back in awe.

Chief Onida Ana said, "This is exactly how Chief Koko described the entrance to the lost city. Now we must be very careful how we walk as she told me about how the entire site is guarded by large snakes and scorpions."

Reverend Small fell to his knees, and offered a short prayer, "Oh Lord, thank you for your mercy. Please lead us safely through this sacred door to our past, and to our future. Amen."

TWENTY-TWO

WARM EMBRACE

P eter stooped down, and peered intensely through the undergrowth directly ahead of the opening. He then raised his rifle, and took aim at something that appeared to move amongst the low level bushes.

He whispered, "Everyone, stay as you are. Don't move. I can see a giant anaconda."

He then prepared to shoot the snake which began to move towards him, and the group.

Chief Onida Ana whispered, "No Peter. Do not shoot. This must be one of the giant snakes left to guard this place."

All the warriors also raised their bows, and aimed at the slowly approaching anaconda. It was about twenty yards away, and as it began to move faster, a lone jaguar appeared from the left, and attacked the snake. It sank its sharp teeth into the neck of the snake, and in the vicious struggle, the snake managed to wrap its tail around the hind legs and torso of the jaguar. As the anaconda began to apply its formidable squeezing pressure, the jaguar was forced to release its grip on its neck. It then fought fiercely to release the tightening hold of the snake by clawing and biting at its tail.

The fight continued for another few minutes as the Chief and her group looked on in astonishment. The anaconda began to extend its hold on the struggling jaguar whose snarls and growls became more of agonising pain than threats.

Chief Onida Ana looked at Peter, and as she nodded, he fired a round at the head of the anaconda, and as it reeled back, its grip began to loosen. The jaguar managed to wrench itself from the snake, and crawled away into the undergrowth. The badly maimed anaconda also turned, and slithered away deeper into the bushes.

The warriors lowered their bows and arrows, and continued to look closely into the bushes ahead, and around the group.

Chief Onida Ana said, "Thank you Peter. I hope that both the anaconda and the jaguar will survive their fight. We must now be much more careful as we move onwards."

Peter looked down at the path they were standing on, and said, "We need to stick to this pathway, and cut through further into the area ahead. Be careful Chief, as the loose stones on this pathway can cause us to trip over."

The group took greater care to chop their way along the pathway which finally led up to a set of stone steps about twelve feet wide, and rising to about twenty feet high. They laboured for at least another hour, and managed to clear away ten flights of stairs which led up to a high stone structure.

Peter called a halt to the work, and suggested that the group should rest on top of the cleared stairway.

He said, "This is really exciting. But it is getting harder for us to clear so much tough vines and bushes. Chief, we will need more help, as this is a vast complex."

Reverend Henry Small clasped his hands as if in prayer, and said, "I thank the Lord for getting us thus far, and in safety. I think that we have seen enough, and we should leave this place now. There must be more jaguars and snakes here, and I am very frightened for all of us."

Chief Onida Ana said, "I agree that it is very dangerous here. But, I need to know more about what is actually ahead of those steps. We can take more rest, and then do some more clearing to get up to the top of this stairway."

Peter said, "OK Chief. We will do as you suggest, but no more on this mission. We can always return to explore more of the structure here, and whatever else is beyond this entrance."

The warriors settled down on a couple of rungs of the stairway speaking amongst themselves in Kayanese. They seemed reluctant to continue with the mission.

Chief Onida Ana addressed the warriors directly, and said, "I know that you are all frightened. But our Great Spirit and Chief Koko are with us, and will continue to protect us all. Please stay with us for a bit more, and then we can return to the settlement tomorrow morning."

Reverend Small said, "Chief Onida Ana and Peter, I am very keen for us to go back this afternoon, and not tomorrow. I do not know what is here, and can attack us at night."

Peter said, "I understand reverend. But we are already very tired, and darkness will catch up with us well before we reach our homes. So, please bear with us, and stay until tomorrow."

The group then continued to work their way up to the top of the stairway, and as they stood at the highest step, they looked around in awe.

Chief Onida Ana smiled, and said, "This is truly amazing! We are at the main gateway of such a vast ancient city. I now feel a great urge to continue."

Peter said, "You are right. It is truly magnificent! This must be Kayana's greatest city!"

Reverend Small dropped to his knees, clasped his hands tightly, and said, "Please Lord God, bless us all for this discovery. This is sacred to all of our peoples of Kayana. Amen."

The warriors also looked around at the vast complex of several huge buildings covered in blankets of trees and plants. They stood quietly, and just absorbed the spectacle of their civilisation spread out around them.

A large flock of blue and yellow macaws rose out of one of the trees covering a building, swirled around, and then alighted onto another one further into the complex. A group of Howler monkeys could be heard further ahead as if they were calling the Chief and her companions forward. A giant sloth lazily hung its long claws along a branch of a large greenheart tree that appeared to be in the middle of an area which could have been a square bustling with the city's dwellers. Beyond the square, stood the magnificent remains of a temple.

Chief Onida Ana said, "As your Chief, I must ask all of you to refrain from discussing this place with anyone, at least until I have spoken with the Piaiman and our elders. This is our secret, and it is strictly forbidden for anyone to trespass here without my permission. There must be a real purpose for this amazing place which belongs to our peoples of Kayana, and we will preserve it for our children to come."

Peter asked for silence, and then pointed ahead of the group.

He said, "The jaguar is alive, and looking at us very closely."

Chief Onida Ana said, "He must be one of our ancestors, and appears to be trying to protect us. I hope that the anaconda is also alive and well. They are the true guardians of the city."

Reverend Small said, "Yes Chief, that jaguar must have been following us all the time."

Peter said, "He is guiding us, and I am very tempted for us to continue with this mission. I feel as if I am being pulled into this place by a strong force."

Chief Onida Ana said, "Well, let us stay here for the night, and we can decide as to what to do in the morning."

The group then completed clearing the top of the steps up to the large doorway, and as the sun dipped in the horizon, they settled down for their evening meal and rest. The warriors continued to chatter in Kayanese until they all succumbed to deep sleep. Peter and Reverend Small agreed to take turns to keep watch through the night. Chief Onida Ana, feeling greatly tired, drifted off into a deep slumber. A cool breeze took everyone by surprise, and they covered themselves with their brown cotton sheets as mosquitoes and other insects began to buzz around them.

TWENTY-THREE

THE TRAIL OF BLOOD

C hief Onida Ana was the first to wake up the next morning, and she quietly walked through the large entrance of the city, looking for any stream or well to have a wash.

Just a few feet away from where the jaguar had lain, she saw droplets of dark red blood, and decided to follow their trail. Within minutes, she was out of sight of the others, and continued walking beside the blood markings on dead leaves covering the stone pathway.

She heard a faint rustle about fifty yards ahead, and paused to withdraw her hunting knife with her right hand. She crouched down, and looked all around her as she carefully took each step forward. She could not see clearly ahead as the bloodstained trail proceeded in the direction of the new sound of a creature in distress.

The tired purring of the wounded jaguar became louder as Chief Onida Ana crept forward. Then, to her utmost shock, she saw the jaguar breathing heavily, and unable to get up from its position as it lay on its left side. The trail of blood ended in a small pool formed directly under the animal's neck where it was bitten by the anaconda. The jaguar tried to growl with its usual threatening menace, but could hardly do so in its very weakened state.

Chief Onida Ana was unsure about getting any closer to the jaguar, and tried to examine its wounds from a safe distance. A wounded and cornered cat is at its most dangerous in such situations.

She stooped down, and said, "Oh great one, you are in such pain. Stay here, and I will bring help."

The jaguar began to close its eyes as its strength continued to wane. Chief Onida Ana looked further behind and beyond where the jaguar lay, and saw a small doorway of another building which was almost covered by vines and other foliage.

She stood up, and carefully walked past the jaguar. The doorway led her down several stone steps into a darkened corridor. The only light was from a narrow opening in the outer wall. Further along, the bright rays were cast directly onto the middle of a six feet wide walkway which led to another wooden door.

Chief Onida Ana stopped before the door which was dry and rotted so much that she only tentatively pushed at it. The door gave way, and small parts of it fell to the ground. She covered her nose and mouth with the palm of her left hand to avoid inhaling the dust from the rotted wood.

Another flight of stone steps led her to a room about twelve feet square. She was curious as to why such secured doors led only to an empty room. She thought that the place must have been looted in the past. She then rubbed some black soot away from the stone wall directly in front of the stairway.

The cleared soot revealed a lever which she turned gently, and as she pushed against the stone, it slowly opened like a door. This inner chamber contained a set of large urns about five feet high. Each had Kayanese words etched near their rims.

Chief Onida Ana's eyes lit up as she peered into one of the urns. It was packed to the top with gold pieces, and jewellery. This was the fortune left by her ancestors, to be used only for rebuilding the great city. Chief Koko had explained this, and Chief Onida Ana smiled with great pride at her discovery.

She turned and strode briskly out of the building, and as she passed by the ailing jaguar, she saw that it was lying quite still.

She said, "Thank you Great Spirit, for leading me to this place. I will now go to get help for you."

Peter was extremely worried when he saw Chief Onida Ana upon her return to the temporary resting place.

He asked, "Chief, where were you? I was so worried. What happened? What took you so long?"

Chief Onida Ana smiled whilst dusting off her clothing, arms and legs, and said, "Come with me with some warriors. We need to save the jaguar who is dying. We must try to revive him."

Peter asked, "What jaguar? We cannot handle such a dangerous creature. What can we do to save him?"

Chief Onida Ana said, "I will explain everything to you later on. Let's go and bring him out, and look after him in the settlement. The Piaiman may know how to heal his wounds."

A hesitant and nervous Peter, along with four warriors, followed the Chief to the place where the jaguar lay. The men quickly lifted the stricken animal onto a makeshift stretcher, and secured it with vines strapped across its shoulders and hind legs. The four warriors lifted the stretcher onto their shoulders, and carried the jaguar as quickly as they could.

The entire group then quietly embarked on their return journey to the settlement. This time, the group was led by the four warriors carrying the jaguar, followed by the six other warriors, and then Reverend Small, Peter, and Chief Onida Ana.

After one hour into the trek, the four warriors were relieved by four others until the group reached the base of the greenheart tree which was used as their resting place. The jaguar was still breathing faintly, and seemed to be drifting in and out of slumber.

Reverend Small leaned over the jaguar, and examined the snake bites.

He looked up at Peter and the Chief, and said, "I don't think that he will survive this. He has lost a lot of blood, and I am not sure about the damage he suffered from the snake's stranglehold. Why not let him die in peace, and we can bury him here?"

Chief Onida Ana said, "No Reverend! He is very important to me, and to all of us. I have a duty to try to save him. Now, let us not waste any more time, and try to get to the settlement as quickly as possible."

Peter said, "OK everyone. Let's get going!"

The elders were standing in front of the entrance to the benab as the group arrived with their unusual patient. The Piaiman hurried across the square to examine the jaguar after it was gently lowered to the ground. Some children quickly gathered around as the other residents formed a large circle around Chief Onida Ana and her companions.

The Piaiman took out a bottle from his pouch, and poured some liquid onto the jaguar's wounds.

He said, "Peter, we need to take him to a secure area, and wait to see if and when he will wake up. If he doesn't, then there is nothing more I can do to save him."

Peter asked the warriors to tidy up the settlement's large chicken coop, and place the jaguar onto some blankets. The chickens were allowed to roam freely for the evening.

Chief Onida Ana lay in her hammock, and could not sleep despite feeling very tired from the extensive trek. The flame from a small lantern on a mahogany side table flickered, and cast shadows around the benab. She thought long and hard about what to do regarding the discovery of the treasure at the lost city. She knew that everything at the site belonged to her peoples across Kayana.

Should she keep this as a special secret until she felt ready to inform everyone else in the settlement and beyond? Will she be able to hide the presence of the ancient city for as long as she was away at her university? What if the warriors and others who know about the city betray her trust, and either return there or give away information about it? Should she come clean, and tell her most trusted mentor, Peter, about the treasure in the hope of ensuring their security? Could she really trust anyone? Should there be permanent guards placed there to prevent any others from raiding, and looting the site? She tried to close her eyes and sleep. But the questions kept coming to her.

She whispered, "Oh Chief Koko, what would you have done? Please tell me what I must do. Please allow me to do the right thing for our people. Please…"

TWENTY-FOUR

HEALING

Very early the next morning, Chief Onida Ana woke up, and headed directly to the chicken coop where the jaguar was safely kept. She peeped through the wire mesh to where it was left by the warriors. To her great surprise the jaguar had moved from the comfort of the blankets.

She whispered, "Hello Great One. Where are you? Are you well?"

The jaguar snarled, and hissed from the back of the coop, and tried to stand up. Unfortunately, it's hind legs were weak, and it could barely sit up.

Chief Onida Ana said, "Never mind my brave friend. We will keep you here until you regain your strength. Then we will set you free to continue to protect us in the forest."

Peter and the Piaiman joined the Chief, and looked at the jaguar closely.

The Piaiman said, "Thank the Great Spirit for saving his life. I will mix some more of the medicine into his water. But he is still in some pain from the damage to his hind legs. All we can do is to make sure that he is given good rest, and allowed to exercise when he is able to do so."

Peter said, "I hope that the anaconda did not crush his bones."

Chief Onida Ana said, "We can only hope that this brave animal can regain enough strength and healing to allow him to at least limp around. His survival is very important to us all."

The Piaiman nodded, and said, "Yes Chief, every jaguar here in Kayana is very important. We must do our best to save all of them."

Shortly afterwards, a group of Howler monkeys appeared in the tall trees around the settlement. Their red-faced cousins also joined them taking care not to clash with each other. Flocks of both the blue, and red and yellow macaws, as well as the native green parrots arrived, and started to squawk noisily. Other birds assembled amongst the lower branches.

The chickens, pigs, tapir, and dogs of the settlement also seemed to be interested in the ill jaguar, and they loitered around the Chief, Peter, and the Piaiman. Onca, who was fully grown into an ageing giant otter, ambled up from the river bank, and looked up at the Chief who was joined by Kassi and Kori.

The younger children of the settlement soon joined the curious gathering, and jostled each other to try to peer through the mesh of the coop to catch a glimpse of the jaguar. The elders and others joined the assembly.

Chief Onida Ana put her right hand up, and said, "Listen everyone. Our great friend, and protector of our forests, has survived from his snake bites. But he is too lame to stand up or to walk. Please allow him time to rest and heal. He is safe with us, but we must also respect his presence."

Peter said, "Yes Chief. You are right. This brave jaguar needs our care, and the Piaiman's medicines. We hope that the Great Spirit and the spirits of our ancestors will heal him well so that we can set him free."

The Piaiman said, "This jaguar has been watching over us for many years now. He has never attacked us or our animals. So, we owe him great love and care until he makes a full recovery. Please do not tease or provoke him. Let him rest peacefully."

One elder said, "The jaguar is the king of these forests. We have learnt to live with them side by side for centuries. If we do not interfere with them, they will not attack us. They are our brave friends."

Reverend Small said, "Yes, all of God's creatures must be treated with respect. Even the anaconda who fought with this jaguar must be protected by us all. Just respect their space, and we will all continue to live in harmony. May the Lord God bless and protect us all. Amen."

Everyone quietly said, "Amen."

Several days later, the jaguar had fully recovered from the wounds, and effects of the snake bites. The Piaiman was very pleased with the results of his concoction which he had used to treat such bites on humans.

Peter said, "Piaiman, your potion should be studied, and produced for sale."

The Piaiman smiled, and said, "Yes, I have thought about this, but I refuse to do so. I believe that some things that are very important to us and this environment, must remain here. We are too tempted to seek happiness through acquiring money wealth. This is not the way of our peoples, and it is one of the many reasons why we have managed to survive here."

Chief Onida Ana, who had also looked at the jaguar, said, "I agree with our Piaiman. We must try to preserve as many of the good things that we have. His potion is most powerful."

An elder joined the group, and said, "Every time our peoples traded with our knowledge, we have been abused, and made to look stupid. Others have come here to study this environment and our peoples, and just stole our ideas. I blame some of our own ancestors who were easily tempted and sweetened by basic gifts given by white invaders, and others."

Peter said, "Yes sir. Alcohol has been the most dangerous foreign drug which has killed so many of our peoples here in Kayana, and other countries. Trading our gold for pots and pans, and alcohol, has been one of the worst things to hurt our peoples. And, just to add salt into our wounds, we picked up their diseases."

Chief Onida Ana nodded, and said, "This is something which I shall try my best to stop. Our own people who have taken jobs in Mr Jennings' gold mine, have become too sweetened by the money they get. Then they go to the mining town, and drink so much rum until they lose their minds. Many of our beautiful young women have also been sucked into that world of sin and shame. Not only are they used, but they are often beaten up, and raped."

Reverend Small appeared, and said, "Good morning dear friends. How is our patient?"

Peter said, "Good morning Reverend. Our jaguar is well, but still a bit lame. We are talking about the situation of our men and women in the mining town."

Reverend Small said, "Thank you. Yes, I hope to meet up with Mr Jennings about that, and I hope that you and our Chief will join me. Just as we have been trying to heal and protect our caged jaguar, we must seek to free our peoples from their cage of hell."

Chief Onida Ana said, "Yes Reverend, we must do this before I leave for my university."

TWENTY-FIVE

THE TOWN OF SIN

John Jennings agreed to a date and time to meet with Chief Onida Ana, Peter, Reverend Small, and the Piaiman. Prior to the meeting, the visitors decided to go into the mining town to see for themselves, what was happening there, and to speak with their fellow Kayanese.

The town was just a collection of two-storey wooden buildings on either side of a dusty main street which was not made with tarmac. The buildings included a small bank, a bar, a general store, a grocery, and a motel. The population was about three to four hundred people of Kayana. During the daylight hours, the town was dull and boring with very little activity. However, as soon as the sun began to set, and the mine workers returned, it came alive with the sounds of the local music and Indian "Bollywood" songs pouring out from the bar. Whilst the majority of the workers were in the bar, the remainder stood in small groups around the other buildings, or at the kerbs of the main street.

Chief Onida Ana and her companions had chosen to visit just after dark, and she led them into the bar. She was immediately subject to suggestive cat calls from the clients.

One African Kayanese miner, already high under the influence of rum, stepped up to the Chief, and pointed at her face.

He staggered slightly, and asked, "So what is a sweet little thing like you doing here? You looking for business?"

Peter stepped forward, and said, "Please show some respect for our Chief."

The man became more agitated, and said, "Go away! I am speaking to the young lady."

Reverend Small asked, "Are you working at the mine?"

The man said, "No Sir. I do my own mining. I am a porknocker, and so are my three friends here. We have come looking for some fun tonight, and then we will return to our work in the morning."

Peter asked, "And who are the miners from the big mine?"

The porknocker said, "Over there. That bunch of buck men are working there. They like the African and East Indian whores here. But me and my friends prefer the beautiful buck girls."

Chief Onida Ana, visibly annoyed by the man's reference to Indigenous Kayanese as buck, said, "We are Kayana people, and you must show us more respect! We are not buck people!"

The porknocker was joined by his friends, and began to rant, "You go to hell! You people are nothing! We have every right to say and do what we like! Now, go back to your hut and stay there!"

Peter said, "Sir, we do not wish to cause any trouble with you and your friends. So, please go back to your drinking, and do not insult us."

The porknocker was held firmly by his friends as he tried to lunge forward at Peter. They dragged him away as he continued to rant and swear at the Chief and her companions.

Reverend Small ensured that the Chief was composed, and then led the group over to where the young Kayanese women were standing at the far end of the bar counter.

He said, "Good evening ladies. Would you mind speaking with us for a while? I am Reverend Small from the settlement. This is our Chief Onida Ana, and to her right is our Piaiman. Next to me is Peter. Why are you here?"

One of the young women said, "To work Sir."

Reverend Small said, "I can see that you are not from our settlement. Where are you from, and how long have you been working here?"

A second young woman, who appeared to be the oldest of the group, said, "Sir, we have been here for two years now. We made good money, and we take it back to our villages. We are poor, and this is our best way to make money."

Chief Onida Ana asked, "How are you treated here?"

The third young woman said, "Sometimes good, and sometimes bad."

Peter asked, "Who looks after you?"

They all pointed to the East Indian Kayanese man serving behind the two feet wide wooden bar counter.

Chief Onida Ana, still intrigued about the young women, asked, "Are there more girls from your villages here? What does your people say about you, and your work here?"

The first young woman, dressed as scantily as her friends, and on six inches high-heeled shoes, a very short floral skirt, and tight-fitting tee shirt, said, "We do not tell anyone what we do here for our money. But we say that we work at the bar and motel as waitresses, and so on."

Peter asked, "How does your boss treat you? Does he take money from you?"

The second young woman glanced over to their boss, and then said, "He is a good man. He gives us our meals, and we stay in our rooms here for free. But if we do not give him his share, he gets angry with us, and threatens to send us away."

The Piaiman asked, "Do you get medical check-ups?"

The third young woman said, "Yes, but not regularly. We take our own precaution. But we are more worried about the men who get too high, and can't control their temper."

Reverend Small asked, "What happens when someone hurts you?"

The first young woman said, "Our boss and some of his friends just bans those clients who behave badly towards us. But we are still very scared, and unhappy here."

Chief Onida Ana said, "Well, the time must come when you have to stop doing this, and go back to your village. This is not a good life for you to lead. Please listen to us, and make up your own minds before it gets any worse, and you get badly hurt. If any of you cannot go back to your village you are most welcome to come to our settlement, and start a new life."

The fourth young woman said, "It is all well and good for you to say this. But we are desperate for help in our villages, and we have no other choice but to come here. Some of our men from the villages come here to work in the big mine, and they are good to us. We can only do what you say if you can help out our villages."

Peter said, "Yes, we understand, and will try to help you."

Early the next morning, Chief Onida Ana and her group walked across the short distance from the town to John Jennings' office. He welcomed them, and offered coffee, and some chocolate biscuits out of a tin imported from Canada.

John Jennings said, "Chief Onida Ana and friends, thank you for coming over to meet with me. What can I do for you today?"

Chief Onida Ana sat upright in her chair, flanked by Peter on her right, and Reverend Small and the Piaiman on her left.

She said, "Sir, we have come to talk to you about our Indigenous people working in your mine, and what is going on in the local mining town. We visited the town last evening, and saw what was happening. We also spoke with some people there."

John Jennings nodded, and asked, "What was it like? I know about the rum drinking, the arguments, the fights, and so on. I only hope that my workers do not get into trouble."

Reverend Small said, "Sir, it's not about the rum drinking, drug taking, and so on. We are more concerned about what happens to our young women who are working as prostitutes there. I do not know how they get into that kind of business, but I would like to see it stopped as soon as possible."

John Jennings took a sip of his coffee, and said, "I understand your worry. But I cannot stop them from doing this especially if they are determined to do it."

Chief Onida Ana frowned, and said, "If we do not try to discourage these young women, they will just carry on, and may even go off to the capital city looking for more of this work. That will be a disaster."

John Jennings said, "Chief, unfortunately this has been happening for decades. Maybe the Minister responsible for Indigenous Peoples' Affairs in Kayana, can do something. I am more than willing to go with you to the city, and discuss the matter with him."

The Piaiman smiled, and said, "Well, that sounds like a good idea, and I am happy to travel with you. But, we need to do more here. I know that we may not be able to stop the rum drinking and drug taking, but you can start by taking some action to scold or sack your workers if they abuse alcohol and drugs. That will send out a clear signal to everyone, about how seriously you and your company regard such behaviour."

John Jennings nodded, and said, "We do have a policy against drunkenness and drug abuse, but I will have another look to see how effective it is. We could ask the Minister to take action to check out the bar business, illegal drug sales, and the application of law and order."

Chief Onida Ana said, "That is very useful. However, I think that we will only be skirting around the problem. I would like to see the mining town completely shut down. Our peoples continue to suffer too much abuse and neglect. Money, drugs, and alcohol do not preserve cultures. They bring gradual but definite destruction of our minds and bodies."

Reverend Small clasped his hands, and said, "Amen."

The Piaiman said, "Mr Jennings, you are one of us, and a very good man. This is not your fault. Our peoples have been suffering like this for hundreds of years. Even my medicine potions cannot halt this disease. Can you please try to, at the very least, stop this prostitution of our girls and women? It hurts us all to see them being used, and abused by everyone they keep calling their clients."

Peter said, "I can understand why our boys and men want to work in your mines. But they also succumb to alcohol, and drug abuse. The other prostitutes must also be curbed. I agree with our Chief that the town should be closed down. This could have a serious impact on our villages and settlements around here and elsewhere."

Chief Onida Ana nodded, and said, "Then, let us check to see what the Minister will do."

Reverend Small shook his head, and said, "Lord, please forgive this town of sin!"

TWENTY-SIX

MORE ACTION THAN WORDS

The delegation to meet the Minister of Indigenous Peoples' Affairs was led by Chief Onida Ana who had just commenced her degree course at the University of Kayana in October 2018. The group also included John Jennings, Peter Thomas, Reverend Small, and the Piaiman.

The three-storey ministerial building was entirely made of the tough greenheart wood, and the design was Dutch in origin. Two armed security guards searched each member of the delegation, and then allowed them through two large iron gates. They used a short concreted pathway that led directly to the imposing main doors. Chief Onida Ana, wearing her Chief's headdress, along with her traditional Kayanese tribal costume, pressed the buzzer once, and there was no response. She did so a few more times, and then the doors were slowly opened by a young woman.

She asked, "Who are you?"

Chief Onida Ana, taken aback by the abruptness of the staff member, said, "I am the Chief Onida Ana, and my colleagues and I are here for a meeting with the Minister."

The staff member asked, "When is your appointment?"

The Chief said, "I have this letter which states that our meeting is set for today in about fifteen minutes' time."

The staff member, still unsmiling, said, "OK. Come in and wait here."

Chief Onida Ana said, "Thank you."

The delegates took their seats on the wooden chairs within the reception area, and waited patiently. The walls of the room were adorned with large portrait pictures of the President of Kayana, the Minister, a map of the country indicating the locations of the main Indigenous settlements across the four regions, and a desk where the staff member sat. A single large fan which was hung from the ceiling, made an irritating rattle as its wooden blades rotated, and offered some respite from the high temperature.

When the appointment time arrived, the Chief stood up, and approached the staff member.

She said, "It is now eleven o'clock. Can we see the Minister?"

The young woman said, "Sit down, and wait until he is ready."

Another fifteen minutes passed before the phone rang, and the staff member suddenly sprang into action.

She said, "Now follow me."

The Minister, of Indigenous Kayanese origin, was a short, middle-aged and overweight man. He stood up from behind his large mahogany desk, and gestured to the Chief and her group, to sit on the leather settees in the middle of the spacious room. He strode over to sit on the single settee opposite his guests. He then poured some icy water from a jug placed on a glass covered centre table, and gestured to the others to do the same.

He sat forward slightly, and smiled as he asked Chief Onida Ana, "So, what can I do for you today?"

Chief Onida Ana took a sip of water from her glass tumbler, and said, "Sir, I am Chief Onida Ana, and thank you for agreeing to meet with us. This is Mr John Jennings the manager of the mine near to our settlement. Here is Reverend Henry Small, my assistant Peter Thomas, and our Piaiman. We would like to talk about the matters we mentioned in our letter to you over two months ago."

The Minister picked up the letter from the centre table, looked at it briefly, and said, "Yes, I have seen this, and I am sorry that I have not yet replied to you. I must do so after our meeting today."

John Jennings said, "Sir, our mining operation has been going on there for over twenty years now, and we have always tried to support all the people living in the area, especially after some incidents like the spillage of mercury a number of years ago. I am also worried about the state of the nearby mining town which is not a good one for all concerned."

Reverend Small leaned forward, and said, "Sir, Mr Jennings and his people are good towards us. But I am very worried about the lawlessness, and bad behaviour by the miners who go there to look for rum, drugs, and prostitutes. This must stop. We need your help."

Peter said, "We are not happy about having the town so near to our villages. It is filthy, rowdy, and a very bad place for our young women to end up in. It is also very bad for our young men who work as miners."

The Piaiman added, "And, the worst thing to happen there, is the spread of nasty sex diseases."

Chief Onida Ana said, "Sir, as you can see, we have many issues with that town which is not even properly organised. It is just a couple of rows of badly built buildings facing a broken road. I want to see that town dismantled."

The Minister sat back, placed his hands on his knees, and said, "I fully understand. I have heard of you Chief Onida Ana, and I do promise to do something to solve these problems. But I will need as much help from you, and all the leaders of the villages."

The Chief said, "Sir, these problems have been there for longer than I can remember, and nothing has been done by you and the others before you. We do not need any more promises. We need real actions, and very quickly. Otherwise we will be destroying our communities, and even worse still, our rainforests."

The Minister, taken aback by the young Chief's show of passion, said, "I understand. I am proud that one as young as you can come forward, and fight for our peoples, and our environment. I will send some of my best people to the town and villages to find out more details of what is happening, and to tell us all what we should do. In fact, now that I have met you all here, I also propose that you join my working group to help take this forward."

John Jennings said, "Sir, I may not get the time to devote to your working group, but I shall try to support it with one of my managers to work with you."

Reverend Small said, "Same here. I am very busy, but I will also try to help as much as I can."

Peter said, "Sir, I am not an educated man, but I am also here to help my Chief, and my people."

The Piaiman smiled, and said, "I will try to find the time, but we cannot travel all the way to this city just to attend meetings, and to do more talking. Maybe your working group can meet in our settlement? Your people need to spend most of the time there. Only then will you get to the truth about what is happening."

The Minister said, "Thank you all. I have also heard about many of the problems at the villages near to the mining towns across Kayana. I am concerned about the increasing number of suicides, the violence by the small-time miners, the rapes and abuse of Indigenous Kayanese girls, the illegal drug dealings and drug-taking, and so on. In fact, I recall the attack on your settlement some years ago. The first thing I wish to do is to secure a police presence in the town, and in the villages. I hope that Mr Jennings' company can help our government to pay for some of this additional security. Then, we can work on the recommendations of our working group. Chief Onida Ana, I know that you will be busy with your studies here in the city, but I would like you to lead the group. You will be paid, and it will be great experience for you as a young Chief."

John Jennings and the others looked across to the Chief, and nodded in approval.

Chief Onida Ana said, "Sir, I am willing to lead the group both here, and on the ground. In fact, I am asking Peter to oversee the work back in our settlement, and your team will be most welcome to stay at our benab. They will get everything that they need. Sir, we will also need more than police help, and I know of three retired soldiers from the Kayana army who may wish to help out."

Peter smiled, and asked, "Are you thinking of Sergeant John Brown, Private Abdul Rasheed, and Private Suresh Nanan?"

John Jennings said, "Well done Peter. I have heard of these soldiers. I hope that they will agree to help us."

Reverend Small said, "Well, we seem to be getting somewhere already. But we do need to keep this momentum going. There is a lot more to do."

Chief Onida Ana said, "I still believe that the mining town should be shut down. If we create the right conditions in all the settlements and villages, and the miners begin to behave themselves, then the situation will improve all around. There will be no need for such towns in the future."

The Minister smiled, and said, "With a leader like Chief Onida Ana here, and such great advisers, I am sure that things will improve. But please be patient, and let me know as soon as you need any further help from myself, or the government."

John Jennings said, "Same here Sir. It is very much in our interest that the peoples and the environment are sustained properly."

Peter said, "Sir, just one more thing before we end this meeting. If our Chief will be based here in the city, and the rest of us have to stay in the settlement, perhaps we could organise a better internet connection."

The Minister said, "Thank you Peter. We can look into that, and see if we can connect you all with Chief Onida Ana, not only for your working group meetings, but also for other matters you may wish to talk about. How does that sound?"

John Jennings said, "Sir, we can fund such a project. Consider it done."

Chief Onida Ana said, "Yes, I always prefer more action than words!"

TWENTY-SEVEN

THE POLITICIAN

C hief Onida Ana successfully led the Minister's working group to research further the issues and problems faced by the people living in the settlements and villages near to the main gold mining operations. During the course of the study, she also managed to perform creditably in her three years' university degree course at the Kayana University. Working closely with the Minister gave her invaluable practical experience of the political science she was studying.

She ensured that as soon as opportunities arose to resolve an issue or problem at any of the gold mines or villages, a solution was put in place. This simple, practical, and uncomplicated approach, won the Chief many admirers and followers, not only from within the Kayana Indigenous communities, but also amongst the other resident Indigenous tribes, and the wider population.

Each of the villages or settlements of the Indigenous tribes elected their own Chief or *Toshao*. Although the Toshaos had a National Council, they were not led by a single unifying Indigenous Chief of Kayana.

The Minister admired the work of Chief Onida Ana, Peter, and the others on the working group, as well as the researchers. He asked the Chief and Peter to join him on his three months' long campaign for re-election to the Kayana Parliament, during May 2020.

The Chief refused to join the political party of the Minister, but agreed to attend the rallies in the villages and settlements across the country. She avoided speaking on the public stage, preferring to personally meet as many of the residents as possible. This brought her much greater popularity, and respect.

The Minister noticed how the Chief was lauded everywhere she went. When his political party won a narrow victory at the general elections, and he was re-instated to his position, he made another attempt at luring her into politics. Chief Onida Ana refused the offer of a significant position by the Minister, and chose to complete her degree course by the following summer.

During her three years of undergraduate studies at the University of Kayana, Chief Onida Ana succeeded in forming two formidable student groups. One was on Human Rights, and the other on the Global Environment. She ensured that both groups included students from all races of Kayana, including African, East Indian, Portuguese, Chinese, Indigenous Kayanese, and people of Mixed Races.

She encouraged members of both groups to go into the rainforests to learn, and experience the way of life of the peoples, the wildlife, and their mutual existence in that environment. The touring parties stayed at the Chief's benab residence, but she took great care to avoid any expeditions from going to the secret location of the lost city.

Chief Onida Ana also kept in close touch with her friends from her High School years. Ruby Smith had excelled in her mathematics degree, and was offered an opportunity to study financial management and accountancy at Kayana's best college located in the capital city. Indra Persaud and Mary Brown extended their studies in botany, and offered the Chief their knowledge, and experience, if and when required.

After the friends' respective graduation ceremonies, they met at a popular American fried chicken and pizza outlet in the main street that ran from the northern beach through to the southern end of the city. This main street connected directly with the motorway that linked up with the country's biggest international airport.

During her public appearances in the city, Chief Onida Ana did not wear her tribal headdress or garments. She chose to wear casual outfits including blue denim jeans, a popular brand of running shoes, and red tee-shirts. Ruby Smith, who had grown taller than the others, also wore similar outfits like the Chief. However, the two new botanists, Indra Persaud and Mary Brown, chose their field research outfits of khaki shirts and trousers, and walking boots.

Chief Onida Ana embraced her three friends, and said to Indra and Mary, "Just look at you two! It seems like you are ready to go off on some major expedition! I am so happy to see you all again!"

Indra said, "Me too! Mary and I are preparing to go into the interior on a fact-finding mission, to look for rare fauna and so on. We are trying to get permission from the Toshao Council, but they seem to be quite reluctant to help us."

Chief Onida Ana said, "Let's order our meals, and then have a chat about that. What will you all have? I am paying for this."

Ruby looked up at the pictures of the fast food menu items, and said, "I will have a large cheeseburger meal. That should be enough for me."

Indra said, "Well, I like the chicken burger meal."

Mary said, "Hmm. I feel so hungry I will have a double beef burger. What will you have Chief?"

Chief Onida Ana said, "I don't really like anything on the menu, but I will settle for some fries, and a banana milkshake."

Ruby asked, "Chief, are you sure that is all you want?"

Chief Onida Ana said, "Yes my friend. That will be more than enough. Let me get the order, and we can have a good chat."

The friends tucked into their meals, and spoke about the main events of their last three years apart. Chief Onida Ana told them about her work with the Ministry, and her travels around the country during the general elections.

Ruby asked, "Chief, will you be going into politics? Our country badly needs someone like you."

Chief Onida Ana said, "I do like the idea, but I am much too young at only twenty-one. I cannot take on more responsibility than I already have as a Chief of my people. I have to get more involved in the work of the National Council of Toshaos, and to build up on my reputation amongst all the tribes of Kayana. This country's problems are far too great for me at the moment."

Indra smiled at the Chief, and said, "Wow! I still cannot believe that I am sitting here with a real Chief! You are so beautiful, and as Ruby has said, you really are the true image of our Kayana!"

Mary nodded, and said, "Yes. Anytime you say that you will be running for President of Kayana, I shall be right by your side. You are truly awesome!"

Chief Onida Ana sucked hard on the straw of her milkshake, and said, "Thank you all. But I am more proud of the three of you who have earned first class degrees in your subjects. You must be thinking of going into higher levels of study."

Ruby said, "Yes Chief, my new course is a professional level qualification, but will also allow me to work in finance as I study."

Indra said, "Mary and I are due to start our Masters in botany, and that is why we want to visit the most remote areas in the rainforest as part of our new research."

The Chief said, "Don't worry about that. I will ask the Council to grant you that permission. I can also ask the Minister of Indigenous Peoples' Affairs to help you with any support you will need. He owes me a lot of favours!"

Ruby laughed, and said, "Spoken like a true politician!"

The friends laughed heartily, and continued to discuss all kinds of topics, including relationships with young men.

Ruby asked the Chief, "Forgive me if I step too far into your personal life. But have you got a handsome young warrior waiting to take you away?"

Chief Onida Ana blushed, and said, "Unfortunately, not as yet. I have not met any such brave young warrior to be by my side. I think that my position as their Chief puts them off. Besides, I have been too busy with my studies, and the work for the Minister. What about you three?"

Indra smiled, and said, "Oh Chief Onida Ana, there you go again with a typical denial from a politician, and celebrity! In fact, from a true Leader!"

Ruby said, "Oh Indra, stop teasing her!"

Mary said, "I believe our Chief. She is honest. And that is a rare quality to have if you are a politician."

Chief Onida Ana nodded, and said, "You are both right. I have seen at first-hand how politicians operate here in Kayana. It is not that they are dishonest. It is more about them having to sacrifice some of their own principles when they have to tow their government's or President's line. I am not ready to do such things as I will be letting my ancestors and people down if I go against their wishes for some kind of short term gain."

Ruby asked, "Chief, what do you think about our current President and Government? We hear so much about how they are corrupt, and only favour their own supporters. If you do not belong to the ruling political party, you stand little chance of getting into certain jobs. How can we get round this without joining a political party?"

Chief Onida Ana said, "This is difficult. This country is gaining much more wealth from the gold and diamond mining, the timber, the agriculture, and the fastest growing source of money from the oil industry. Do not believe what you read, see, or hear in the Press. Our President and Government are working very hard towards uplifting all Kayanese, and our country."

Ruby asked, "Are you suggesting that all of these industries have their own avenues to use? Even if we do not belong to political parties?"

Chief Onida Ana said, "Yes. I do not believe that there is widespread corruption, but I think that we can avoid this through pursuing our education, and using our special talents. It is a tough route, but one worth considering. In this way, when we succeed we do not have to be obligated to anyone, or to any particular political doctrine."

Indra said, "Wow Chief! You are really smart! But, you have just promised to use your own political contacts to help me and Mary. Is that not a form of corruption?"

Chief Onida Ana said, "No. That is an honest use of a network, and only in a situation where others will not be disadvantaged. Besides, the Minister thought that by having my presence on his campaign, he was also being smart. I realised what his motives were, but I also used the situation for my own gains."

Indra sighed, and said, "Yes Chief Onida Ana!"

Ruby said, "You are our hero! You are a politician!"

TWENTY-EIGHT

THE MODEL SCHOOL

C hief Onida Ana was given a special welcome upon her return to her settlement. Indra and Mary had taken the opportunity to travel with her, and to begin their research. Peter strode forward to greet the Chief with wide open arms, and the broadest of smiles. They embraced each other.

The Piaiman stood at the entrance to the benab, and was flanked by five elders. He then led the group in a smoke ceremony witnessed by all the residents who formed a large circle around the ceremonial. When the Piaiman completed his prayers, the women and girls commenced singing songs of welcome for the return of their Chief.

Reverend Small offered a blessing for the Chief and her companions. The Piaiman asked everyone to enjoy the specially laid out feast of several meats and vegetables, and the local piwari drink. The children and young people were offered bottled water with their meals.

At the end of the feast, Chief Onida Ana was invited to address her people. Peter placed her feathered headdress on her shining black hair. She stood between Peter and the Piaiman, and said, "Today I feel that I am really at the place where I belong. Thank you all for such a great Kayana welcome. I wish to also thank the Piaiman, Reverend Small, Peter, our elders, and all of you for keeping our settlement so well looked after whilst I was away. You have always been in my mind, and I would also like to thank all of you who had helped and supported the Minister's working group. That report is with him and his government, and I anxiously await their actions to implement all of the recommendations. I intend to follow this up as one of my most important priorities as your Chief."

One of the elders shouted, "Long live Chief Onida Ana!"

The audience replied, "Long live Chief Onida Ana!"

The Chief smiled, and raised her hands to acknowledge her people, and for them to pause whilst she continued to speak.

She said, "From time to time I will have to go to the city and other places in order to represent you all, and I know that Peter, the Piaiman, and our elders, will be here to help you as they have done over the last three years. I am proud of my degree from the University of Kayana. This piece of paper gives me more authority to speak out in government circles, and other important places. My time at University showed me just how important our way of life is, how we see this environment, and how much more the world needs to know about us. We are very fortunate to have, and to preserve what we have here around us. This is also what I will fight to keep. Our true wealth is this very simple life. We do not need mansions and skyscrapers. Our humble homes are our palaces, and this tall canopy is our protection."

The audience continued to listen in awe. Kassi and Kori who had been kept by Peter whilst the Chief was away, recognised her, and flew to take up their places on her shoulders. Onca could be heard calling out from his family home on the bank of the tributary. The Chief's tapir, now fully grown, ambled up to stand near her feet.

Chief Onida Ana continued, "I am even more determined than ever, for us to work harder to protect our community of animals, birds, and other species, not only here, but across Kayana. My two friends, Indra Persaud and Mary Brown, are to be treated as our own sisters as they continue to do their research on our plants and trees in our environment. All of these things are only on loan to us by our Great Spirit and our ancestors. My friends will be advised by our Piaiman who knows everything about our plants and trees, and how they look after us. They have provided us all with food and medications for centuries, and we need to pass on their secrets to all of our peoples here in Kayana, and around the world."

The Piaiman nodded in agreement, and said, "Thank you Chief."

The Chief continued, "There is no reason for all of these things not to make us stronger and richer. Stronger in the sense that we will continue to survive anything, and richer because we have the answers to so many of the problems of this country, and the world. But we can also destroy all of this, and ourselves, if we are not careful. The temptations of alcohol and bad drugs are very strong, and I have seen how some of our brothers and sisters, and their families, have been destroyed by abusing these two wretched curses."

Reverend Small clasped his hands, and said, "Give me an Amen!"

Everyone said, "Amen!"

The Chief nodded, and said, "If we do not look after ourselves, our families, and our communities, as well as our environment, we will have nothing to show the world. The future is in our own hands. We must not look to others to save ourselves, and our environment. We have been fortunate to have the Great Spirit and our ancestors to guide us along the right path. This is our destiny."

The audience erupted in a spontaneous round of loud applause, accompanied by the women and girls' native shrieking cries.

One of the elders said, "Long live our Chief Onida Ana!"

Everyone repeated, "Long live Chief Onida Ana!"

The Chief paused, took a sip from a bottle of water, and said, "I want all of our children and young people to begin to take education about our own history, our language, our environment, and our customs and religion, as priorities alongside the education that is being offered by Kayana. I am asking our Reverend Small, the Piaiman, and Peter, to put together the courses of study in each of these traditional subjects with practical experience to commence here in the benab, as soon as possible. I shall also ask our Minister of Education and Mr Jennings, to fund, and build a new school along these lines. A good mix of our tradition as well as the modern education is a better way for us to develop as a people, a settlement, and a nation. I am also asking my dear friends Indra and Mary to help us with some teaching whilst they are here."

Indra and Mary smiled, and nodded in agreement.

The Chief continued, "These are just the start of the plans that I wish to implement here with all of your help. I cannot do any of this on my own, but I can lead us forward. Besides, these ideas were given to me by my great grandmother Chief Koko. Her vision for the future is what we must all work towards."

John Jennings, although not being invited to the welcome home party, arrived with one of his managers, and took up a position next to Chief Onida Ana. She turned towards him, and acknowledged his presence.

She said, "I am very happy that Mr Jennings has chosen to come here today. I hope to speak with him about my proposal to build our model school here, and maybe his company will also build such schools in the other villages and settlements where they operate. I see no reason why all the large mining companies should not invest more in our peoples' education, and environment. I also hope that the Kayana government will agree with my idea. I have said much to you today, and I hope that you will all continue to work with me towards a better future."

The people applauded their Chief, and then quietly dispersed. Chief Onida Ana gestured to the Piaiman, Reverend Small, Peter, the five elders, and John Jennings, to join her in the benab. Indra and Mary followed the Chief and her guests. Everyone sat on the available chairs and small wooden benches facing the Chief. The manager who had accompanied John Jennings, stood behind the group.

Chief Onida Ana said, "I have spoken at length about our plans for now and the future. And now that you are all here, I propose that you join me as a committee or council to help plan the work for the new model school, starting with the classes here in the benab, until it is built."

John Jennings said, "I like your idea Chief, and my manager here, Mr Abraham Campbell, who is Indigenous Kayanese, will be my representative on your committee. He has the authority to help you in any way you wish, and I am personally donating some money in a budget to help you build the school and furnish it, as soon as you get the go ahead from the Minister. I will also speak with my contacts in the Kayana government, and take your bigger idea forwards alongside the help of the other mining companies. Abraham will keep me informed about progress here, and you and I can meet regularly."

Chief Onida Ana smiled, and said, "Thank you Mr Jennings. We will build our model school."

TWENTY-NINE

HAPPINESS

In defiance of the Kayana government's refusal to allow Chief Onida Ana to build the new school for her community, she proceeded to commission the construction with funding for, and support by, John Jennings and the mining company. The curriculum which was taught temporarily in the benab, proved to be very popular with the students and parents, and included the formal teaching of the Kayanese language, customs, spirituality, and the protection of the environment, alongside the national english-based curriculum subjects.

The space in the benab was too small to accommodate all the children at once, and some classes were held outside in the square, and on field trips into the forest. Jacob Holmes, the Headteacher of the Chief's former high school, provided teaching support by offering the services of some of his junior teachers on a subject by subject basis, and through an agreed rota. The Piaiman took full responsibility for teaching culture, religion, and the environment. Peter taught practical building construction, hunting, and survival skills. The Reverend Small held Sunday school for christianity. Indra Persaud and Mary Brown taught botany.

Such a rich, and varied curriculum offered to the children, quickly brought immense joy amongst the entire population, and many of the women began to offer their services to formally teach the girls crafts such as basket weaving.

The opening of the school in time for the new academic year from September 2022, was a most joyous occasion for the community and their supporters, such as John Jennings and Jacob Holmes.

The children and their teachers quickly settled into their new school building which was constructed on eight feet high concrete stilts. The main body of the structure was of tough greenheart, and the furniture and other fittings were made of mahogany. The sloping roof was covered by corrugated aluminium sheets, and painted green to blend in with the dominant colour of the forest. The exterior of the building, including the access stairs, was whitewashed. Every able-bodied resident had given their labour and skills freely in support to the trained builders and carpenters provided by John Jennings.

Chief Onida Ana did not invite anyone from the Kayana government, preferring not to draw attention to the school project. The ceremonial opening was simple, and conducted by the Piaiman, and with blessings by Reverend Small.

The Chief and her committee met regularly in order to check on progress, and to deal with any problems that arose. She was always very keen to tackle any issue as quickly as possible, and would often take matters into her own hands to do the tasks. Her people were always full of admiration for her, and every time she left the benab, some of the youngest children would rush up to hug her, and then walk proudly alongside her. This new joy and peacefulness was infectious, and everyone went about their daily lives with much greater enthusiasm and purposefulness.

During one of her regular meetings with John Jennings, the Chief explored some thoughts on how her community, and the wider Indigenous Peoples across Kayana, could become more self-sufficient then, and into the future.

She asked, "Mr Jennings, our new school is already inspiring our people in the settlement, but I am not sure as to what will be required to take advantage of this important development. Can you offer any suggestions?"

John Jennings leaned back into his grand office chair, and said, "Chief, I have also been thinking about the future. It seems that we are both thinking alike. It is certainly good to have some kind of vision for the future, and then if others agree with this, we can work back from that point in order to be clear as to what to do now, next year, and in the years to come."

Chief Onida Ana said, "Chief Koko had already told me what the vision is for all of our Indigenous Peoples here in Kayana. This must also include all the other peoples of this country as we are all wrapped up in this future together."

John Jennings took a drink from his bottle of cold water, and said, "You are right. The future of any country must involve everyone. So, what is this vision of yours?"

The Chief said, "It is simply about building a Kayana where everyone can be happy."

John Jennings smiled, and asked, "Is that it? Is that all? To be happy?"

The Chief frowned, and said, "Sir, happiness is not only a personal thing. It should be a goal for all others, and not at anyone else's expense. Do you feel happy?"

John Jennings said, "I am not sure. At times, I do feel happy. But at other times, I feel sad."

The Chief asked, "Can you say when was the last time that you felt really happy, and why?"

John Jennings paused for a moment, and said, "Well, I felt very happy when we opened the new school in the settlement."

Chief Onida Ana smiled, and said, "You were not the only one who was happy. The entire community was really happy, and that sweet feeling is still with them. This happiness is because of the things that you did, and how you helped us to accomplish that dream. Now, this is the kind of happiness that Chief Koko's vision is about. We need to think about how this wonderful state can be maintained, and secured into the future. That is why I asked the first question."

John Jennings sat up, and said, "Yes, I think I understand where you are coming from. This happiness is not only about building massive wealth, skyscrapers, huge mansions, and so on. It is about what will keep the communities self-sufficient, and in harmony with their environment now, and into the future."

The Chief said, "Sir, that is not all. Our peoples must not lose their communities. Our talented young people are drifting away, and are being seduced by that fake wealth. They may be happy to some extent, but their true happiness is here, with their elders, families, and friends. This disconnection drives them to seek comfort elsewhere, and that is often in the form of alcohol and illegal drugs. This can never replace the strength of togetherness."

John Jennings said, "So you mean that we must continue to build on that togetherness at a rate that is at the right level, and pace. There are some basic things that we can do, and I am happy to help. First of all, clean drinking water, and proper sanitation. This would be at the top of my list."

The Chief smiled, and said, "That is a very good idea. But it is typical of western so-called civilised people. Our peoples, and yours, have lived and survived here in the rainforest without the chemically cleaned water, and sanitation, for centuries. I am not saying that we must not change some of our habits, but that there are other priorities for us. We should ask the people what they think that they need now. Of course, clean water and sanitation will always be important."

John Jennings, although surprised by the Chief's views, said, "You are so right. I, as a half Indigenous person, should know better than to assume that we always know what is best for others. I would love to join you for your consultation with the people. It has to be the best way to help them. But we must also recognise the causes of some illnesses, and try to find ways to prevent them. Using the clean rain water collected in the tanks that we installed years ago, has been helpful."

Chief Onida Ana smiled, and said, "Sir, you will be most welcome to join the meeting, and who knows, if the majority of the people ask for better and cleaner water supplies, and sanitation, then so be it. But my feeling is that they may propose some things that we have not yet thought about. This is how our peoples have always behaved. Their opinions always matter, and I as their Chief, have to try my very best to help them to achieve their wishes. Of course, at times Chiefs have had to disagree, and tell the people why."

John Jennings said, "This is a much fairer system, and we in the so-called modern democratic societies, can learn from this. Chief, have you thought about entering politics?"

The Chief shook her head, and said, "Oh no, not again! I have no intention of entering politics here or elsewhere. I have a very big job of leading my people, and I do not agree with other Chiefs who have joined with one or other political parties here in Kayana. People in the government have asked me to join up, and represent Indigenous Peoples in parliament. But, I have principles handed down for over five hundred years, and I do not wish to compromise any of them. I shall attend the National Council for Indigenous Peoples, but not any other political arena. As you know fully well, there is still a lot more to do here for my people, our community, and others as well. I need to get on with this."

John Jennings said, "Thank you Chief. You are quite right to stand by your principles. My company and I will continue to do all we can to support you and your people here. I have asked Abraham Campbell to continue to work with you and your committee at the settlement, and to keep me well informed. You and I must also continue to meet like this so that we can keep the vision alive. Besides, I am learning from you."

They both stood up, shook hands, and laughed. The Chief paused at the door, and said, "Learning from each other is a good source of happiness."

THIRTY

PRIORITIES

E veryone in the settlement answered their Chief's call for a full open meeting in the square, to consider their opinions as to the most urgent, and important things to be done for the benefit of all.

Reverend Small was asked by the Chief to video the meeting so that the committee would not miss any idea or suggestion made. She intended to pay heed to everything, and asked Abraham Campbell to make a list of the suggestions. The committee will then decide on the priorities.

One elder said, "Chief, now that we all have good houses, and a nice new school, our people need to have more space to do sports and games, especially our traditional ones. We seem to have more time to idle."

Chief Onida Ana said, "That is a very good idea. What sport do you have in mind?"

Another elder said, "Football for all the children to play in a more organised way, rather than them running about, and kicking the ball aimlessly."

An older woman, who had been teaching Kayanese crafts at the school, said, "We need a space to sell our products to visitors. A small shop will be a good start."

Another elder asked, "Why are we so keen on making money? This is the source of all evil."

The woman said, "We do not have to sell for money. We could use the shop to exchange for goods that we need."

A young man said, "Chief, me and my friends are bored with too much hunting and fishing. We would like to play football in a proper ground with goal posts and so on. Also, we need more contact with the outside world. Can we have a large TV for the settlement?"

The first elder frowned, and said, "The world is right here. We need to preserve our own way of life, and avoid all those useless goods being advertised on the TV. Maybe we can have a TV screen to teach us things we need to learn, and not a commercial outlet for rubbish. How can boxes of frozen fish be any better than our fresh catch?"

A beautiful young lady stepped forward nervously, and asked, "Can we have a celebration of our peoples and culture? My friends would like to put on a show of singing, music, dancing, and a beauty parade."

The first elder shrugged his shoulders, and said, "I think that a cultural show will be nice, but I do not wish to see a beauty parade."

Chief Onida Ana said, "Our people are beautiful, and everyone can see this. We do not need to copy others, and do beauty parades. But, we could have both boys and girls showing off our beautiful traditional costumes which are made here."

The young lady smiled, and said, "Thank you Chief. We love you."

Reverend Small said, "Chief, our church needs some repairs and repainting. I hope that we can get some help for this."

John Jennings said, "Consider that done Reverend."

Peter said, "We should expand the mooring, and widen the road from the bank to the square. Also, it would be good to build a new road from here to the mining area, and the airfield there. That mining town needs to be torn down, or, re-developed into something much better, and safer for all."

John Jennings said, "I agree that you need a better mooring and roads. But you can continue to use the river instead of cutting down so much of the forest. We need to think more clearly about these good ideas, but with regard to preserving our environment."

The audience continued to offer many more suggestions for the Chief and her committee to consider.

Chief Onida Ana said, "We already have some very good ideas to think about, and some we can do fairly quickly. If anyone has any more ideas, no matter how small, or big, please come to me, and we will consider them."

John Jennings smiled, and said, "Chief, you are right about the issue of water, toilets, and sanitation. No one spoke about these. But I still think that as we get more visitors, and people who want to live here, we will have to improve on what we have."

The Piaiman said, "I know that I am relied upon for dealing with a lot of illnesses and worries. But I think that we need a small community clinic which can serve the basic medicinal needs, and offer my potions as well. We can practice both types of medicine here."

The first elder said, "That is a very good idea. We also need faster transportation to take our very ill up river to the bigger community hospital there. The access to Mr Jennings' airfield will help us to get the very seriously ill people to the great hospital in the city. Also, whilst we are on this topic, I think that we need to tidy up, and expand the area of our cemetery."

Chief Onida Ana turned to John Jennings, and said, "You see Sir, it seems that we are being asked to develop the entire settlement, and to expand it into something that could become a much more established small town in the future. We should therefore ask the surrounding villages and settlements what they need for now, and into the future. I am very pleased to hear our people saying that they want to stay here, take more care of our environment, and develop a settlement which has the right facilities for the residents, and for visitors."

John Jennings said, "I agree with you Chief, and I shall do whatever is necessary to help you achieve this vision. I am beginning to feel even happier every time I meet up with you, and your wonderful people. You certainly think differently about these matters, and I continue to learn from you. I will share these thoughts and suggestions with my company's bosses back in Canada. My own people there can also learn from you all."

Reverend Small clasped his hands, and said, "Amen."

Peter said, "Chief, we have a lot of work ahead of us."

Chief Onida Ana raised her eyes above and beyond the forest, and said, "Yes Peter, there is a lot to do."

That evening, a tired but very pleased Chief Onida Ana lay in her hammock looking up through the converged rafters of the benab, and stared at it until she fell into a deep slumber.

A crackling noise caused Chief Onida Ana to wake up suddenly. She scanned the room, and saw everyone else still fast asleep. She carefully stepped down onto the wooden floor, and tiptoed over to the door. As soon as she opened the door, she was confronted by the dark red flames leaping out of the school building. Peter ran towards her and the benab. His eyes were wild with sheer terror.

The entire settlement was woken up, and the residents stirred into action by forming a line leading from the school gates to the water's edge by the mooring. Buckets of water were passed on by each person through to the head of the line. Then, with great effort, the water was poured onto the nearest flames. Other residents ran towards the rain water tanks beside their houses, and fetched buckets of water to be thrown at the fire.

The collective effort of everyone was in vain as the fire swept through the wooden structure, and engulfed the entire building in a very short time. The residents then took the precaution of dampening the houses which were nearest to the school building.

Chief Onida Ana, who had joined the line throughout the firefighting effort, slumped to her knees with exhaustion, and tears rolled down from her reddened eyes to her blackened cheeks.

Peter crouched down beside her, and said, "I am so sorry Chief. But at least no one was hurt. We will rebuild this."

Suddenly, an elder shouted, "Look! There is someone running away! He must have started the fire! Get him!"

Peter and the Chief mustered up as much energy as possible, and joined the chase into the darkness of the forest. The person being chased, was very nimble, and after a few minutes, he disappeared from view. The chasers gave up through sheer tiredness.

THIRTY-ONE

PAINFUL TRUTH

T he mood in the settlement was sombre, and sadness filled the air as the entire community stood helplessly staring at the charred remains of the school. Small puffs of smoke rose silently as the solid greenheart beams smouldered.

Chief Onida Ana, still also shaken by the events of the evening, and with some of the soot evident on her face and arms, called the people together.

Peter, the Piaiman, Reverend Small, Abraham Campbell, and the elders, stood beside her as she beckoned the others to gather around more closely.

She said, "Thank you all for your hard work last night. We will find out who did this, and why. The person who ran away from here cannot be too far away, and we will track him down. We know that he headed into the forest, and away from the river. So, if he is not from our area, we can still catch up with him."

The Piaiman said, "Chief, please be careful. That man, if cornered, could become as dangerous as a jaguar. He may also be armed with guns."

Chief Onida Ana said, "Yes, we will be very cautious, and try to keep our distance. Our warriors are strong, and very skilful. Peter will carry his rifle, and we will catch the culprit. I want him alive."

Reverend Small said, "Yes Chief, please try your best to catch this person. We need to know who is behind this evil act. I cannot believe that it was one person only. I hope that no one here is involved. This is a very sad day for us all, and I pray to the Lord to guide us at this time. I pray also for the safety of our Chief and others who will go on this mission. Amen."

The Piaiman said, "Oh Great Spirit, please heal our wounded hearts. Help us to stand firmly together, and rebuild our school, and our happiness. Oh ancestral spirits, help us all to lift our arms and our heads higher than ever."

Peter said, "Chief, we must go on the hunt now. Everyone, please listen to our elders and Mr Campbell, and help to clear this site. We should get back here in a few hours. Mr Jennings will come over soon to help to guide the work, and the plans to rebuild our school. We know that this was a criminal act, and we wish to deal with the culprit ourselves. We do not need to involve the police or the military, at least until we return. So, please do not discuss this fire with anyone else."

Chief Onida Ana and Peter then led the search party of five of the best young warriors of the settlement. They took the one track leading out from the main square, and into the dense jungle. A group of Howler monkeys accompanied them by staying higher up into the canopy, and moving in the same direction as if they knew what the search was about. They were quick to respond to Howler calls from further ahead, and the search party responded by increasing their speed.

The warriors moved ahead of Chief Onida Ana and Peter as they cleared any overgrowth on the path. They soon reached the base of the giant greenheart tree which was always used as a first resting point in the past, and they noticed signs of the person being tracked.

The Chief, breathing more heavily, paused, and said, "I am feeling very tired, but we cannot afford to waste any more time here. He cannot be too far away from here as these broken stems are still very fresh."

Peter said, "Chief, please stay here with one of our men. I can go ahead more quickly, and catch the culprit."

The Chief took a long drink from her water bottle, sprinkled some onto her perspiring face, and signalled the search party to move on. The Howler monkey troop became more agitated, and this spurred the searchers onwards at a brisker pace.

Within fifteen minutes, Peter spotted some movement just off the track ahead. He asked everyone to stop, and to stoop down as he inched forward with his rifle pointing ahead of him.

Chief Onida Ana whispered, "Don't shoot him."

Peter peered through the base of some bushes, and as he saw the man's feet and legs, he ordered him to surrender.

The man, with his face covered in black soot, sprung out from his hiding place, and started firing his pistol wildly. The shots rang out, and this caused the Howler monkeys and birds to scatter in utter panic. The hunting party crept even lower to avoid being hit.

Peter composed himself, and with one decisive turn, shot at the legs of the gunman who fell down almost immediately, screaming in pain. A return shot from the gunman grazed the left arm of Peter, and he also fell to the ground. The warriors rushed over to the wounded fugitive. They quickly disarmed him, lifted him up, and brought him out of his hiding place. They then laid him down on the track. Chief Onida Ana stooped over Peter, and began to tend to his wound.

Peter grimaced, and said, "I'm OK Chief. It's just a bruise. Let's get this man out of here. He won't be able to walk."

The warriors quickly made a stretcher with two six feet long pieces of bamboo and tough vines. They tied a handkerchief tightly above the wound just below the man's left knee to stop further blood loss. Then they eased him onto the stretcher.

The Chief stepped over to have a closer look at the suspect, and realised that he was a fellow Indigenous Kayanese from outside the area. Although she knew that it was important to take him to the settlement, and then on to the community hospital for further treatment, she decided to ask him a few questions.

She asked, "Who are you? Where have you come from?"

The man, still in some pain, said, "I don't want to talk to you."

The Chief said, "Look here, I have no time to waste with you. Tell me!"

Peter stood over the man, raised his rifle, and pointed it towards the man's chest.

The Chief said, "If you do not wish to tell me who you are, and say why you burnt down our school, we will leave you here to be eaten by the jaguars or snakes. The choice is yours."

The man, fearing for his life, said, "Please do not leave me here. I was given money by a man to burn down the school."

Peter asked, "Who?"

The man said, "I can't say. They will kill me."

The Chief said, "Well it seems that your options are getting worse. Either you tell us, and you get saved, or you stay quiet, and die anyway!"

The man said, "I don't care anymore."

Peter, now more visibly angry at the man's refusal to answer, grabbed his neck as if to strangle him, and growled, "Look scumbag, tell us or I'll put you out of your misery right now!"

Peter squeezed at the man's neck harder, and caused him to choke.

The man coughed, and then said, "Yes I will. It was a man from the government. He wanted that school burnt down at all costs. I am sorry. I am a poor man. I need the money."

The Chief said, "Well, this is not a good way for you to get rich. I don't need to know more from you. Peter, let's get him out of here."

The warriors lifted the stretcher, and carried the man ahead as the Chief paused to look back beyond the spot where they apprehended him. The pathway which led to the old city, was once again overgrown with bushes and vines over the three years since its discovery.

Peter asked, "Chief, are you OK?"

The Chief whispered, "Yes, I am. I hope that our secret city is still a secret. I wanted to have a look. But since the pathway is overgrown, I can assume that no one has come this way."

Peter also whispered, "I agree Chief. We have all kept very quiet about our secret, and I have never allowed anyone to use this track. Even the Piaiman takes his students through a new one away from here. Our researchers, Indra and Mary, do not know of this place."

The Chief said, "Thank you Peter. I know that I can always trust you. Let's get back to the settlement as quickly as possible. How is your shoulder?"

Peter said, "It hurts a bit, but I am fine. I will go with the prisoner to the community hospital, and I will get some treatment."

Chief Onida Ana, taking longer strides to keep up with the warriors who were trotting with their patient, said, "Yes, when you go to the hospital, just hand him over to the authorities. We do not need to bring any charges onto him, as long as he stays away from here."

Peter took a sip from his water bottle, and said, "Chief, you will have to tackle the government people to find out more about this crime."

The Chief said, "No, we will keep the government out of this, and rebuild our school. I will deal with those responsible when I am ready. We must not draw more attention to this, and any other project that we do. This is all our business, and as long as we get the right help, we must use that as much as possible."

Peter shrugged his shoulders, and said, "Chief, I am sure that you know what you are doing. I am more than happy to keep supporting you."

The injured man groaned in pain as the warriors carried him over the bumpy terrain.

He murmured, "Ow! You're killing me!"

THIRTY-TWO

MORE TO DO

Less than three years later, on the first of January 2025, Chief Onida Ana's twenty-fifth birthday was set to be celebrated by her entire community, and invitees from all the other Indigenous tribes across Kayana. The event was carefully planned by Peter and members of the village council. The Chief knew that plans were being discussed, but she was not allowed any involvement. Invitations were also sent to leaders of Indigenous Peoples from other countries, and John Jennings was asked by his Inuit people, to represent Canada. Members of Kayana's government were encouraged to attend.

Chief Onida Ana's settlement had grown substantially in population, as well as area covered. The attraction was inspired by news of the new developments, and the Chief's leadership.

A new mooring was built to allow for larger river boats. Onca's growing family was given greater protected space along the river bank. A wide road was built from the mooring to the square in the settlement, and tarmac was used to ensure greater stability instead of large potholes which used to appear after heavy rainfall.

The school was rebuilt, and extended to accommodate the rising demand for places. Indra Persaud and Mary Brown decided to stay on as teachers upon the completion of their research. Their laboratory which was sited at the school, became a source of study for students across the region, and was funded by the Kayana government.

John Jennings kept his promise to build a new road from the settlement to the mining company's airfield so that critically ill villagers could be quickly flown out to the community hospital up river, or to the large public hospital in the capital city.

The mining town was also substantially rebuilt, and subject to a greater presence of security personnel overseen by the three retirees from the Kayana army; John Brown, Abdul Rasheed, and Suresh

Nanan. The unit also employed, and trained security officers from amongst the Indigenous population.

The women weavers of the village formed a local cooperative to produce, and exchange their Kayana designed baskets, table mats, wooden plates, jugs, and a large array of costume jewellery, for their most needed goods including clothing and foodstuff not available at the settlement.

The mining company and the Kayana government collaborated on the provision of affordable electricity, and the supply of clean water for the settlement and all the other villages nearby. Due to the relative remoteness of the settlement and the mining town, a dedicated sanitation unit was built to allow for more modern toilets.

A playing field was established next to the school, and football soon became the most popular sport which encouraged young boys and girls to play on the same teams. The man who had set fire to the old school, was forgiven by Chief Onida Ana, and was employed as the caretaker for the new school, and groundsman for the football pitch, as well as the person responsible for maintenance of the small pavilion.

Chief Onida Ana had successfully negotiated for the formal approval of the school, and for its running costs, with the Kayana government. She had taken advantage of knowing who had instigated the destruction of the old school, and used this very skilfully, to obtain all the support she needed from the government. The Minister of Education was invited as guest of honour to the birthday celebrations.

Due to the large number of residents and guests attending the celebration, it was decided that the new pavilion and sports ground would be used for the day's activities. Many guests were offered accommodation at the extended benab, individual homes, and the new motel in the mining town. Others who did not opt to stay over, returned to their homes using an array of passenger boats hired specifically for the day.

The Minister of Education formally opened the programme of speeches, entertainment, fashion parade, and a grand feast.

He said, "Today is an important landmark in the history of our Indigenous Peoples of Kayana. It is not only a celebration of Chief Onida Ana's twenty-fifth birthday, but the establishment of an exciting model of living for all of our Indigenous communities across Kayana, and for our other peoples. I am very impressed with the new approach to education here, not only for the benefit of you the Indigenous Peoples, but for all Kayanese peoples in our multi-racial and multi-cultural country. You are teaching us all about why it is so important to protect our precious environment. Our government wants to continue to work with you all in doing the right things to allow our rainforests to breathe life into the atmosphere. We are also aware that the operations of our extractive industries here on land, need to be monitored more closely, and I am happy that Mr Jennings and his company are leading the way. But, we also need to be much more watchful about the pollution risks of the extensive oil production taking place offshore in the Ocean, and the impact of this on our coastlands, and here in the interior."

John Jennings nodded in approval, and smiled at Chief Onida Ana and the other delegates sitting alongside each other on the stage facing the crowded pavilion, and those spectators using the open ground spaces.

The Minister continued, "So, my fellow Kayanese, and guests from elsewhere, let us acclaim our beautiful Chief Onida Ana on her special birthday, and for her demonstration of mature and far-sighted leadership! Long live Chief Onida Ana!"

The entire audience responded with, "Long live Chief Onida Ana!"

John Jennings stood up to address the gathering.

He said, "Today is a new day of a new year, and a new dawn, not only for us all, but for this wonderful and gifted young woman whom I have grown to respect. Happy 25th Birthday Chief Onida Ana! May you live to lead us all for very many more years to come. I bring you these special wishes from my own Inuit and other peoples of Canada, and from our gold mining company. Thank you for a vision of a future that is far more important than the making of huge profits from exploiting the planet's natural resources. Your views are strong, and come from the amazing survival of your peoples, despite the last five hundred years of wanton destruction of millions of your gracious peoples by foreigners who should have never set foot on these lands, or on these rivers."

The audience stood up to applaud John Jennings, and he raised his hands above his head to ask them to take their seats.

He continued, "We can offer apologies for the spread of terrible diseases which were brought from Europe, and killed millions of your ancestors across the Americas and the Caribbean. We cannot reverse this genocide, but we can all strive to rebuild the paradise that Indigenous Peoples found here, and know how to protect. Let us salute our Chief Onida Ana who has begun to bring happiness to everyone! God bless Chief Onida Ana!"

The Piaiman took his turn to speak, and started with a traditional Kayanese verse of praise for the Chief, and for wishing her a long and fruitful life.

He raised his hands aloft, and said, "Oh Great Spirit and spirits of our ancestors, especially Chief Koko. Today we seek your blessings for a young woman of great intelligence, grace, and heart. May our Chief Onida Ana continue her great work with and for us all, and for the future generations to come. May our love for, and loyalty to our Chief never diminish. And, may our community continue to live in peace and in harmony with everyone, and everything around us."

Reverend Small said, "Amen!", and the audience replied with "Amen!"

Peter stood up, and said, "Now that we have heard such good wishes for our Chief, I would also like to wish her a very happy birthday, and long may she walk with us. Now, we will enjoy a specially assembled fashion show by our young people who have worked very hard on their costumes, and their presentations!"

The fashion show lasted for about fifteen minutes, and the young people displayed a beautiful collection of imaginative outfits blending traditional designs with more modern styles. The guests and audience were very impressed, and could not wait to purchase all the available stock, and refreshments on offer. A group of Ecuadorian native flute players and drummers provided the musical entertainment on stage.

Upon the resumption of more official speeches, Peter asked Jacob Holmes to say a few words.

Jacob Holmes rose to spontaneous applause, and said, "Thank you all! I shall not take up much of your time as we wish to continue to enjoy the entertainment, food, and refreshments. But today is indeed a very special one for all of us who have seen this beautiful young person grow into such a formidable leader. If I am allowed to say this, I wish our Chief Onida Ana a very special landmark birthday, and may the Great Spirit continue to give her the strength and guidance to achieve even greater things in the years to come. Chief, I wish you every success in whatever you put your mind to. Happy birthday my dear friend!"

Chief Onida Ana wiped away some tears from her eyes and cheeks, adjusted her headdress, and stood up to a deafening ovation with chants of "Long Live Chief Onida Ana!"

She said, "Thank you all for your very kind words. I have enjoyed everything you have done to make this day even more special for me. Thank you also for making this settlement grow into such a wonderful, and happy place. Some people say that it has become a small town. But whatever you call it, let it continue to glow with this warmth, and welcoming spirit. Chief Koko must love what we have here, and this is part of her grand vision. So, we have more work to do, and will need everyone's help. What we have achieved so far, is the basis for our future, not only here, but for all of our peoples throughout Kayana. Now, let us all enjoy the party!"

One of the elders climbed up the steps to the stage, and offered the Chief a beautiful floral garland. He then hugged her as the audience continued to cheer.

Shortly after the official celebrations ended, the Chief and Peter escorted the Minister of Education to the mooring, and before she could bid him farewell, he turned around to face her.

He asked, "Chief, will you consider joining our party, and running for election to the Kayana parliament? I am more than willing to endorse you. What do you say?"

The Chief said, "Sir, I wish to stay as I am, and to carry on with my work here. There is still a lot more for me and my people to do. Thank you for coming here, and supporting us. I wish you well in this year's general election."

THIRTY-THREE

BLOODY ENCOUNTER

The villagers continued to enjoy what was left of the party well into the afternoon, and up to dusk as darkness quickly descended on the settlement. All the guests who were from within Kayana, had taken advantage of daylight, and left by way of the boats operating as one-off river taxis. The other guests agreed to join Chief Onida Ana in her benab, for a final round of refreshments before retiring to their accommodation in the houses in the village, and in the motel in the mining town.

John Jennings took the opportunity to speak with the Chief alone, and aside from her guests.

He said, "Chief, I know that this is not the right time and place to have this chat with you. But I felt that before you hear any news about this, I need to discuss with you, a proposal being made by my company, to expand our gold mining operations here."

A very alarmed Chief Onida Ana arched back in her chair, and said, "Well, that is a really big surprise to me! We will need to talk about this as soon as possible, and I mean tomorrow morning. I can tell you straight away that I will strongly object to such a plan!"

John Jennings said, "I had to mention this to you as soon as I could, and we can meet first thing tomorrow morning. Good night Chief. Sleep well."

Later that evening, Chief Onida Ana lay in her hammock when all of her guests had left, and was so troubled by the shock news that she could not sleep. Her mind was racing with thoughts about what John Jennings' news could mean for all the peoples of Kayana.

The country's sudden acquired wealth from the most lucrative oil exploration in its history, had created a hugely rich group of people who were able to take full advantage of the windfall. The general economy grew at its fastest rate ever, and was well above those of its neighbours. Many ex-patriot Kayanese returned to the country looking for opportunities to share in the bonanza. With this rapid growth in wealth, greater demands were being made for the country's high quality gold and diamonds. This caused the mining companies to seek approval to expand their operations.

Chief Onida Ana felt that the Kayana government would succumb to the pressures from its supporters, for the production of more gold and diamonds to meet the growing local demand. Refusing permits to expand mining would run contrary to the need to stay in power for as long as possible. Chief Onida Ana finally felt very tired, and fell asleep.

Very early the next morning, Chief Onida Ana and her guests in the benab were woken up by the din caused by a major clean up of the settlement. She hurriedly drank some coffee after her usual dip in the inland creek. She then took a motorised canoe to meet John Jennings at his office.

He welcomed her, and said, "Thank you for coming over to see me this morning. I am sure that you must have thought long and hard about what I said regarding an expansion of our operations here."

Chief Onida Ana frowned, and said, "Yes, I could hardly sleep. I could not understand why you of all people, would want to expand what you are doing here. How much more are you planning to ask for? Have you not taken enough of our flesh and blood?"

John Jennings coughed slightly, and said, "About double our current operations. This is just to meet so much more demand by Kayanese, for our gold."

The Chief opened her eyes widely, and asked, "Double?"

John Jennings said, "Yes, Chief."

Chief Onida Ana rose up from her chair, placed both palms onto John Jennings' desk, and said, "No way! Not a single square foot! This cannot happen here! This cannot be allowed! Is anyone else asking for expansion?"

John Jennings said quietly, "Yes Chief, all the mining companies operating here in Kayana."

She asked, "Please tell me, why do you wish to destroy so much more of our rainforest and lands? I thought that you believed in our vision. Why do you now want to do this? And, to break all of your promises? I still cannot understand this."

147

John Jennings leaned forward slightly, and said, "Chief, I am opposed to this move by my company. I have offered to resign my position, but this has been refused. I am caught up in a very difficult situation, and I am also having sleepless nights."

Chief Onida Ana asked, "So, what will you do now?"

John Jennings said, "Unfortunately, I will have to do as my boss commands. What will you be doing?"

Chief Onida Ana said, "Sir, I cannot tell you. It is now very hard for me to trust you. What will happen with the support that you have been giving us?"

John Jennings said, "I will continue to support the projects that we have started. My company wanted me to stop, but I have refused to do so as a condition of staying on here."

She said, "I am very grateful for that. But I now need to go, and discuss this with my people."

John Jennings stood up, and said, "Chief, I am really sorry. I do understand how you feel. Myself and the other General Managers of the other mining companies will be meeting the President of Kayana next Monday morning. This was meant to be kept as a secret."

Chief Onida Ana, still very angry, turned around, and left the office without uttering a word.

As soon as she arrived at the settlement, the Chief called Peter, the Piaiman, Reverend Small, the five elders, Indra Persaud, and Mary Brown, for a meeting in the benab. She had excluded Abraham Campbell to avoid any news about her plans from going back to John Jennings.

Chief Onida Ana sat at the head of the long dining table which could accommodate up to twenty persons.

She said, "Today, I am deeply sad, and angry to have to tell you about something which will be the worst event to hit us in decades. Mr Jennings just told me about a secret meeting between the General Managers of all the mining operations here in Kayana, and the President of Kayana, to be held next Monday morning. They will be asking the President for permission to expand the gold and diamond operations across the country."

Everyone was stunned by the announcement, and just stared in disbelief at the Chief.

She said, "Let me say that Mr Jennings does not agree with his company, and he told me about the secret meeting. He will continue to support all of our projects. But we must keep this whole matter as quiet as possible. What do you all think that we should do?"

Peter said, "Chief, we have to stop the mining companies at all cost!"

Reverend Small asked, "Why do they want to destroy so much more of our precious rainforests?"

Chief Onida Ana said, "There is now a huge demand for more gold and diamonds by the stinking rich people of Kayana who have been milking wealth from the oil industry. They now only want more Kayana gold and diamonds."

One elder said, "We have to stop this plan. This is war!"

Reverend Small said, "This must not be a physical fight, as we will never win. I am so shocked by this greed of some of our Kayanese people."

The Piaiman said, "We cannot engage in a physical fight. This is not our way. We are peaceful people. We must be guided by our wisdom, and the Great Spirit."

The Chief said, "Yes, we must oppose this plan, and I think that all of us, and the other Chiefs must go to the city, and protest peacefully at the President's Palace. If you all agree, I will now contact the Chiefs, and make the arrangements. I will also seek legal advice as to our rights in these matters. This must include our right to be properly consulted by the mining companies as part of what is called Free Prior Informed Consent, or FPIC, before the beginning of such development on our ancestral land, or using resources within our territory."

Peter said, "Chief, I am sure that you will do the right legal things. Meanwhile, I will tell the security guards and all of our best warriors to help keep an eye on matters here. Let us travel together on Sunday, and then we can start our vigil first thing on Monday morning."

Everyone nodded in agreement to the plan for a peaceful protest.

Just after dawn on the following Monday morning, the peaceful protest of about one hundred Chiefs and other supporters, dressed in their various tribal costumes, and with face and body markings, stood quietly in front of the grand main gates of the Presidential Palace, located in the heart of the city. Chief Onida Ana took her position at the head of the protest group, and was approached by one of the two heavily armed security police of the Palace.

He asked firmly, "Why are you here?"

Chief Onida Ana looked at him straight at his eyes, and said, "We are the leaders of all of our Indigenous Peoples, and we have come in peace to protest at a plan to destroy our rainforests."

The Security Officer asked, "Have you any permission for this?"

The Chief said, "Sir, this is still a free country, and we are a peaceful people. All we are doing here is standing on this land of ours, to protest against something that will affect the lives of all of our peoples of Kayana. We just wish to continue to stand here."

The Security Officer said, "That may be so, but you all need permission to stand here. As you do not have this, I am asking you to leave this place now."

An enraged Peter stepped forward, and said, "Sir, this soil belongs to all of us, and we can stand anywhere we wish! We will not be moving from here!"

The Security Officer, clearly outnumbered, returned to his post, and made a phone call.

Chief Onida Ana said to her companions, "Please stay calm, and do not say anything. I will do all the talking."

Within a few minutes, the entire area in front of the Presidential Palace gates, was surrounded by scores of police cars, and armed military personnel. A Police Chief, as head of the operation, approached Chief Onida Ana.

He asked, "Are you the leader of this assembly?"

The Chief said, "Yes Sir. I am Chief Onida Ana, and most of the people here are Chiefs of our Indigenous Peoples from all parts of Kayana. We have come here in peace to protest at a plan to destroy our rainforests, and lives."

A procession of black limousines rolled up to the main gates, and Chief Onida Ana spotted John Jennings in one of the cars. He nodded when he saw her.

As the gates of the Presidential Palace slowly opened to allow the vehicles to enter, a group of protesters could not resist the temptation to storm through. The Chief and Peter rushed forward to try to stop the protesters.

During the ensuing scuffle and confusion, the group of Chiefs, along with Chief Onida Ana and Peter, were arrested, and bundled into a waiting police van. The Chief and Peter tried to explain to the officers that they were just trying to stop the invasion of the Presidential Palace grounds.

The remainder of the protesters were then pushed away from the gates and the immediate surrounds, by the aggressive, and heavily armed police. A small group of press photographers and TV reporters appeared on the scene, and tried to interview and film the protesters who refused to speak, and quietly drifted away.

At the prison, the duty officer spoke to each of the arrested protesters, took their details and belongings, and asked for them to be kept in the same prison cell. Chief Onida Ana felt humiliated, and angry at the way they were being treated. She demanded to speak to a higher level officer, and this was denied by the duty officer.

Chief Onida Ana took off her headdress, and felt a burning sensation by her left eye. Peter took his handkerchief, and tied it across her head to stem the flow of blood.

THIRTY-FOUR

CUSTODIAL SENTENCE

T hat evening, the local TV and Radio media covered the story of the protest at the Presidential Palace, and the arrests of Chief Onida Ana, Peter, and four of the other Chiefs who were accused of trying to breach security. The event quickly became the headline news, and a major talking point across the country.

Chief Onida Ana requested legal representation to counter the serious charges of unlawful protest, and breach of security, that were made by the police. A large crowd of local people gathered outside the grand Law Courts as the handcuffed accused were ushered in from the prison.

One group was very hostile towards the accused, and shouts of "Go back to your jungle!", "Useless *buck* people!", and "Give us our gold and diamonds!", were heard above the noise.

Another group, in support of Chief Onida Ana's actions, shouted their slogans of "Long Live Chief Onida Ana!", "Long Live our Indigenous Peoples!", "Hands off our true Kayanese Peoples!". Some of the Chiefs who had decided to stay on in the city, stood beside this group of supporters, and nervously watched the commotion.

The police formed a cordon between the opposing factions, and repeatedly asked them to disperse. This time, in the full view of the TV cameras, the officers did not resort to the use of force.

The Magistrate listened to the charges brought against Chief Onida Ana, and her companions. He then asked for their defence.

Chief Onida Ana, still wearing the bloodied headband, stood up, and the packed gallery gazed at her in awe.

She said, "Your honour, my peoples and I are sorry for causing any disturbance yesterday. We came here in peace, to show our solidarity against a much greater threat to the rainforests of Kayana. Sir, my peoples have suffered in silence for hundreds of years as our lands have been taken away for mining and logging. We are not the ones who crave after wealth. We do not want the gold and diamonds. But we only use a very small amount of timber. We have never used more than we ever needed for our survival, and our existence."

The Magistrate, an elderly African Kayanese, wearing his spectacles just over the tip of his long nose, peered over them, and nodded as Chief Onida Ana continued to speak.

She said, "Sir, I apologise to you and the President for holding a peaceful protest without the necessary permission to do so. But we had no time to apply for this, as we only heard about the meeting with the General Managers of the mining companies, a very short time before yesterday. I also apologise for my fellow Chiefs here, who tried to force their way past the security people. Peter Thomas and I tried to stop them, but we were all grabbed by the police. Sir, we do not wish to complain about the police action, and prefer to leave that to the Chief of Police to deal with. I also promise that our peoples will always try to uphold the laws of our country, now and in the future. All we want is to be treated with respect, and fairly."

The Magistrate intervened, and asked, "Chief, you have a bandage across your forehead. Has that been seen by a doctor?"

Chief Onida Ana said, "No Sir. No one has looked at the bruising I received from a police officer when I did not even try to resist arrest. My friend Peter was also hit hard on his back and legs by another police officer."

Members of the audience shouted, "Shame! No way to treat peaceful people!"

The Magistrate looked up at the audience, and said, "Please keep quiet! Any other further comment or interruption will be dealt with! Go ahead Chief."

Chief Onida Ana said, "Thank you Sir. Finally, my people standing here with me, do not wish to plead, and I request to be punished for being responsible for the protest, and the disruption."

The Magistrate said, "Chief Onida Ana, I shall be the sole judge as to the outcome of this case. I fully empathise with the reasons for your protest. I also record that I am unhappy about the way that you and your people were treated up to now. I do believe that you and Peter Thomas tried to stop the actions of your fellow Chiefs. Since you have accepted full responsibility for this whole episode, I dismiss your colleagues, and I am asking for you to serve a custodial sentence of two weeks. I am also asking for your injury to be treated urgently. This court is dismissed."

Members of the audience supporting Chief Onida Ana and her colleagues, shouted, "Shame on Kayana!"

Tears streamed down from Chief Onida Ana's eyes as she was escorted out of the court, and placed into the prison van, amongst other prisoners.

Peter shouted just before the van sped away, "Chief, I will wait here in the city! I will meet you at the jail!"

Chief Onida Ana was the only female amongst the prisoners in the van. She tried her best to avoid their intimidating, but curious, gazes. Upon arrival at the city prison, she was met by a nurse who treated the bruising at the side of her left eye, and placed a new bandage to cover the wound. She was then taken away by a female prison officer to have a shower, and then escorted to her prison cell.

She sat on the edge of the mattress in her cell, and began to sob. The bland grey clothes she was told to wear, added to the unexpected humiliation.

All the Chiefs and Peter who remained in the city, gathered just outside the main prison gates, and were quickly told to move away by the police. However, they were given permission to wait in an open space about one hundred yards from the prison. The Piaiman from Chief Onida Ana's community, arrived at the space, and asked everyone to gather around him for prayers.

He said, "I am here to be with you for as long as our Chief Onida Ana is held in prison. Let us keep a quiet vigil, obey the authorities, and any instructions we get from the police. A businessman here in the city, is sending us some blankets and canvas tents to be used during our stay. Food and refreshments will also be brought for us. Most of the people here are now in support of our Chief Onida Ana, and we will always show our gratitude towards them. Also, if anyone from the press approaches you, please direct them to me as we must always speak with one voice. Some people may come here to taunt us, call us names, and try to provoke a reaction. Please stay calm."

Peter said, "Thank you Piaiman. Only one of us will be allowed to go and visit the Chief, and I am happy to do so. If you wish to send her any message, please tell me, and I will let her know. I have been told that she is very upset, but is safe in her own cell. She will not be allowed to mix with the other prisoners, and will be under close watch. I think that this instruction was from the President of Kayana."

The Piaiman said, "The President is a smart man. He has seen how most of the Kayanese people have now become supportive of Chief Onida Ana, and our peoples. Of course, there are still others who simply do not like us. Some of those are the new multi-millionaires who have benefitted from Kayana's oil riches, and are in favour of the expansion of the gold and diamond operations."

One of the Chiefs asked, "Does anyone know as to whether the mining companies have been granted their wish to expand?"

Peter said, "No. We will have to wait and see. I think that at least for now, our protest has worked. When Chief Onida Ana is released, she will advise us as to what to do next. I will now go over to see if I could get to meet her."

The Piaiman said, "Be careful Peter. Be calm, and try not to respond to any harsh word or provocation from the prison staff."

Chief Onida Ana was delighted to see Peter who was allowed to meet her for one hour. They exchanged greetings, and words about how each other felt since the sentencing. She was happy to learn about the continuing vigil by the Chiefs, and the other protesters. She hated the food served to her, and the way she was spoken to. Peter suggested that she must stay composed, and that the time will soon be up for her release.

Chief Onida Ana said, "Peter, please pass on my thanks to everyone who is camped outside. Also, tell our people in our settlement that I am fine, and will be back with them very soon. Our protest has awakened most Kayanese about what is happening in the rainforests of our country. This is all I can say for now."

Peter nodded, and said, "I understand Chief. I will do as you have asked. Please try to get as much rest as possible. I can see that the bruising is improving."

The Chief smiled, and asked, "And how about you? Are you feeling better?"

Peter said, "Yes Chief. The swellings on my back and legs are now just black bruises. The Piaiman has been treating my wounds."

That evening, and every subsequent evening, the protesters lit one bonfire, and sat around it chanting and praying to the Great Spirit for the wellbeing of the young Chief. Their sound carried to the prison, and they were warned by the police to lower the volume of their singing. Chief Onida Ana told Peter during his next visit that she heard the chanting, and it made her feel more at ease in her stark cell.

On the morning of the Chief's release from prison, Peter, the Piaiman, and all those who had kept the vigil, gathered around in front of the main gate. Members of the press and TV media also secured good vantage points to witness the emergence of the Chief. Another gathering of ordinary Kayanese people stood across the street with many holding hastily prepared placards in support of the stance against further damage to the rainforests, and potential harm to the people living near the mines.

Chief Onida Ana, wearing her headdress, and full Kayana costume, smiled radiantly as she stepped through the gate, and into the first group who greeted her with hugs and kisses. She raised her right fist in a show of defiance, and the entire gathering erupted in loud acclaim. Someone started a chant of "Long Live Chief Onida Ana!", and this was repeated several times before she raised both arms to stop the chanting.

She said, at the top of her voice, "Thank you all, my fellow Kayanese! Thank you for your amazing support, and good wishes! You made my time in prison a lot easier than it would have been without such solidarity. My fellow Chiefs and peoples, you must all be very tired now, and I suggest that we all go back to our homes, villages, and communities to tell the people what has happened here, as we await the outcome of the mining companies' request. If they get their way, then we will have to continue to protest, and get our message across both here, and internationally. This rape of our environment must stop, and we must try our best to do so!"

The crowd applauded the Chief as she led the way towards the transportation which was arranged for the departure from the city. Members of the press chased after her, shouting questions about her plans, and she repeatedly answered, "No comment!"

THIRTY-FIVE

FIRST STEPS TO FREEDOM

C hief Onida Ana, Peter, and the Piaiman, were greeted by the entire community upon their arrival at the small harbour of their settlement. The Chief's pet animals and birds also found their way to the edge of the mooring, and she stooped down to accept their warm welcome. The ageing Onca splashed about in the water alongside his family of giant otters. Kassi and Kori took up their usual positions on the Chief's shoulders, as the tapir and other animals displayed their sense of great joy. The band of Howler monkeys sent out their message across the surrounding canopy.

The reawakening of public interest in the protection of the rainforests caused by the protest led by Chief Onida Ana, and her incarceration, caught the imagination of the local Kayanese people, and those abroad. The President of Kayana felt the mood of the population, and requested an urgent meeting with Chief Onida Ana. Instead of risking another long trip to the city, and being aware of a need to avoid more public attention so soon after the protest, she decided to ask the President to meet her, and the community council, at the benab.

The President agreed, and after a month of careful planning, a private trip was undertaken. No formal publicity was given by the Office of the President, and the low-key journey lasting about three hours, took place without mishap.

The President and his small support team of security guards, and assistants, landed at the harbour, and were warmly welcomed by Chief Onida Ana, Peter, the Piaiman, Reverend Small, and John Jennings. A special lunch was served at the long table in the benab, and most of the residents gathered outside in silence.

The Piaiman and Reverend Small blessed the meeting with prayers, and the parties settled down to speak with each other.

Chief Onida Ana said, "Mr President and guests, welcome to our humble abode. I trust that you enjoyed the meal and refreshments offered, and please accept a bottle of our own specially fermented, and best quality *casareep*!"

Everyone cheered as the President gratefully accepted the Chief's gift.

She continued, "Sir, as you can see, we have all worked for many years, and with good support from your government and Mr Jennings' mining company, to develop our model settlement within this mining area. You are also aware about our protest against any further expansion of mining operations here, and across Kayana. My peoples do not see the need for greater production, and exploration for gold and diamonds. Our country has gained a lot through the oil production, and that wealth should not be squandered on obscene private collections of gold and diamonds. This country needs better healthcare, roads, factories, farming, education, sanitation, electricity, sea defences, and protection of this special gift of our rainforests. My people and I love where, and how we live, and we want to continue to do so with only a small amount of basic needs. We need better sanitation, cleaner water, and medical supplies. We do not wish to become millionaires. Our wealth is right here, and these rainforests provide enough oxygen for the whole of Kayana."

The President, who was a middle-aged man of medium height and build, was very impressed by the young Chief's clear thinking, and eloquence.

He smiled, and said, "Chief Onida Ana, I believe in everything you have just said. I also apologise for the way that you and your fellow Chiefs, and others were treated in the city. You, and this environment are special gifts to Kayana from the Great Spirit, and the God to whom I pray. You have already inspired most of the peoples of Kayana, and I personally admire your show of great vision, and leadership. I have come here today to announce that I have rejected the request for expansion of all extractive mines here in Kayana, for at least the next five years to 2030. You are the first to know this, and so is Mr Jennings who can inform his delegation about my decision. I shall send them a formal notice about this."

Everyone in the Chief's group applauded the President's announcement. John Jennings looked across at the Chief, and they both smiled at each other. He gave her a "thumbs up" signal, and she responded likewise.

The President continued, "Chief Onida Ana, I also wish to make you an offer. I am asking you to chair a special committee to look at a new strategy for Kayana's rainforests, Indigenous Peoples, and a long term development programme across the country. I am, like you, a champion of the natural environment, and I want to see the vision that you have spoken about, come to fruition. You do not have to leave this community to work with me, and I shall provide all the support you need here to conduct the review, and deliver the strategy. I shall also provide all the expertise needed, and use a specially earmarked budget for this. What do you say?"

Chief Onida Ana said, "Sir, I do not wish to enter into any form of politics. I have said many times before, that I have a lot of work to do here with my people, and across Kayana. I cannot accept your kind offer, and I do not wish to be seen supporting you, and your political party."

The President said, "Chief, that is precisely the reason why I believe that you are the best person to lead this work. You are a neutral, and that will be respected everywhere. I know, and understand why you do not trust politicians like me. But I sincerely want you to believe, in front of everyone here, that I have no political motive in asking for your help."

John Jennings said, "Chief, I accept the President's decision, and as I have done before, I promise to give you as much support that you and the committee will need to produce a strategy such as this. Please accept the President's offer."

The Piaiman said, "Yes, I agree that such work is really important for all the peoples of Kayana, and for the world that is looking at us. This could be our best chance to deliver that vision we have held on to for hundreds of years."

Peter smiled, and said, "Chief, this is a very important moment in our history, and that of Kayana."

An elder, sitting next to Chief Onida Ana, said, "Yes, this is the first time in all my eighty years, that someone has come here to ask us to help develop this beautiful country of Kayana. The Great Spirit, and the spirits of our ancestors, will guide you Chief, and all who work on this plan. I am nearer to my physical end here, and this news makes me want to live on for many more years!"

159

The other four elders nodded in agreement.

Peter looked at Chief Onida Ana, and said, "A proper strategy for Kayana's Indigenous Peoples must also include all the other African, East Indian, Chinese, Portuguese, and Mixed Race folks. This is a country designed for all Kayanese. I am so happy that the President of our country has chosen you Chief Onida Ana, and all of us here, to lead this work, and show everyone our vision for now, and the future."

Chief Onida Ana's eyes filled up with tears of joy, and as she wiped them away, she said, "Maybe now is the time for me to take our peoples of Kayana further forward. You all have expressed sound reasons to believe our President's good intentions, and so I am willing to accept this offer. However, I will need the sanction of all the other Chiefs across Kayana, and if you do not mind, I shall do this first. Otherwise, without their wisdom, experience, knowledge, and support, we will not have a proper strategy and plan. Mr President, I hope that you will understand this."

The President smiled, and said, "Chief Onida Ana, that is the right and proper way to do things. I had thought of this, and spoke with most of the Chiefs who all supported the idea of you leading the committee. They are all willing to participate in the review. Indeed, they would like to have you present the first draft of the strategy at the next annual convention of the Chiefs in the city. So, they are asking for the work to commence as soon as possible. I also plan to be there to endorse the strategy which will then go to the Kayana parliament for approval."

The Chief looked a little worried, and asked, "Sir, I would prefer that a Chief for each Region presents their own part of the strategy. Will that be OK?"

The President said, "Yes Chief, I agree. It is clear that you are already thinking about how this important work should be done. Thank you. If you do not mind, two of my officials will stay here to help you set up all that is required for the review and research, for the strategy and plan. I also plan to visit you every three months to discuss how things are progressing. They will not be public visits, and I am looking forward to spending some vacation time here with my family so that we can all appreciate, and experience what it is like to live here."

Chief Onida Ana said, "Thank you Sir. You and your family will be most welcome. In fact, I should also ask our dear friend Mr Jennings to bring his family from Canada to spend their vacation here."

John Jennings smiled, and said, "Yes, of course Chief! I should have done so a long time ago!"

Reverend Small said, "Mr President, thank you for coming here personally to meet with us, and to see for yourself, how true Kayanese people can live in such close harmony with what the Good Lord has provided. If this is what Heaven looks and feels like, then I thank the Lord for this gift. Chief Onida Ana, and fellow brothers and sisters, this is a truly blessed moment in our long and challenging history. This is a great opportunity for us to take more responsibility for the future of Kayana, and all its peoples. To everyone who will now embark on the first steps to true freedom and betterment, I ask the Lord God to bless us all with the right answers for all the issues we face now, and will face into the future. Amen."

Everyone repeated, "Amen" as the Chief brought the meeting to a close. She invited the President to accompany her to meet with the large gathering just outside the benab.

The Piaiman raised his arms aloft, and said, "Dear brothers and sisters, our President of Kayana has enjoyed our hospitality, and has asked our Chief to lead a major project which will help to develop the whole of Kayana, and our peoples, well into the future. I bless them through the Great Spirit, and now ask the President to say a few words before he leaves us."

The President, smiling with great satisfaction, said, "Fellow citizens of Kayana, thank you for making me and my team feel so happy here. You are living in a situation which I envy, and I shall do more to help you with your immediate problems. Chief Onida Ana and her team will help me to propose the right vision and plan for Kayana. Instead of waiting for a whole year from now, I wish to announce that my government will fund your water, sanitation, and electric power needs from today!"

Everyone applauded and shouted with sheer delight at the news.

The President said, "Thank you, and I hope to return soon with my family, to spend our vacation here. God bless you all."

Chief Onida Ana and the President embraced each other, and she said, "Thank you Mr President. We are truly honoured by your presence, and are really happy about your great support. Do have a safe journey back to the city."

The Piaiman joined the community as they waved the President and his team goodbye.

The Piaiman smiled, and looked up to the patches of clear blue sky through the gaps in the canopy, and said, "Oh Great Spirit, thank you for the first steps to our vision of a united, and peaceful Kayana. Thank you for opening our hearts and eyes to the dreams of our ancestors. Thank you for Chief Onida Ana."

THIRTY-SIX

CRIMINAL GANGS

Chief Onida Ana wasted no time in assembling her team to work on the President's project. She was delighted to welcome back her former high school friend Ruby Smith to lead on the analytical modelling work using her outstanding mathematical and financial skills. Indra Persaud and Mary Brown took on the issues relating to the environment, mining, and the lumber industries. John Jennings' manager, Abraham Campbell, and Peter Thomas, worked together on the social and cultural elements, and issues of the Indigenous Peoples across the country.

The President, as promised, sent a team to construct a dedicated water and sanitation system for the mining town and the settlement. Electricity was harnessed from the industrial generators used by the mining operation. The costs of the supply of electricity, clean water, and sanitation, was funded out of the contractual payments from the mining company, to the Kayana government. There was however, a new problem which emerged from the news of the developments to the mining town, and the settlement. Small-time independent miners, of African, East Indian, and Indigenous heritage, began to operate on the outer fringes of the large mining area, much to John Jennings' annoyance.

The new mining gangs, or porknockers, began to attract bandits and robbers from across Kayana's borders, and the first attack on a small group, was brutal. The criminal gang demanded all the gold that the porknockers had found, their money, and other valuables. When the miners refused, the gang shot and killed the five men, and took the spoils. This episode sent shockwaves across the country.

Chief Onida Ana's immediate response to the news of the attack, was to appeal directly to the President, for more security services to the mining town and the surrounding villages. The retired soldiers,

John Brown, Abdul Rasheed, and Suresh Nanan, had managed to protect the mining town and the Chief's settlement, with their continuing presence, and the training of local young warriors. However, the Chief requested further help for all Indigenous villages and settlements across Kayana.

The President advised Chief Onida Ana that such a request was unaffordable, and opted to ask for the country's army to do more patrols in and around all the mining operations. The Chief accepted this, and indicated that the safety of Indigenous Peoples, and all others who worked in the hinterland, must feature as an important priority for the strategy she was leading on. The President in turn, decided to meet with the leaders of Kayana's borders, to ensure that they worked together to control, and stop the activities of the criminal gangs.

Chief Onida Ana's tendency to act quickly to prevent, and, or deal with issues of real concern for her Indigenous Peoples, and other Kayanese, greatly enhanced her status and reputation as a Chief. Her popularity spread widely, and was further extended when as part of the President's project, she decided to visit all the villages and settlements to speak with the Chiefs, and their communities. She took Peter, Ruby Smith, and the Piaiman on her epic mission. Peter acted as guide and bodyguard. Ruby kept detailed records of the information they gathered about each village, settlement, and industrial operation they encountered. The Piaiman shared his knowledge, and acquired more from his fellow spiritual leaders. Such a comprehensive study and record about all the Indigenous Peoples of Kayana, had never been undertaken before.

Chief Onida Ana was always greeted with great warmth and affection at each village, and other places that she and her companions entered. At one remote Indigenous village, deep into the south-west region of Kayana which had recently attracted attention due to a rumour of gold to be found in the shallow edges of the nearby river, she was told about regular attacks by small-time miners from across the borders of Kayana, and by criminal gangs. The miners would often enter the village demanding food, and sexual favours of the young women. When the criminal gang members arrived, they in turn, bullied the miners, and also entered the village to do the same as the latter.

The village Chief, with tears in his tired eyes, pleaded with Chief Onida Ana to do something about the plight of his community. They had become extremely frustrated, and were fed up with having to move from one location to another, only to be attacked again. The entire population of only about one hundred frightened men, women, and children gathered around the visitors. They could not smile as they were so consumed with sadness.

Chief Onida Ana said, "I feel for you. I will get help for you, and try to stop the illegal mining and the criminal gangs, as soon as possible. You do not need to move away from here yet again. This is your land, and people must respect you for looking after it. Have you lost anyone from this community?"

The village Chief said, "Yes Chief. Every time one of our people is killed, we bury him or her, and we move away. We burn our homes and other belongings before we leave so that the attackers can see that we have nothing left. But they still come after us. We can fight them, but we only have poison arrows, and they have guns. We are peaceful people, and all we want is to live here, and to be happy. Now, we are sad, and we are being killed. Please help us quickly."

Chief Onida Ana, Peter, Ruby, and the Piaiman all wiped tears streaming down their cheeks. Ruby took notes of the most important things needed by the villagers, and as they turned to walk away, the village Chief led slow, and appreciative applause. The Chief and her group stopped, turned around once more, and waved goodbye. She then paused once more, and decided to take action.

In the absence of good and reliable phone signals, the Chief could not communicate immediately with the President's office, and she feared for the lives of the villagers. Peter then volunteered to trek back to the nearest location from where he could make the phone call for some security, and much needed supplies to be delivered by helicopter.

Chief Onida Ana and the others decided to stay behind at the village Chief's benab whilst Peter set off on his attempt to get help. The village Chief offered Peter the support of a young warrior from the village.

The village Chief said, "Peter, this is our bravest and best young warrior. He knows a lot about this whole area, and how to find a place with a phone. Take some cassava bread and water with you, as it is about one day and night from here."

Within a few hours of Peter's departure, a gang of five robbers entered the village. They fired their pistols in the air, and caused the villagers to stop everything that they were doing, and flee for their lives. Chief Onida Ana and her companions heard the commotion, and she stepped outside the benab to confront the attackers.

The leader of the gang stood in front of his four men, and faced up to Chief Onida Ana. He was a short, stocky, and dark-skinned man. He wore a black kerchief over his nose and mouth. His brown eyes were opened widely with the surprise of meeting someone prepared to stand up to him.

He asked, in a gruff voice, "Who the hell are you?"

Chief Onida Ana, with her right hand on the handle of her hunting knife still in its shaft, said, "I am Chief Onida Ana. I am asking you and your gang to leave us alone. We have nothing to give you."

The gang leader turned to his men, and laughed out mockingly. They joined in with his taunt.

He said, "Well, if you have nothing to give us, we will take you away! You are a great prize. Let me see. A ransom for you could fetch us thousands of American dollars!"

Chief Onida Ana said, "You will have to kill me. I am not going anywhere with you."

The gang leader turned to his men, and laughed out loudly again.

He said, "Well, we will stay here, and wait till your friend comes back. Then we will send him away to tell the world that you and your friends have been kidnapped. Our ransom will be brought here, and you, the great hope of Kayana, will be set free. Simple! Now, get back into the house, and order some food!"

The gang leader held his pistol to Chief Onida Ana's back, and wrenched her knife from her waist, as they entered the benab. His four gang members stood outside as guards. All the remaining villagers took the opportunity to flee into the surrounding forest.

THIRTY-SEVEN

HEADLESS SNAKE

The gang leader rested his pistol on the small dining table. He ordered Chief Onida Ana, the local Chief of the village, Ruby Smith, and the Piaiman, to sit down opposite him. Chief Onida Ana studied the position of the pistol from the corner of her eyes, and mentally weighed up the risks of trying to grab it, and overcome her captor who was busy scoffing some food which was placed before him.

He paused after a large mouthful, looked up at his prisoners, and pointed to the gun.

He said, "Don't even think about grabbing my gun! You will get nowhere, and my men will shoot to kill!"

Chief Onida Ana said, "You are wasting your time here. We have nothing to give you. Also, no one will give you any money to free me and my friends. So, why don't you just eat up, and go away?"

The gang leader said, "I have heard about you. Everyone is talking about how great you are. How you are the most important Indigenous Kayanese in this country. You must be worth a fortune, and I am going to get a lot of money for you."

He laughed loudly, spitting bits of his food in front of him. The other gang members copied his mockery.

A few hours passed whilst the gang leader became increasingly impatient, and fidgety. He picked up his pistol, and pointed it at Chief Onida Ana. She stared back defiantly at his tired looking eyes.

He asked, "When is your friend coming back here?"

Chief Onida Ana said, "I don't know. Maybe tomorrow. Maybe next week. I don't know."

He angrily slammed his left fist on the table, and his empty aluminium bowl bounced up, spun around, and then finally settled. Chief Onida Ana did not flinch as she continued to stare at him.

He snorted, wiped away bits of food from around his mouth with his left hand, and said, "So you think that you are so smart? Let me see how you cope with this old good-for-nothing Chief!"

The old Chief arched back in his chair, and pleaded, "Sir, please do not beat us up. We do not have any money or gold anymore. People have gone to bring food for us. That is all we need. Please listen to Chief Onida Ana, and go in peace."

The whirring sound of a helicopter's blade became increasingly louder as it reached nearer to the village. Within minutes, it became deafening as it encircled the site before hovering over the small open square. A large plume of dust rose up from the ground, and was whipped around, and into the surrounding houses. The four guards began to open fire at the large and imposing vehicle, as they ran away towards the jungle.

The gang leader grabbed Chief Onida Ana firmly by her right arm, and forcibly pushed her ahead, with his gun aimed at her neck.

He shouted at the helicopter pilot, and gestured for him to fly away. The pilot ignored the instruction, reached for his pistol, opened the pilot's door, and moved towards the hostage taker.

The increasingly frustrated and angry gang leader tightened his grip on Chief Onida Ana, and pulled her closer to himself. Chief Onida Ana winced in pain, but managed to use her right leg to trip over her captor. He fell clumsily to the ground as his pistol was fired. The pilot stopped for a moment, and then fell to the ground.

Peter and his warrior companion quickly emerged from the helicopter, and they grappled with the gang leader. They disarmed him, and managed to tie his hands firmly behind his back. The pilot slowly stood up holding his left arm where some blood was oozing from his gunshot wound.

The Piaiman quickly ran across to the pilot, and after a quick examination, tied a cotton kerchief over a poultice of herbal leaves from his pouch, around the wound.

Chief Onida Ana walked over to the wounded pilot, and said, "Thank you for coming so quickly, and for saving our lives. Please come into the benab, and have some rest and something to drink."

The pilot said, "Chief, it is better for me to offload all the provisions I have brought for the village, and to return to base as quickly as possible. I shall check to see if the helicopter was hit by any of the gunfire, and then take this prisoner to the authorities. I also need to get this wound sorted out."

The Piaiman said, "Sir, my treatment will work well for you."

The pilot said, "Thank you. I know it will work. I am a half-Indigenous Kayanese."

The village Chief said, "Thank you for coming to help us, and to save our lives. Now that you know where we are, please tell the government to send us more help."

Chief Onida Ana said, "Please also take my message to the President, and let him know what has happened here. Me and my team will now make our way back to our own settlement, as soon as the villagers here come back to their homes."

Peter asked, "Chief, what must we do about the four gangsters who ran away? They are still armed, and dangerous!"

Chief Onida Ana said, "No snake is dangerous without its head. Let them rot in hell."

The pilot drank some water from his water bottle, inspected the body of the helicopter, and then climbed back into the cockpit. As the powerful engine and rotors started up, some of the villagers began to cautiously re-enter the village. Chief Onida Ana and the others stepped back into the benab as the helicopter took off, and began to climb out of the clearing, and above the canopy.

A few minutes of calmness descended on the village after the helicopter disappeared from view. The remainder of the villagers emerged from their hiding places, and nervously returned to the village square.

Chief Onida Ana, the Piaiman, Ruby, Peter, and the old village Chief stepped out of the benab, and they quietly greeted and hugged as many of the villagers as they could. The dignified calmness, and friendliness of all the people of the village, greatly moved Chief Onida Ana and her companions.

She said, "My dear brothers and sisters, I hope that from now onwards you will not have to leave this place, and keep running away. This land, forest, river, and all else here belong to you and your children, and to those yet to come. I will make sure that you will continue to get the help you need to live here peacefully, and happily. Me and my people will always be there for you. Thank you Chief. We will now leave you to get back to your normal lives."

The village Chief, with tears of joy in his weary eyes, and a broad smile, hugged Chief Onida Ana, and bade her farewell.

He said, "Chief, may the Great Spirit continue to walk with you, and guide you in everything you do for Kayana."

The entire gathering applauded Chief Onida Ana and her companions as they left the village, and disappeared into the forest.

THIRTY-EIGHT

A NEW KAYANA

The general elections for the Presidency of Kayana was due to be held in late 2025. The President and his political party held a slender lead by only two members of parliament, and delayed the voting until the following May 2026. He urged Chief Onida Ana and her working group, to complete the project on the country's Indigenous Peoples, and aimed to use the report as an important plank of his strategy and manifesto to develop Kayana for the benefit of all the peoples.

Chief Onida Ana duly completed the first draft of her report, and led her team to meet the President to discuss its findings, and recommendations. A special session was arranged for her to do a formal presentation to the President and his cabinet, at the newly and extensively refurbished Presidential Palace in the city.

Chief Onida Ana chose to wear her tribal crown, and beautiful Kayana costume embellished with an exquisite necklace, and armbands created by the women's group of her settlement. She stood up at the President's invitation, and everyone was astonished at her statuesque presence, and beauty.

She smiled, and said, "Thank you Mr President, and honourable ministers. I have been most privileged, and delighted to have been asked to lead this research with the help of an amazing team of experts who are all here with me. I wish to thank them all for their hard work, and their great insights which made my task a lot easier than it would have been otherwise. I also wish to thank all of my peoples, and other Kayanese whom we met, and listened to, across the country over the last year. This report reflects their views, and ideas for the future development of Kayana. It is our great hope that the government and the people of Kayana can embrace this report in its entirety, and work together to help build a better, and happier country."

The meeting applauded the Chief's introduction, and she then proceeded to discuss the findings about all aspects of the lives of the Indigenous Peoples from village to village, and region to region. She also reflected on the state of the country's rainforests, rivers, highlands, and lowlands, urging her audience to preserve such gifts, and to significantly cut back on the level of exploitation. Her report pointed out that Kayana's agricultural activities were under threat by severe competition from other countries around the world, new scientific advances which reduced reliance on fertile land, and trade restrictions on Kayana's products.

Chief Onida Ana spoke about the general lack of development of newer and better infrastructure for transport, education, healthcare, social care, businesses, sports, and eco-tourism promised by successive Presidents, and their governments.

She paused to take a sip of cold water, and then continued after receiving a nod from the President.

Chief Onida Ana explained that her research also found examples of good initiatives and progressive enterprises by the people, with and without the support of the governments of the past, and the present. She cited her own model settlement and local mining town, their junior and senior high schools teaching the country's curriculum as well as the environment, and the Kayana language. She welcomed the expansion of new businesses encouraged by investments from profits of the extractive industries, and by the Kayanese returning from abroad.

She pointed out that the country had tremendous potential with brilliant people, and all the resources it needed to become fully developed. Excellent small enterprises were good for the local economy in the areas they served, but some of these should be further expanded to cover trade across Kayana, and contribute to exports abroad. She was however, very critical about any attempts by global corporations to exploit the mineral reserves, and lumber. She emphasised that Kayanese had enough gold and diamonds for their needs. More emphasis should be placed on the use of alternative materials for housebuilding, instead of reliance on Kayana's timber.

Her report also commented on some negative social aspects of the country, and in particular, the growing criminal activities including fraud, corruption, armed robberies, domestic violence, alcohol and drug misuse, suicides, and increasing attacks on Indigenous Peoples.

She cited the need for stronger legal responses alongside more directed education, suitable job opportunities, the rebuilding of racial trust, and religious tolerance, amongst all the peoples of Kayana.

The President led the applause to acknowledge the report's findings, and then gestured for the Chief to continue with her presentation.

She said, "Kayana, despite its problems, still remains a very beautiful country which has managed to retain most of its natural life-giving rainforests, rivers, and contrasting landscape. But, our geologists and environmental specialists have warned us about the uncontrollable threat that our entire coastland faces from nature's increasingly violent storms and hurricanes. Indeed, we are also potentially subject to a severe earthquake which can cause exceptional havoc, and destruction. Mr President, instead of waiting for these things to happen, our report recommends that we seriously consider a relocation of our capital city, and all the other towns on the coastland, to sites further towards the hinterland. Too much of our national budget is being wasted on patching up and repairing sea defences, and our poor irrigation systems. These continue to cause severe flooding along the entire coastland and river banks, every time heavy rains come. We need to act now."

Chief Onida Ana paused once again, to take another sip of water, and continued, "Whilst we strive to rebuild a new and progressive Kayana, we must also embrace, and seek to take a much more proactive approach to the adoption of the fastest growing economic revolution that is happening around the world. We need to invest in research into how best we can adopt Artificial Intelligence or AI, to suit our needs here in Kayana. We have many bright young people who are keen to explore the entrepreneurial benefits of using AI, and we must invest in them."

The audience was captivated by the Chief's forthright presentation which was amply supported by impressive statistical, and other evidence for the findings. She seemed to have a very good grasp of the complex data and information, and this confidence served to make the report much more convincing, and influential.

She then used the final quarter of her allotted time, to spell out the recommendations for the development of Kayana over the next ten, and twenty years. The recommendations covered infrastructure development including better and more environmentally friendly power supplies, cleaner water, and new sanitation systems to fit in with the worldwide targets by 2030. There were recommendations for more efficient air and ground transportation systems, a new eco-university to be located in the hinterland, more schools, hospitals, community clinics, and free supplies of medicines. Chief Onida Ana emphasised that the investments would create more jobs for local Kayanese.

Her call for the relocation of the capital city and other coastal towns demanded the most finance, and she justified this by the savings from lesser expenditure on maintenance of the almost broken sea defences and irrigation systems. The report recognised also, that such dramatic changes in the environment of the coastal communities will need careful handling, and planning over at least the next twenty years, and if possible, before any devastation hits the areas in the future.

Chief Onida Ana's report also recommended a review of all contracts with foreign owned global corporations exploiting the mining, timber, and oil industries, and negotiating for greater shares of the profits. She concluded her presentation by calling for a stronger Kayana in all aspects of its development, and its peoples. Alongside the economic regeneration, she wanted to see a healthier and happier population to benefit from bigger and better cultural institutions, and sports facilities. She raised a few eyebrows when she mentioned that as a growing population, the culture, and main language of the Indigenous Peoples should be invested in, and shared across the country.

Chief Onida Ana stood more upright as she made her final remarks, "As a more prosperous nation, we must consider strengthening our military capability in order to enhance our security from any type of internal and external threat. Likewise, our defence must also be strong enough to withstand any cyber threat, as we develop our technological base for all of our activities. Thank you for listening to me, and I commend this report to you Mr President, and your government."

The President, and all the attendees at the meeting, rose to give the Chief a sustained ovation.

He said, "Thank you Chief Onida Ana. Today, I should call you Queen Onida Ana! You have set out a most compelling vision, and challenge for us all. The insights shown by you, your team, and the people of Kayana you spoke with, as well as your recommendations, are truly remarkable, and awe-inspiring. I may not agree with everything you have suggested, but you have given me much to ponder, and I shall take this to the Kayanese peoples over my campaign in the general elections. If I return as President, I shall take that as an endorsement of this plan by the Kayanese peoples. I know that you do not wish to enter into politics, and to be part of any political party here in Kayana. But I hope that I can call on your support to lead on many of these recommendations. I am proud to have you as our youngest, bravest, and most inspirational of leaders. I hope that you and your team will accept this offer. Indeed, I hope that you can start from now on, so that this new Kayana can be built, even if I do not continue as your President."

THIRTY-NINE

MOTHER OF ALL STORMS

The results of the general election in Kayana, in May 2026, saw the re-election of the President, alongside a landslide victory by his political party. The President was overjoyed, and the mood of the country became one of greater optimism, and expectation. He immediately contacted Chief Onida Ana by phone, and thanked her and her team for the development strategy of Kayana.

The peoples of Kayana liked what they heard and read about the strategy that was adopted as the main manifesto for the President and his government. He wasted no time in personally leading the development plans, and offered Chief Onida Ana the principal strategic development role alongside himself, and key ministers in his government. He also reached out to the main opposition political parties, and requested their involvement in the rebuilding plans.

The next few years marked substantial development and improvements across Kayana. The President's popularity had grown to legendary status. The people of Kayana also noticed the emergence of the beautiful, and articulate Chief Onida Ana, whose own popularity across the country closely rivalled the President's.

The Chiefs of the National Council for the Indigenous Peoples of Kayana, also embraced Chief Onida Ana, and at the Annual Conference of Chiefs, they unanimously elected her as their overall Chief of Chiefs. She in turn, ensured that all developments promised in the strategy, and in particular those directly relating to Indigenous Peoples and their environment, were fully implemented.

She took every opportunity to attend the launch of every project for the benefit of the people. She also ensured that she was seen to support the initiatives which were for the benefit of the people who were from the areas that had voted against the President.

Chief Onida Ana's settlement which continued to grow in size and population, managed to retain its charm and simplicity despite extensive modernisation. The people, especially the elders, insisted on wearing their Kayana costumes, and the new uniform of the school was of Kayana design.

As the first of January 2030 neared, all the surrounding villages, and the mining town, were decorated with special banners proclaiming the advent of Chief Onida Ana's thirtieth birthday. A lavish celebration was planned by Peter and the village council. The benab was virtually rebuilt and extended along the lines of the traditional design, but also included some essential modern facilities. More rooms were created to house the Chief's guests.

Her friends, Ruby Smith, Indra Persaud, and Mary Brown were married, and chose to have their own homes built within the settlement as they continued to work for the government agencies dealing with the conservation of the rainforests, and the environment. Chief Onida Ana was proud to act as godmother to the children of her friends. She was also continuously urged by Peter and her friends to get married, and to settle down. She rebuffed them by suggesting that all the young men of her age were too much in awe of her, and she was not prepared to enter into a relationship under such circumstances. She wished to continue to dedicate her life to serving her people across Kayana, and all others in the country.

The President chose to attend Chief Onida Ana's new year and birthday celebrations, and asked for the events to be covered by the local television and radio stations. The entire cabinet of his government also attended whilst the remainder of the country heralded the new year with hundreds of parties.

Just after midnight, when everyone had welcomed in the new year, dark clouds appeared across the entire coastland, and soon a torrential rainstorm dampened the revelling in the streets as everyone headed back to shelter in their homes. The weather forecasters had warned about the impending storm, but no one expected such a wild and dangerous one. The wind picked up speed, and the ocean waves grew in their intensity as they crashed into, and splashed over the seawalls.

The President and his colleagues kept in touch with his office in the capital city, and stayed up to follow the television and radio broadcasts which were all concentrated on the storm. The celebrations at the settlement petered out, and everyone returned to their homes. Chief Onida Ana's visitors also gathered around the large television screen in the benab, and closely observed pictures and commentaries about the storm. The pictures of the seawall of the city were cause for real concern as the powerful waves lashed the defences, and broke through down the main streets in a way that was never seen before.

The President turned to his ministers, and said, "This is not looking good. I think that we need to get back to the city as soon as possible."

Chief Onida Ana said, "Sir, that will now be impossible, as the airports have been shut down. You must stay here, and try to monitor the operations of the emergency services. The storm is getting worse, and the weather people are saying that the winds are now up to hurricane levels. This could be the mother of all storms that we have been warned about."

The President nodded in agreement, and took up a seat at the head of the extensive dining table. Chief Onida Ana sat next to him to his right, and the ministers took up the remaining seats.

He said, "Since we cannot travel back to the city, I think that we have to treat this benab as our emergency control room. In fact, due to the increasing intensity of the storm, and the news of the widespread flooding across the entire coastland, as well as breaches over the banks of the three biggest rivers, I now officially declare a national emergency. We will continue to be directly linked to the control room at the Presidential Palace where the heads of the Armed Forces, police, fire service, and health service, are organising the responses on the ground there."

Chief Onida Ana asked, "Sir, what happens if the Palace is also flooded, and power supplies are cut off?"

The President, appearing more distressed and tired as the events unfolded, said, "Chief, we have no other emergency back up."

The Minister for Home Affairs said, "Sir, all of our emergency rooms in the city and the other coastland towns, have also been knocked out by flood waters, and have suffered extensive damage to the buildings. Due to the pitch darkness, and loss of power, we are not seeing the real extent of the damage being caused. Another few hours of this, and I dread to think of the true impact of this national disaster."

Everyone in the benab looked on in awe at the television screen as a lone reporter tried to cover the only pictures of the raging storm. He could not stand up any longer as the wind lashed out wildly, and he sought refuge within the TV studios. The only live picture was from a camera scanning the scene of devastation outside the building. The TV presenter then announced the President's declaration of a state of emergency, and his message for everyone to stay within the confines of their homes.

Unfortunately, some citizens who chose to ignore the President's warning, stepped out of their homes, and tried to save their pets and livestock. Several incidents of drowning were reported on the radio. Messages were continuously relayed for the public to remain calm, seek shelter, and not venture out into the storm. Some people chose to ignore the warnings, and decided to loot stores in the cities and towns affected by the storm.

Strangely, at dawn the next day, the winds and rain had died down, and an eerie calmness prevailed under the cloudless blue skies. Darkness gave way to bright, and hot sunshine. Residents began to emerge from their shelters. They looked around at the incredible amount of damage with debris scattered on and near the roadways, the flooded terrain, and the broken wooden posts which carried the electric cables. Tall coconut trees which could withstand such powerful winds, lost many of their branches in the mayhem, and they stood out amongst several other trees which were toppled over, and those still standing with broken branches. Most of the zinc roofs of the older wooden houses were ripped off, and scattered hundreds of yards around.

Throughout the day, news was relayed about the damage caused by the storm all along the coastline of over two hundred miles, and also miles inwards along the river banks. These were the most populated areas of Kayana, and soon the news included the large numbers of casualties, and the severely injured who were languishing at the main hospitals and health clinics which were overwhelmed.

The scenes of terrible devastation were being shown on television channels operating from neighbouring countries. Large swathes of sugar and rice fields were mostly under several feet of brown and heavily silted water from the sea and the rainfall. The owners and workers stood helplessly staring at the flooded areas around the fields, and villagers tried to retrieve any useful items they could muster.

The flood waters turned streets and roads into lakes and streams, and survivors who lost their entire homes, began desperate calls for help. The emergency response across Kayana was woefully inadequate, and members of the Armed Forces tried to encourage survivors to abandon their properties, gather up as much belongings they could find, and head further into the higher levels inland.

The news of the storm and floods drew international attention, and the President was able to appeal directly to neighbouring governments for help with basic medicines, clean drinking water, tents and other forms of shelter, clothing, and, some foodstuff. He insisted on travelling back to the Presidential Palace, but Chief Onida Ana and others advised him to stay at the benab. The Armed Forces and police began to work closely with international agencies which were flying in the items requested by the President.

Chief Onida Ana and her group of helpers managed to contact the other Chiefs of Kayana, and, in an unprecedented effort, they organised hundreds of boats and canoes filled with provisions, blankets, and clean water. The fleets of boats and canoes used the inland waterways and rivers to head towards the areas of the flooding. Chief Onida Ana and the President could see how the operation was progressing via pictures relayed back to the TV channels by drones, and helicopters.

Although such an operation would take many days to reach some destinations, the President and his ministers were greatly moved by the immense gesture of Kayana's Indigenous Peoples. Tears streamed down his face as he embraced Chief Onida Ana.

The Piaiman raised his arms aloft, and said, "May the Great Spirit save all of our peoples of Kayana from the ravages of this mother of all storms, and take the flood waters back to the ocean."

Reverend Henry Small clasped his hands, lowered his head, and said, "May the Lord God bless and protect all of Kayana today, and forever more. Amen."

FORTY

THE AMAZING DREAM

The emergency relief from several international agencies, and countries, continued to pour into Kayana as the true extent of the destruction, and loss of life, became more evident. The sea defence walls along the coastland were severely breached in many places, and work was already underway to mend them. Most of the buildings and farms nearest to the sea defences were completely destroyed, along with the loss of several hundreds of lives. The country's burial and cremation facilities were overwhelmed. Hospitals and clinics were under severe pressures which were only being relieved by foreign medical staff, and medicines being especially flown into the country.

The President and his cabinet finally reached the Palace in the city which was in utter chaos. Desperate people took to the streets when the flood waters began to subside, and large scale looting of abandoned grocery and retail stores was out of control, despite the curfew in place.

Chief Onida Ana and her team had decided to accompany one of the fleets of boats and canoes taking provisions up to, and along the coastland. People made homeless by the floods, were given priority as each vessel moored at the harbours and jetties of the three main rivers. As soon as each boat was off-loaded, it was re-fuelled before heading back for more provisions. Unfortunately, stocks of fuel were also running out, and this threatened the continuation of the rescue operation. Chief Onida Ana requested more supplies of oil from the President's own committee overseeing the emergency.

The President took the earliest opportunity to address the Kayana people via television and radio, as soon as the media was restored. He extended his heartfelt condolences to all who had lost loved ones, and promised to do everything to help care for the injured. He declared a week of mourning. He then assured the people about the rescue and reconstruction work already underway, and asked for more patience regarding some essential supplies, and shelter. The President pleaded with those committing theft and other crimes, to stop this, and warned that the Armed Forces as well as the police had begun to clamp down hard on such activities. He warned that those convicted of rioting and looting, would be required to do hard labour on the reconstruction projects, instead of being put in the overcrowded prisons.

All schools in the affected areas remained closed, except for being used as spaces for temporary shelter. Church halls, Temples, and Mosques were also used for shelter, and the respective members of each congregation opened and ran kitchens to provide food for their residents, and all others who needed such help. The Kayanese people showed great resilience, generosity, and caring for their fellow citizens.

Kayanese people living and working abroad were deeply moved by the impact of the devastation to so much of their homeland, and they quickly began to raise funds, and send supplies directly to the villages and towns affected. This was greatly aided by the respective Kayana embassies, Kayanese run charities, and, individuals.

Good progress with the repairs and restorations of the sea defences, kokers, drainage of the flood waters, repairs to roads and bridges, and the rebuilding of houses, allowed the people affected the most, to resume a level of normal living. However, the extent of personal loss, and the impact on the Kayana economy, were considerable. Those opposed to the government expressed their discontent through protests on the streets, and via the media.

The President summoned Chief Onida Ana and her team for a meeting along with his cabinet, at the restored Presidential Palace.

He said, "Chief Onida Ana, thank you and your team, and all the Indigenous Peoples of Kayana, for your outstanding help in our country's worst ever disaster. I would like you to join me on my next television and radio broadcast to the nation. I appreciate that you, as Chief of Chiefs, are very well known across the country, and you represent a figure of great calm and healing for our peoples. Will you do this?"

Chief Onida Ana, looking quite drawn and tired, said, "Yes Mr President. Thank you for your appreciation. The Indigenous Peoples have demonstrated their love for our country, and all its peoples. We are guided by our Great Spirit, and the spirits of our ancestors. We want to see a happy and peaceful Kayana, and will always stand beside our brothers and sisters of Kayana."

The President smiled, and said, "Thank you. I also want you to work beside me in leading the redevelopment of Kayana over the next five years of this my final term as President. I would like you to be based here in the city, and everything you need will be provided. All of your flights to and from your village will also be paid for, as and when you need them. Also, do not worry about me asking you to join any political party. Indeed, it is far better for you to remain neutral, and non-political in this role. Kayana needs you."

Chief Onida Ana and her friends had enjoyed the last five years of development programmes initiated by her report. She felt that the proposition to move the capital city to a safer place inland, should be treated as a major long term priority. Kayana's coastland and river bank settlements had become much more threatened, and vulnerable.

She said, "Mr President, I can only accept your offer and request, if you begin to seriously address the problem of our unviable capital city, and most important hub for the country. We have to find the best place, and start building the city that can serve the needs of Kayana for decades, or even centuries to come. We owe this to our peoples now, and to our future generations."

The President sat back, smiled, and said, "Chief of Chiefs, I knew that you would bring forward the vision of a new Kayana built around a modern, and safe capital city. We cannot afford such a huge project now, but whilst we rebuild what has been lost or damaged, there is no reason why we cannot plan for a new capital city fit for this twenty-first century, and beyond. The time is right to have this conversation in government, and with the people. After all, they have heard me speak about such a project during the last election campaign. So, let us set the ball rolling!"

Chief Onida Ana sat forward, smiled, and said, "Thank you very much Mr President! I suggest that we set up a most representative research and action committee with all the right experts, to work on this proposal, and come forward with a feasibility study for you and parliament to debate, and decide upon. This work will take a fairly long time. Regular reports on progress will have to be made, and presented to you and parliament. We will need to consider a number of options for such a city, and will need to think well into the future."

The President said, "You are right. We cannot afford to rush such a project, but at the same time, I am mindful of the dangers we face, and how costly it will become if we persist with what we have. I do not wish to witness any more suffering and despair as we are seeing now, over the rest of my term of office, and, the remainder of my life."

Chief Onida Ana said, "Sir, that is also my wish. It is incumbent on my generation to plan and build a future that will make you proud, as well as all those to come. I know that my ancestors will be very proud of this."

The Piaiman said, "Sir, our ancestors had a vision for cities to merge with the environment, and to work with nature to preserve what we have. I hope that here in Kayana, we can build something for the world to admire, and imitate. I hope that we can use nature's natural sources of power, and its healing elements across such a city. Of course, we cannot ignore the power of modern technology. So, I hope that we can find the right mix of ancient, modern, and future knowledge to build a city fit for the next thousand years!"

The President looked around at everyone sitting at the large cabinet meeting table, and said, "Now, that is a truly compelling vision! Some of these things exist in cities around the world. So, I expect that Chief Onida Ana and her team will need to travel around to pick out the best solutions that will fit in with our vision. I do not think that there is a city with all of these elements working together. But the great challenge is for us to build this vision as economically as possible. We do not have the billions or trillions of American dollars like other countries. So, our solutions will have to be the smartest. We will need to encourage our best people both here and abroad, to work together, and deliver this amazing dream."

FORTY-ONE

DOWN WITH THE PRESIDENT

O ver the next two years into 2032, the Kayanese people who had lost property and farming land due to the savage storms, tried to rebuild their lives where they could. Others who had fled their villages to higher ground further into the interior, were too afraid to risk returning to an environment that was subject to so much uncertainty. They built temporary houses made of timber, concrete, and with aluminium roofs. Such areas were called shanty towns.

The President and his government were very concerned about the illegal occupation of the land by the shanty town dwellers, and the unsafe way that the areas were established without careful planning, and infrastructure to support them. He pressed Chief Onida Ana and her committee to speed up their research, and to present their options for the new capital city, and other towns. His intention was to remove the shanty towns, and provide better accommodation and facilities for the displaced people.

Despite the foreign aid and charitable contributions to Kayana, the country's economy continued to worsen. Shortages of basic foods caused prices to rise on a daily basis. The poorest and most vulnerable could not afford to buy staple foods such as rice, sugar, butter, and cooking oil. Relatives from abroad tried to help by sending barrels of such provisions, clothing, and other goods by air, and sea cargoes. Yet, more people took to the streets begging for help, from house to house, village to village, and town to town.

Protests against the President and his government became more frequent, spontaneous, and increasingly agitated as the citizens defied the curfews, and the presence of the army and police force. Every day, the local people gathered outside the main gates of the Presidential Palace calling for him to step down. Similar protests were being made at all governmental ministries, and other prominent government buildings, including the parliament.

This new movement was leaderless, and not formally established as a political party. But, as time passed, and more protesters became known and popular amongst ordinary Kayanese people, some individuals began to emerge as spokespersons. The movement relied heavily on the expert use of social media, and were always ahead of the authorities in the planning of the protests, the sites, the dates, and the timings. By the time the army and police arrived onto a protest, it was too late as the speeches were already completed, and the press had taken their pictures, and conducted their interviews.

The President called his cabinet to an emergency meeting at the Presidential Palace. The protest movement quickly realised what was happening, and after a few ministerial cars had arrived at the main gates, hundreds of protesters gathered around to shout their slogans, including, "Down with the President!" and, "Resign Mr President!"

The security services, the army, and the police, quickly waded into the crowd, and arrested all those who refused to disperse. The protesters soon realised that it was pointless to resist, and most of them quietly left the scene.

The President and his cabinet had heard the protest chants before the meeting. He was visibly upset by the demands for him to resign.

He said, "This crisis in Kayana was not caused by us. But, we must share some of the blame for not doing enough to rebuild our country, and the lives of people who had lost so much because of that storm. We have done quite a lot in these past two years, but obviously not enough. I do apologise to you for this failure. I must take full responsibility for my actions. And today, I have come to the conclusion that it is better for me to step down as your President, and to call an election as soon as possible."

The entire cabinet was shocked by the announcement. They all growled, "No! No! No!"

The Minister for the Environment said, "Sir, I am sure that my colleagues here disagree with you. This is not the time for you to leave. All you need to do is to tell Kayana what other projects will be done to help ordinary people."

The Minister of Finance shrugged her shoulders, and said, "Sir, you must stay and see this through! We have the finances to do more for the people, and you must announce this as soon as possible. Our National Bank can issue more bonds and currency into our system. Our oil revenues can allow us to be more generous in allowing us to freeze the price for gasoline, pay for the subsidised electricity in full, and the supply of emergency bottled clean water for everyone in the shanty towns and others in need. We can even offer pay rises for all essential workers to give them the opportunity to cope with price rises."

The President listened intently, and said, "Thank you. What else can we do to ease the rising tension? Who can I speak with from amongst the protesters? They do not have a leader!"

The Minister for Housing said, "Sir, we can relax on the attempts to move the people from the shanty towns, and try to work out some kind of deal with them. We could offer to allocate plots of the land to them for the period up to the time we would like to move them to the new city and towns."

The Chief of the Armed Forces said, "Sir, we should ease up on breaking up the illegal protests, and release those arrested today as a goodwill gesture. You can announce this as part of your speech about the immediate actions as advised by the ministers. You can also lift the State of Emergency and curfew measures, and offer to speak with the leading protesters."

The President leaned forward, and asked, "What if they refuse to stop their protests?"

The Chief of the Armed Forces said, "Sir, we must allow the people to protest, and stand well back from the crowd. We will only act if they become violent, and damage property. We are monitoring the social media that they use, and are better informed of their protest plans. Some of our personnel have also managed to infiltrate the groups. This is now working very well for us."

The President smiled, and said, "Smart move. You are now behaving just like our neighbours who are operating like dictators in police states. Kayana must never be seen like this. I have to ask you to stop the spying activities as soon as order is restored."

He turned to all the others around the table, and said, "Let us firm up these ideas and proposals, and I shall announce them in a special sitting of parliament in a day's time. If you have to stay here at the Palace overnight please do so, and let me see the draft speech by midday tomorrow. Now, please get down to work!"

Chief Onida Ana and her team who were still resident at the Palace, offered to help the ministers and their aides to put together the package of helpful measures for the people, and the first draft of the President's speech.

At the special meeting of the parliament the next afternoon, the opposition leader who was given a copy of the President's speech only one hour before the sitting, walked out of the chambers with his small group of party representatives. They stood briefly at the grand balcony of the parliament building, and encouraged the large crowd of protesters to shout out their disapproval of the President and his government. The opposition leader then tore up his copy of the speech, and threw it into the air amidst loud cheers.

A large television screen which was placed high up within the foreground of the parliament building, showed the President standing up to deliver his speech. The crowd immediately raised the tone of their protest, almost drowning out the speech that was being broadcast for their benefit.

Then, as the President announced the measures to relieve hardship of the people, the protest voices gradually stopped. The promises simply astonished the crowd, and suddenly the people began to listen more attentively, reading the subtitled highlights of each announcement. The crowd began to applaud as the President continued, and then erupted in joyful celebration when he ended by saying that from that moment, the curfews were to be lifted, and the State of Emergency ended.

One young protester shouted, "Long live Kayana! Long live our President!"

The entire crowd applauded, and began shouting, "We want the President! We want the President!"

The President ended his speech, and along with his ministers, he walked out to the balcony to acknowledge the rapturous applause.

He shouted, "Let's get Kayana moving again! God bless you all! God bless Kayana!"

FORTY-TWO

AMBUSH

N ews of an armed attack and siege at Chief Onida Ana's settlement came as a complete surprise to her, and her team She hastily made arrangements to travel back from the city, but was advised by the President, to stay at the Presidential Palace.

The President summoned the Chief of the Armed Forces to an emergency meeting with the cabinet, including Chief Onida Ana, and her team. Information about the attack was relayed by a young warrior from the settlement. He indicated that the invading gang were about ten, from across the border with Kayana. They had killed John Brown, Abdul Rasheed, and Suresh Nanan in what their leader called revenge for his father who had been executed by the former.

The gang leader and his men held all the elders at the benab, and were demanding a multimillion Kayana dollars ransom. He wanted the money to be taken to him by Chief Onida Ana personally.

The President asked the Chief of the Armed Forces, "Sir, how long will it take to send a rescue unit to the settlement? This will inform us as to how long we can use any delay tactics until your people get there."

The Chief of the Armed Forces said, "Sir, we have a small unit further up the Great River, and they have already been briefed to go to the settlement using speed boats and a helicopter. They should reach the outskirts of the site within a couple of hours."

Chief Onida Ana said, "Please be careful, as those criminals have already killed our best security people, and can easily harm others. Mr President, are you sending the money in cash?"

The President frowned, and said, "Chief, I am sending them thousands of bullets, and not one dollar! I also hope to send them in body bags to their country's President, with a strong message for him to deal with the criminal gangs that come over to Kayana to rob and kill our people."

Chief Onida Ana said, "Sir, please do not rush in as we do not wish to lose our elders, or anyone else there."

The Chief of the Armed Forces said, "Chief, please do not worry. Our troops are commandos, and very good at ambush, and will take the gunmen out with ease. We are sending highly trained snipers with powerful rifles which can kill from hundreds of yards away."

The Piaiman said, "Sir, I have every confidence in you and your troops. But each one of our elders is so precious to our peoples."

The helicopter landed safely in the nearby mining town, and five snipers immediately set off towards the settlement, with a local warrior as their guide. The drivers of the speedboats shut down the motors about three hundred yards away, and the commandos began to paddle towards the harbour, as quietly as possible. The heavily camouflaged combat troops carefully stepped onto the muddy river bank near to the mooring, and sneaked into the areas of undergrowth surrounding the settlement.

When the snipers and the commandos finally met up to within yards of the perimeter of the settlement, they fanned out into a horseshoe shape to block every path into the jungle, and leaving only one possible escape route for the gunmen, via the river. Each speedboat waited in camouflage with their driver, and more snipers took aim to intercept any attempt at escape.

Onca, and all the members of his giant otter family residing on the bank beside the mooring, seemed to sense the tension in the air. He led them to swim around the boats and canoes tied to the mooring. The troop of Howler monkeys who had been agitated by the commotion caused by the criminal gang, stayed high up in the canopy surrounding the settlement, and continued to create enough noise to express their anger at the siege. Chief Onida Ana's pet toucan, Kassi, and Kori the macaw, stood on their perches within the benab, and squawked constantly to show their displeasure with the captors.

Apart from the elders held captive, most of the residents had fled into the jungle, and some up the river, leaving the settlement almost deserted. Eight of the ten gang members stood outside and around the benab, armed with rifles. The leader of the gang, and one other, sat in front of the elders on the long table normally used for meals and meetings. The commander of the army unit reminded his troops to lie low, and to keep quiet.

Late in the afternoon, the gang leader called in two of the guards from outside the benab, and asked them to follow two elders to the nearest house to prepare and fetch food for the gang.

The commander sent two of his commandos to ambush the guards. The troops executed the plan perfectly by creeping up behind the gang members, and slitting their throats. They then took and wore the clothing of their victims, and followed the elders back to the benab. As soon as the two elders placed a pot of corn soup and a basket of cassava bread on the table, the two commandos quietly, and stealthily killed the two captors. The other six gang members turned around as soon as they heard the sound of an aluminium cup fall with the gang leader. The commander immediately signalled his snipers to kill the gang members before they could take cover or run away. The siege was over.

Chief Onida Ana and her team were on their way to the settlement when news of the success of the rescue mission was relayed to her by the commander. She expressed her gratitude to him and his troops. Upon arrival at the mooring, she was delighted to see a happy Onca and his family clambering up to the river bank, and heading to the edge of the harbour to welcome her. Kassi and Kori flew quickly to land on the Chief's shoulders.

The commander saluted, and then shook Chief Onida Ana by her right hand. His unit formed two short lines, and stood to attention as the Chief and her entourage passed through towards the benab. The bodies of the gang members were already bagged up, and loaded onto a large motor boat to be transported to the capital city, prior to them being airlifted back to their country.

The people of the settlement slowly and silently returned to the square where the bodies of John Brown, Abdul Rasheed, and Suresh Nanan were placed in newly made mahogany coffins. The President had requested for the flag of Kayana to be draped over each coffin. They were to be specially flown to the city for a joint, and unprecedented state funeral.

Thousands of Kayanese lined the streets leading from the President's Palace, to the National Veteran's cemetery. Chief Onida Ana stood beside the President and the First Lady as they followed the three hearses, and, separate vehicles carrying the near relations of John Brown, Abdul Rasheed, and Suresh Nanan.

At the cemetery, the final prayers for John Brown was led by the Head of the Christian Church of Kayana. Abdul Rasheed's final resting place was allocated within the special section for Muslims, and the *janaaza* was led by the *Imam* of the Association of Muslims of Kayana. Suresh Nanan's funeral was led by the most prominent *Pandit* of Kayana, before a special Hindu cremation ceremony. The family was supported in taking the ashes to be strewn at the mouth of the Great River, according to Hindu custom.

One month later, a special bronze plaque bearing the names of the three heroes, was erected in the central seating area within Chief Onida Ana's settlement square. Chief Onida Ana led the special ceremony for John Brown, Abdul Rasheed, and Suresh Nanan.

She said, "My fellow citizens of Kayana, we are gathered here to celebrate, and honour the valour of these brave brothers of our people. The Piaiman will say a special prayer in our Kayana language, to inscribe their names in our hearts, and for their brave spirits which I am sure are here with us. These men, our brothers, could have had a very quiet life in their retirement with their families. But, they answered my call to come, and help to protect us. We as a people, cherish such bravery, and sacrifice. Long may they live in our memories, in our hearts, and in this settlement."

The Piaiman delivered his chant, and then asked the Chief to unveil the plaque. He raised his arms aloft, and completed his final chant.

He then said, "Today, and always, we will come here, and pay homage to you John Brown, Abdul Rasheed, and Sunil Nanan. You are our brothers, and we will never forget what you did for us, and how you gave your lives for our safety, and survival."

Reverend Henry Small clasped his hands, and said, "May the Lord Jesus always walk with you John Brown. May you Abdul Rasheed, enter Paradise on the Day of Judgement, and may your soul, Suresh Nanan, reach its final state of fulfilment. Amen."

The entire gathering solemnly said, "Amen."

FORTY-THREE

THE FIGHT FOR PEACE

The President of Kayana tried to implement his promise of sending the bodies of the invading criminal gang, back to their country. The ten corpses were placed in coffins, and loaded onto a pontoon which was towed by a small barge along the Great River, and out to the coastal edge of the ocean through to the nearest harbour on the border.

The officials at the border refused to accept the bodies, and they called for a naval gunboat to escort the barge and pontoon back out to sea. The President of Kayana was extremely angry at the rejection, and called his counterpart to discuss the matter. He was met with fierce counter arguments, and both men failed to agree as to what should happen with the corpses.

The incident sparked open, and hostile reactions in both countries, culminating in a threat of an invasion by the larger, and better equipped Armed Forces of Kayana's neighbour.

The President of Kayana summoned an emergency meeting with the Chief of the Armed Forces, and instructed him to deploy part of the Kayana army, navy, and air force in defensive positions at the borders in the interior, and along the coastland. He then made an urgent request for help from the President of the United States of America, and the Prime Ministers of Canada, and the United Kingdom.

The standoff continued as the President of Kayana asked for an intervention by the Security Council of the United Nations. A warning was given to the aggressor, with a threat of intervention if Kayana's sovereignty was breached. American fighter jets arrived at the main international airport of Kayana, and the country began to brace itself for a war.

The President of Kayana, upon returning from his brief trip to the UN in New York, stood up to address the parliament of Kayana.

He said, "My fellow Kayanese, I stand before you here at a time of grave concern for our country. We are a peace-loving nation, and we are asking our neighbour to desist from trying to bully us. We have noticed the aggressive build-up of their Armed Forces on our borders, and their navy near to the edge of our maritime waters. Our Armed Forces are no match compared to theirs, and I am grateful for the presence of our three great allies of the United States of America, the UK, and Canada, who are supported by the UN. Our offshore oilfields, and other inland installations such as the oil refineries, are well guarded by our international friends. I ask all Kayanese to remain calm, and to be vigilant. If you see something or anyone threatening our safety and security, please report this to our emergency line which is being announced in the Press and TV as I speak. Mr Speaker, I am asking for this parliament to approve my request for young and able-bodied Kayanese to volunteer to defend our country, and to report to their nearest police station as soon as possible. I am so proud to announce that our Chief of Chiefs, Onida Ana, has asked all of the Indigenous Peoples to make themselves available to defend their villages and settlements across Kayana. Chief Onida Ana and her peoples also wish to live in peace, but are wary of constant attacks by criminal gangs from across our borders. I could not stand idly by, and allow this to continue. Whilst all of this is happening, I still ask for a peaceful resolution, and an avoidance of conflict."

The entire chamber of the parliament stood up in support of the President, and applauded his announcement. The leader of the opposition confirmed his party's support for the President and government, and offered to help in the execution of the plans to defend the country. He proposed a joint all party committee for the crisis.

The Minister for the Environment announced measures to conserve power, water supplies, petrol and other fuel, and, food provisions, until further notice. New curfew hours were introduced. Neighbourhoods were also encouraged to form vigilante groups to help defend their areas from local criminal gangs seeking to take advantage of the situation.

Chief Onida Ana and her team returned to their settlement in order to take command of the defence preparations there, the mining town, and all the other Indigenous Peoples' villages and settlements across the country. The warriors ensured that more young people were recruited, and trained in the arts of self-defence. Chief Onida Ana called a meeting of all the Kayana Chiefs, to assemble at her settlement. The school was temporarily closed, and used to accommodate the two hundred guests. The grand hall was used for the meeting.

Other special guests including John Jennings and his senior manager, Abraham Campbell, Jacob Holmes, the Headteacher of the High School, and Isobel Rodrigues, the history teacher, were invited to support Chief Onida Ana and her team. A traditional welcome prayer was led by the Piaiman, and this was followed by a short blessing by the Reverend Small.

Chief Onida Ana, fully attired with her tribal headdress and costume, and special face and body markings in red and black, stood up at the head of the grand table which included one Chief from each of the other main Indigenous tribes of Kayana.

Everyone in the hall stood up to render the National Anthem of Kayana, and then took their seats to listen to the Chief of Chiefs.

She said, "Welcome to my brothers and sisters from all over our dear land of Kayana. We are facing the greatest threat to our peoples for over five hundred years. Whilst our President of Kayana and the rest of the United Nation's international community are doing whatever is necessary to prevent a war here, we must be prepared to defend ourselves, and this sacred land of ours. Members of our Kayana Armed Forces are on their way to join us in all of our two hundred villages and settlements. Please make sure that you welcome them, and look after them with your usual hospitality. However, please be mindful that they are almost all young men, and do not encourage any fraternising with our young women."

Chief Onida Ana paused, took a sip of water, and continued, "Our own young warriors are training others in the arts of survival, and defence. But, apart from our poison darts and arrows, and a few hunting rifles, we are not properly equipped to fight a large and strong invading army. So, I ask them to stand and support our Kayana Armed Forces who will need our knowledge of the rainforests, and how to cope with all the dangers they may encounter. Please also make sure that you store extra provisions so that you can feed yourselves, and the Kayana army and navy personnel stationed in your villages and settlements. They will bring medical supplies, and personnel to support our defence.

When this crisis is over, the Armed Forces will leave any supplies left over with the Chiefs."

Chief Onida Ana paused for a few moments, pointed at the TV and Radio crews, and said, "I will now ask you from the media to stop recording and filming until I give you permission to continue. What I am about to say should not be broadcast as we do not wish for our enemy to learn about our plans."

The media duly obliged, and Chief Onida Ana continued, "Thank you. I am asking our best warriors to move up to the borders in the jungle, and observe what our enemy is up to. They will not engage the invaders, but relay messages back to our Kayana Armed Forces about what they discover. Our warriors are best equipped to survive in this environment, and they can travel very quickly and quietly. If any conflict arises, they are very capable of hand to hand fights, and in the use of the poison weapons. They are also well trained in the use of combat knives. I wish all of our warriors, good fortune, and great success. Now, people from the media can resume your reporting."

One Chief from the border areas stood up, and said, "Thank you Chief of Chiefs. There is one big problem with your plans. As you know, me and my people all along the borders have been travelling freely from one country to the other without anyone stopping us. We do not even know where these borders begin and end. Besides, the enemy country also uses our brothers and sisters who reside there, and they will also support their country's Armed Forces. We will be spying on each other. And, we might be fighting with each other, in a war which is not our own. How can we deal with this problem?"

The gathering started to speak amongst themselves as Chief Onida Ana asked for calm.

She said, "That is a very important point. I agree with our brothers who come from, and live along the border areas. I have reached out to the Chiefs there, and they are aware as to why this war might begin. They have also had to endure invasions by criminal gangs of that country, and are not willing to help the Armed Forces there. Members of the media, once again, please do not report on this, and stop recording."

The border Chief said, "Yes, we will try to keep in touch, and share information which will help our Kayana cause."

196

John Jennings stood up beside Chief Onida Ana, and said, "Chief Onida Ana, and peoples of Kayana, I wish to announce that Canada, my country, has offered to help Kayana with military, and other aid. Most of the gold mining operations here are run by Canadian companies like mine, and it is very much in the interests of my government that our businesses are not affected by the criminal gangs."

The border Chief said, "Your presence here is the main cause of these actions by the criminals who also peddle drugs and alcohol in your towns. You need to clean up your act, and even close down your gold mining as this is causing us more harm than good."

The gathering agreed with the border Chief, and applauded him.

John Jennings said, "Whilst I do not agree with everything you have said, I wish to make a special plea to the young men who are increasingly engaged in taking hard drugs, misusing alcohol, and even getting into petty crimes to feed their addiction. This has been caused by so much unemployment here, and I am announcing a new project to offer full training at our mining operations, and with good pay. This is also part of Chief Onida Ana's plan, and we are happy to play our role in this. Despite our presence here, drug and alcohol abuse is a very serious problem for Kayana, and I hope that we are able to help in some way. This is as big a battle as any we are faced with. I hope we can win both of them."

One of the five elders raised his right hand, and said, "Chief Onida Ana, the problems with our young men need to be dealt with. Me and my brothers and sisters here, and in many other villages are seeing how these addicts are not even listening to us. They are behaving as if taken over by evil spirits, and do not care about others. They need help."

Chief Onida Ana said, "Well, we have two big battles to fight, and this threat of war by our neighbours has helped to open our eyes. Thank you all for your advice and support at this difficult time. Let us stand together, and defeat our enemies both within, and at our borders."

A few days later, the President called Chief Onida Ana, and thanked her and her peoples for their contributions to the defence of Kayana. He told her that under the great weight and influence of Kayana's allies and the United Nation, the threat to Kayana was resolved peacefully. Chief Onida Ana thanked the President, and told him that whilst a terrible war was averted, Kayana's own internal battles needed urgent action.

FORTY-FOUR

RISE AND FALL

The next three years to 2035, and just before the Kayana general elections, were relatively peaceful. Kayana's redevelopment programmes funded principally from substantial oil revenues, included a reinforcement of the coastal sea defences, a rehousing of all those who had lost their properties and land through the great floods of 2030, the construction of new settlements further inland, and a building of new and faster highways through to the interior mining towns with connections to the Indigenous villages and settlements. Thousands of new jobs were created for all of Kayana's people, and a new problem of shortages of skilled and unskilled labour, saw an influx of expatriot Kayanese from around the world, as well as new migrants from the badly hit economies of the Caribbean islands.

Greater wealth creation across all sectors of the Kayana economy also contributed to the strategic redevelopment of key infrastructure to accommodate the rapid rise in the country's population. New and bigger hospitals, schools, housing estates, water supplies, and sewerage plants were being built as the country moved towards becoming a more developed state with even greater potential. However, the age old curse of crime continued to plague the country, and its people.

The President introduced new, and tougher measures to deal with the cancer of violent armed assaults by criminals who were heavily involved in drug trafficking. He created a specially trained, and heavily armed police unit for the sole purpose of hunting down, and prosecuting all drug dealers and users. Severe prison sentences were imposed on the guilty, and this was accompanied by intense counselling, and community service. The approach adopted to deal with the drugs and alcohol problem of the young Indigenous Kayanese was more preventative. Counselling and job opportunities were offered instead of custodial sentences.

Full employment, visible development, and a more orderly society resulted in a very attractive Kayana. The people of several races and cultures were more content as differences were respected, and celebrated. The President was highly optimistic about the prospect of his political party winning the next elections, and his personal popularity was evident as he attracted large crowds of supporters wherever he visited.

However, Kayana's continuing problems of flooding after heavy rainfall, and pressures from competition in the world markets for its agricultural products, caused severe hardships for the plantation owners, farmers, and their workers. The President and the Minister of Agriculture devised a new strategy for the sector, based on only producing foods for the country's rising population needs, introducing new technological food production which placed less reliance on the land, and an inefficient irrigation system.

The President, encouraged by Chief Onida Ana, agreed to build a new Kayana Institute of Technology with strong links to others around the world, and this was to be located near to her settlement. This was the most revolutionary idea presented to parliament. The opposing party attacked the proposition mainly on the grounds of difficulties with travelling to, and from the remote area. The leaders of the University of Kayana, sensing unfair competition, also criticised the President for not offering the same institution as an extension to their University's base.

The President persisted with the idea, and finally, parliament voted for building the new Institute as proposed. Chief Onida Ana and her team were delighted with the outcome. She nominated Jacob Holmes and Ruby Smith to join the committee to plan, and build the Institute. This was to be chaired by the Minister of Education.

Kayanese loved sports, especially Cricket and Football. Prior to the discovery and production of oil, these sports were in decline due to the lack of excellent facilities, poor pay for the players and coaches, and a continuing drift of young talent to the USA and Canada. The latter were in the form of lucrative scholarships with the prospect of successful players graduating to the biggest leagues for American Football, Basketball, and Athletics. An economic and politically motivated migration from Kayana was still high even though the economy was providing more opportunities locally.

The Indigenous Peoples of Kayana loved Football, but there were no proper facilities to encourage, and support the development of the players. The President, who was a former Cricket and Football player, ensured that the Minister of Sport's budget was substantially increased to build new facilities in schools, villages, and towns. The returning Kayanese expatriots also demanded top class facilities for the sports that they enjoyed playing, or watching.

Kayana's new status as the top economy in the region, excepting Brazil, drew much more interest from the fastest growing economies of the world, including India, China, and Japan. The UK stepped up its presence and influence by offering its expertise in the Finance and Banking Industry, as well as in higher Education. African countries such as Ghana, Nigeria, and South Africa also took greater notice of the growing gold and diamond industry of Kayana, and offered technical support, especially to the small and medium sized operators.

The President's commitment to the protection of the environment alongside harnessing power from water and solar sources, and the plan to build the world's first Eco-University alongside the Institute of Technology, drew special attention from the major institutions and organisations intent on saving the planet. He was proclaimed as a "Champion of the Earth".

The only tourism that occurred in Kayana was limited, and strictly restricted, to the promotion of the protection of the rainforests, and the related environment. Although there was a growth in recreational sites for clients to enjoy many of the natural creeks and smaller waterfalls, these were also subject to tight control.

The rich variety of the cultures of Kayana's races and mixed races was more openly embraced, and celebrated by all Kayanese. The historical racial tensions between East Indian and African Kayanese had begun to subside, and a new education curriculum was introduced to reflect the strength in diversity of the nation. This included the teaching of the Indigenous culture, and the native Kayana language, alongside East Indian, African, Chinese and Portuguese history, culture, and languages.

Chief Onida Ana enjoyed extensive popularity amongst all of the peoples of Kayana. She became a regular speaker at major Kayanese and International conferences about her Indigenous Peoples. She strongly advocated for all Indigenous Peoples to embrace education in their home countries, and to participate in all aspects of their country's political, economic, and other activities.

She spoke out about the abuse of drugs and alcohol by some of the younger Indigenous Peoples, and their increasing involvement in criminal activities to feed their habits. Chief Onida Ana also championed for the rights of Indigenous women and young girls who were being forced into prostitution in Kayana, and abroad. She called for the elders to step up, and emphasise their positions of respect and authority in their own homes, villages, settlements, and regions.

Chief Onida Ana, with the support of the President, set up a TV and Radio studio in her settlement, and appeared on regular broadcasts to the other Indigenous villages and settlements across Kayana. The stations' wide variety of programmes covered most aspects of Indigenous cultures, religion, languages, and other activities as a way of raising greater awareness of her peoples. Although the Chief steered well clear of the local Kayana politics, she encouraged debates on current issues affecting the peoples locally, and internationally. This interaction provided her with even greater popularity.

Just before the general election campaign began in 2035, the President suddenly collapsed with a suspected heart attack. He was rushed to the privately run specialist cardiology unit in the city. Every effort was made to revive him, but within two hours of his admission, the President was pronounced dead.

FORTY-FIVE

ALL IS WELL

The sudden demise of the President plunged Kayana into a deep state of grief. A state funeral was quickly planned, including a period of two weeks of lying in state to allow Kayanese of all backgrounds to pay their final respects to their greatest leader.

On the day of the funeral, tens of thousands of Kayanese lined the route from the Presidential Palace, through the tree-lined mall, past the parliament buildings, and then via the drive to the National Cemetery for heroes, and those who served in high political positions for the country.

One month later, following the postponement of the elections that were due in May of 2035, a new date was chosen, and political campaigning began. The President's sudden passing threw his ruling party into chaos. When a suitable replacement candidate was finally chosen to run for President, support for the party flagged considerably.

The leader of the main opposition party was also very unpopular especially amongst minority groups including the Indigenous Peoples in all four regions. The Press, TV and Radio stations put out news which severely discredited the two main candidates, and there was a call for a third option.

The younger population also highlighted the need for a change from the politics of the old guard, and they used social media to harness support for an alternative, and a more youthful government to take the country further forward.

The new migrants, and the wealthier expatriot Kayanese who began to settle in the country, aligned themselves to the populist movement, and strongly advocated for an independent candidate. The constitution of Kayana allowed for this, and, as the appeals via the internet took place, a group of likeminded independents gathered together, and decided to travel to meet Chief Onida Ana.

When the group arrived at the mooring of the settlement, the local Press, TV and Radio reporters followed them as they made their way to the benab. The residents gathered around in the square, and faced the entrance to the benab. The independents comprising of young men and women of African, Chinese, East Indian, Portuguese, and mixed race Kayanese, were warmly welcomed by the Chief.

The leader and main spokesperson of the delegation sat directly opposite Chief Onida Ana who was flanked by the Piaiman, Peter, Ruby, Indra, Mary, and five elders.

Chief Onida Ana welcomed the group, and introduced her team. She then asked the leader of the delegation to introduce herself and her colleagues. The leader was an African Kayanese young woman in her early twenties.

She leaned forward, and said, "Thank you Chief Onida Ana, for agreeing to meet with me and my colleagues. You may be aware that we have begun a huge campaign to mobilise support for, and advocate for a new kind of politics here in Kayana. We have a following of almost half the population of Kayana, and these are mostly young people of eighteen to twenty-five years old. Our followers come from all backgrounds, races, and cultures, both here and abroad."

Chief Onida Ana smiled, and said, "That is very impressive, and remarkable. Why do you want to change the politics of Kayana? Surely our recent President led us into substantial growth as an economy? Why change what we have now, and are aiming for?"

The leader said, "Chief, we have been discussing the progress that is being made, and we welcome this. However, we believe that we, as a country and nation, are not moving forward fast enough. We also discussed the report that you and your team had produced for the last President, and we do like most of the proposals. But, unfortunately there are still too many older politicians from both of the main parties who are effectively blocking the pace of progress that we really need."

Chief Onida Ana said, "I can understand that, and I have also noticed this all the way through our study, as well as during some of the implementation of our development plans. There is one thing that you seem to have neglected in your movement."

The leader smiled, and asked, "And what is that?"

Chief Onida Ana said, "You do not seem to have engaged with the Indigenous Peoples of Kayana."

The leader smiled, and said, "Aha! We accept this, and that is why we are here speaking openly with you!"

Chief Onida Ana asked, "And how am I going to be of use to you, and the movement?"

The leader said, "Chief, you are the one young leader who have had experience of leading your peoples, and who is now the most popular, and iconic figure not only of your people, but of all Kayanese, both here and abroad! In fact, we are in absolute awe of you, and your popularity across the world! You are our best prospective leader of Kayana!"

Chief Onida Ana looked at the delegation, and at her own team, with surprise etched on her face.

The Piaiman said, "Chief, I think that this is your moment. I believe that the Great Spirit has led these amazing young people to us, and we must respond very positively."

The leader asked, "Sir, who is the Great Spirit?"

The Piaiman said, "The Great Spirit is our peoples' spiritual supreme leader. You refer to God, or Allah, or Bhagwan, and we appreciate this unseen power and force which guides us all. This is the energy that binds us all together, along with everything we see, hear, and feel around us."

The leader smiled, and said, "Wow! That is awesome! Kayana needs this force right now!"

One of the elders sitting just to the left of Chief Onida Ana, said, "The Great Spirit is guiding us all, and I feel that this is the moment for our Chief to step forward, and lead Kayana. Please accept the offer, and message of these amazing young people."

The leader said, "Thank you, sir. You speak with such wisdom. You know the answers. Dear Chief Onida Ana, what do you say?"

Chief Onida Ana said, "This has come as a complete surprise to me. I have always steered well clear of politics in this country, and preferred to lead my people as their Chief of Chiefs. But it seems that the vast majority of Kayanese want change, and a newer younger leadership. I am pleased that you think so highly of me. But…"

The Piaiman leant forward, and said, "Chief, this is no time for "Ifs" and "Buts". We need you now, and you already have the support of most Kayanese. Please accept this request, and we will all be behind you."

Chief Onida Ana said, "I cannot agree to do this until I discuss the matter with our Council of Chiefs. So, if you do not mind, I shall speak with them, and let you know the outcome. In the meantime, please do not disclose what we have discussed here today. The Press, TV, and Radio people must not find out about this. I also need to think about what this all means from here onwards."

The leader smiled, and said, "Thank you very much Chief Onida Ana. I know that you are the best person to lead a new Kayana, and you have the backing of most of the people in this country. We will not disclose or discuss this with anyone until we hear from you."

That evening, after a sumptuous meal of corn soup, cassava pie, boiled sweet potatoes, and fried catfish, Chief Onida Ana retired to her hammock. All the other residents of the benab respectfully kept quiet, and slept soundly. She later woke up, and after a brief stroll around the square which was lit up by a full moon, she returned to her hammock.

She thought about the question and request posed to her by the delegation, and wondered what Chief Koko would have advised. Should she accept this immense responsibility so early? What will be the outcome for Kayana and the Kayanese people if she refused? Must she go against the wishes of her thrusted advisers? Will such an opportunity to lead the country ever come again? How will the Chiefs respond? Will they also advise her to accept?"

Chief Onida Ana found great difficulty to sleep that evening. Every time she began to drift into a slumber, she was awoken by more questions. Then finally, she succumbed to sheer tiredness, and fell into a deep sleep. A cool soothing breeze entered the benab, and calmness prevailed.

The Chief's eyes opened slightly, and in her daze, she saw the outline of a figure standing over her feet at the end of the hammock.

Chief Onida Ana whispered, "Who? Who is there?"

The figure responded, "It's me. It's Chief Koko."

Chief Onida Ana said, "No. You cannot be. Go away."

The voice said, "You asked for me. So, I have come. What do you want?"

Chief Onida Ana, still trying to open her groggy eyes, said, "If you are Chief Koko, I need to know what to do."

Chief Koko asked, "To do what? To lead your peoples? To lead Kayana?"

Chief Onida Ana said, "I already lead our peoples. I am too young to take on Kayana. I cannot do this."

Chief Koko said, "You must lead. That is why you are here. It is a command from the Great Spirit."

Someone coughed slightly, and asked, "Who's there?"

Chief Onida Ana said, "It's only me. All is well."

FORTY-SIX

A SHINING LIGHT

C hief Onida Ana called a meeting of the Chiefs. Those who could not travel to her settlement at such short notice, were encouraged to participate through an internet connection, and by a shared phone link. She opened the meeting by welcoming the Chiefs in the grand hall of the school. She described the request for her to campaign as an independent candidate in the general election.

Some of the delegates raised concerns about their people fighting for seats in parliament when they were already supporting members of the two main political parties. They felt that their issues were being well represented within the existing system, and to change their alliances would be tantamount to betrayal. They also noted that Chief Onida Ana, as Chief of Chiefs, had been representing Kayana's Indigenous Peoples with great success, and that it was much better for her to stay away from the politics of the country, and to continue to use her existing influence as a neutral force.

Others were much more vocal about the need for leaders within the Indigenous community to step up, take more responsibility in politics, and all other aspects of life in Kayana. They felt that, on balance, no political leader, with the exception of the most recent President, had managed to progress their issues, and resolve their problems. They were being used, and bribed just for their votes. The time had come for them to use their votes to extract more sustainable development, not only for themselves, but for all peoples of Kayana. They encouraged Chief Onida Ana to stand for all the peoples of Kayana, as a strong, young, and influential independent candidate who was best placed to unite the country, and to preserve the environment alongside respect for the culture of the Indigenous Peoples.

The Chiefs, who were always gentle and peace-loving people, continued to argue their positions for, or against the idea of Chief

Onida Ana running for President. At times, the exchanges became very heated, and the Piaiman had to call for order.

Peter raised his right hand for permission to speak, and Chief Onida Ana allowed him to air his views.

He stood up, and as the Chiefs and the other members of the audience fell silent, he took a sip of water from his bottle.

He said, "My dear and honourable brothers and sisters, I have listened to you all today, and I think that you have missed a number of very important issues. First of all, we as a people, have managed to survive for over five centuries after most of our ancestors were brutally destroyed. We were told to stay here, and wait for the time to come when we must take our rightful place in this country, and in all other countries on this planet. We have endured more pain, and suffering until the last thirty-five years or so when a new light began to shine for us. Secondly, I had been given the greatest honour, and responsibility by our last great Chief Koko, to guide and support this shining light. Thirdly, as I am now getting too old, I believe that my work has been done. The Great Spirit and the spirits of our ancestors, have asked us to stand firmly alongside this beacon who is here to lead us to our promised future. Long live Chief Onida Ana!"

The entire gathering replied with, "Long live Chief Onida Ana!", and applauded Peter as he sat down.

The Piaiman stood up, and said, "Dear brothers and sisters, since you have all shown your appreciation for Chief Onida Ana, can I assume that you are agreeing for her to run for the Presidency?"

The Chiefs raised their right hands in a unanimous show of support.

Chief Onida Ana stood up, wiped away some tears from her eyes, and said, "Thank you all for your overwhelming support. I have listened to those who made strong arguments against this decision, and I shall do my best to take your concerns into account. I do not have the kind of money to launch a major campaign in this election. So, I will need all of your help alongside those young people who have already organised a brilliant campaign using social media. I have travelled far and wide across this country, and I hope that many, if not all of you, will join me again. This time I shall reach out to all Kayanese, and to listen to them. I am very fortunate to have a strong and loyal team here with me, and I hope that they will also join me in planning and running this campaign."

Ruby, Indra, and Mary smiled, and signalled a "thumbs up" to Chief Onida Ana.

Peter stepped forward, and embraced the Chief.

He whispered in her left ear, "President Chief Onida Ana, our Daughter of the Great River, sounds very nice."

The leader of the independent group was delighted to hear of Chief Onida Ana's decision to run for the Presidency as the representative of the movement.

She called Chief Onida Ana, and said, "Hello Chief! This is Janet Gladstone who made the proposal to you. I am over the moon that you agreed to lead our movement. My group and I would like to meet you at the benab, and to start our planning. Will this be O K?"

Chief Onida Ana said, "Of course. You should come over as soon as possible before the news gets out. We need to put together a formal statement for the people running the election, and for the Kayanese people. We have a lot of work to do, especially without much funding."

Janet said, "No problem Chief. We will be there first thing tomorrow. As for funding, we can raise money very easily by asking our internet followers here and abroad, to give whatever they could afford. Ruby Smith, your expert on finance, can organise this within the electoral rules, and so on. We as a group are all volunteers, and there are many more who will join us in our campaigning. This will be the most cost-effective operation in Kayana's election history."

Bright and early the next morning, the sun broke through the gaps in the canopy, and spread golden shafts of light through to the forest floor. The open square in front of the benab was brightly lit up, and everyone in the settlement was busy with their daily chores. The pets and livestock joined in the melee. Chief Onida Ana, Ruby, Indra, and Mary tiptoed down to the creek to enjoy their usual early morning swim. They began to playfully splash the cold water upon each other just as they had done as schoolfriends many years ago.

Later on, Janet Gladstone and her group arrived at the benab, closely followed by a large contingent of local and international press personnel. Chief Onida Ana emerged from the benab, and stepped forward to warmly embrace Janet and some of her colleagues.

The Chief said, "Dear fellow Kayanese, and other guests, welcome to our humble settlement. I hope that after I have spoken, you will stay on, and indulge in some of our local dishes and refreshment which have been prepared for you. Today, I wish to inform you that upon a request by the young people's movement instigated by Janet Gladstone and her friends, and, the unanimous approval of all the Chiefs of our Indigenous Peoples, I am hereby declaring my intention to run for the Presidency in these elections. We do not have a formal political party, but have registered our Kayana Peoples Movement or KPM, as such. We already have the support of over half the voting population, and we are now campaigning to win the hearts and minds of all of our peoples of Kayana, and also our brothers and sisters living abroad. Our last President had started to rebuild and develop our country, and now we need to move further up, and faster. We do share his vision for Kayana, and we need to lift our country to a place amongst the most advanced nations in the world. We will continue with the most progressive protection of our beautiful environment. Both must go hand in hand so that we can all enjoy a most peaceful, and happy coexistence. I am sure that all Kayanese people will join us in this march towards a new Kayana. Thank you."

Everyone gathered in the square gave Chief Onida Ana a resounding cheer along with sustained applause.

The first TV reporter asked, "Chief Onida Ana, we can see how popular this decision is. What do you say to the notion that the vision you have just promised is all but a dream? A case of "Pie in the sky"?"

Chief Onida Ana smiled, adjusted her headdress, and said, "If you look up into that clear blue sky, you will not see pies. If you close your eyes, and try to imagine what Kayana should look like, you will probably come up with the same dream as half of our population already aspire to. None of what I have said will happen overnight. If we all work with the same resolve, we can attain our vision within the next twenty years."

A second reporter asked, "Chief Onida Ana, you and your movement, the KPM, seem to have only our younger people and voters as your base. What about our older hardworking Kayanese people? How are you and your KPM going to win their support away from the political parties that they have voted for over many decades?"

Chief Onida Ana said, "The KPM is for all the peoples of Kayana. Our manifesto will spell out our plans for all Kayanese, with particular focus on those who are most in need, and most vulnerable. We are not exclusive. We are inclusive. Everyone matters to us. Of course, there will always be people who will not support us, but we are honestly committed to everyone. You do not have to be members of KPM. In fact, there is no such thing as membership."

A third reporter asked, "Chief Onida Ana, none of you and your team have any experience in politics or in running any business or public sector service. How can you govern this diverse country?"

Chief Onida Ana smiled, and said, "Yes, you are right. We do not pretend that we have experience of governing or running things. But, when you look at all the hundreds of politicians who have preceded us, and you look at the state of Kayana, can you honestly say that they used their knowledge and experience wisely? We will be open to the best Kayanese talent here and from abroad, and many of these people already have amazing skills and experience. Let's see how this will work. Believe me, my team and I are very well qualified, and experienced in planning and running things. We have been doing so in support of our last President for a number of years now. We researched, and wrote Kayana's Strategy and Development Plan."

FORTY-SEVEN

REACH FOR THE STARS

C hief Onida Ana, Janet Gladstone, and the team worked incredibly hard to produce a manifesto for the next five years to 2040. They planned an inexpensive publicity programme based on the Kayana Peoples Movement's extensive use of social media. This was backed up by teams organised to visit individual households across the country. Chief Onida Ana led the visits in every district across the four regions of the country. Her "soapbox" style public meetings were extremely popular as Kayanese flocked to see, and listen to the Chief who insisted on wearing her headdress, and native Kayana costume.

The two main opposition parties could not stop the rising swell of support for Chief Onida Ana and the KPM. They resorted to spreading false stories and smears about the Chief and her guiding spirits, accusing her of being a nonbeliever in God. They tried to paint the Indigenous Peoples as heathens and cannibals who indulged in eating monkeys, and spreading terrible diseases. They also hired supporters to attend the KPM rallies, and tried to disrupt the meetings by provoking fights with the movement's supporters. The police tended to stand by, and do nothing to stop the harassment.

Despite the disruptions, Chief Onida Ana and her team continued relentlessly with their campaign programme. She would commence her speeches with calls for peace, and a show of love amongst her audiences, as a way of minimising the impact of heckling by opposition supporters. She advised her followers to restrain themselves, and not to retaliate. This tactic began to work very well as the orchestrated disruptions began to be ineffective. The popular election polls showed that Chief Onida Ana and the KPM commanded growing support into about seventy percent of the electorate. This signalled the potential for a massive landslide victory.

Chief Onida Ana and her team reached the final leg of their campaign, and their rally was organised at the large open area in front of the Kayana parliament. Tens of thousands of supporters crammed into every available space along the grand mall that led from the Presidential Palace to the parliament building.

She stood up on a specially built wooden platform, and when she raised her arms aloft, the crowd screamed their approval whilst frantically waving several sizes of the multi-coloured Kayana flag, and the yellow banners of the KPM. She clasped her hands to signal her full appreciation for such adulation.

She said, "Thank you Kayana! You look beautiful from here! Thank you all for your support for me, and for a better, more peaceful, and more prosperous Kayana! This beautiful country belongs to us all in equal measure. We are true Kayana brothers and sisters, and let no one divide us. We stand together hand in hand, side by side, for one Kayana."

The crowd erupted in more screaming and applause.

Chief Onida Ana raised her right hand, and continued, "Today we have come together for one thing. We want to see greater progress. This is what I promise to you. Our vision goes far beyond what we can see here. But it is also a vision which our ancestors had for us all. They wanted to see the end of violence amongst our peoples, the end of suppression by others over us, the end of enslavement by masters who do not respect us, the end of corruption by those we entrust with Kayana's wealth, and, the end of discrimination by those who believe they are superior to others. We must work together to defeat these evils, and reach together for the stars!"

More applause rang out.

Chief Onida Ana said, "If we win in the next few days, it will be a victory for all Kayanese. We will embrace our friends who support us, and also those who oppose us. Finally, whilst we aim to build large and high, we must also work harder to understand, appreciate, and sustain our precious environment. Our land of many waters, is breathing because of our evergreen rainforests. We are truly blessed with the presence of some of the world's rarest, and most endangered species of animals, birds, insects, and plants. This amazing balance of nature is for us all to respect, and protect for our children, and for those yet to come."

Suddenly, the applause began to be increasingly drowned out by the high-pitched sirens from several police cars and fire trucks racing past in the street parallel to the mall. People began to scream as thick black smoke could be seen rising above buildings in the main shopping area only hundreds of yards away from the gathering. Pockets of the crowd became more unsettled as people began to flee in sheer panic.

Chief Onida Ana was forced to cut short her speech, and she began to plea for calm. She raised her normally dulcet voice to call for her supporters to stay together. But as the dark plumes became more visibly intense, the crowd began to disperse away from the area.

Chief Onida Ana remained on the platform, and raised her arms aloft in another gesture for calm. Then the sound of what appeared to be firecrackers became closer as she fell amongst members of her team and security personnel. Janet Gladstone and others flung their arms in the air, and screamed.

The Piaiman shouted, "Quick! Get an ambulance! Peter and Chief Onida Ana have been shot! Quick! Help us!"

The people nearest to the platform screamed uncontrollably, and rushed up to the podium. Others stood in utter shock with tears streaming down their confused faces. The loud stuttering of a helicopter flew along the path of the mall causing great confusion as people were scattered in fear. The helicopter hovered above the platform, and within minutes, the bodies of Chief Onida Ana and Peter were hoisted into the hold. The aircraft then sped away towards the casualty unit of the newly built public hospital. The other members of the Chief's entourage quickly stepped down from the platform, and scrambled into cars which had taken them to the rally. Police outriders led the group of black hire cars towards the hospital.

The thousands of KPM supporters dispersed in all directions away from the scene of the fires. The poorly equipped, and small number of fire trucks were fully deployed in an effort to stop the spread of the fires, by dousing other mainly wooden buildings nearest to those being engulfed by the raging flames.

The helicopter landed safely onto the helipad, and a group of medical personnel and porters quickly took the bloodstained bodies of Chief Onida Ana and Peter, and pushed the trolleys with great urgency through to the two operating theatres.

Some press personnel gathered just outside the main gates of the hospital, and dozens of the Chief's supporters began to arrive, having run as quickly as they could from the mall area. Chief Onida Ana's team had arrived a few minutes earlier, and they were ushered into a specially cleared waiting area outside the operating theatres. Everyone sat down in a state of shock.

The Piaiman, with fresh blood stains on his white cotton shirt, clasped his hands, and closed his eyes. He mumbled his prayers in Kayanese, as the others looked on in disbelief.

He opened his bleary and tearful eyes, and said, "Please Great Spirit! Spare the lives of our beloved Chief Onida Ana and Peter. Please heal their wounds, and do not take them away from us. Please save us all."

The waiting room remained quiet, and the only voices to be heard were from the growing crowd of supporters and onlookers gathered at the main gates which were only about one hundred yards away.

The wait for news about Chief Onida Ana and Peter seemed like eternity. Everyone in the waiting room did not speak, and just stared blankly in front of themselves. Occasionally, they would wipe away their tears with bare hands, or with handkerchiefs.

Eventually, a very tired consultant surgeon who was leading the two teams of operating personnel, stepped into the waiting room. He was of Portuguese Kayanese heritage, about six feet tall, and with a slight stoop.

He said, "Thank you for your patience. The very bad news I have to give you is that whilst Chief Onida Ana's life was saved by Peter stepping in front of her when she was being shot at, the wounds to his chest were too great, and sadly we could not save his life."

The Piaiman said, "Thank you, sir. That is terrible news. Peter was such a brave man. A true and loyal warrior. May the Great Spirit look after his soul."

The surgeon said, "Thankfully, we were able to save Chief Onida Ana as the wounds she got were less life-threatening. She has survived because of Peter's bravery, and sacrifice. But, she needs rest, and a period of good rehabilitation in order to get back to full fitness."

Janet Gladstone said, "Thank you, sir. Please extend our gratitude to all of your team. Peter's sacrifice makes him a martyr. We are truly grateful to you and your team for all your hard work. We need to plan for Peter's funeral now, and will consider all options for Chief Onida Ana's care. We are so grateful that she will recover fully."

Everyone in the waiting room began to speak with each other. They were all very saddened to learn of Peter's demise. Then they began to speculate on who shot the Chief and Peter, and why.

Janet Gladstone said, "My friends, let us remain calm, and leave the authorities to investigate this terrible crime. We must keep our focus, and reach for the stars as our dear leader said. Firstly, lets plan for Peter's interment to take place at his beloved settlement. Myself and Ruby, Indra, and Mary should stay here to look after the Chief. Our Piaiman and Reverend Small should accompany Peter's body to the settlement, and ask the elders to make the preparations. We will suspend our election campaign, and allow our supporters to grieve over the next few days. Our capital city has become a dark and dangerous place full of fear caused by a few."

Chief Onida Ana's recovery was remarkably quick, and she was able to leave the city for the funeral of her dearest friend and mentor, who had paid the ultimate price in doing his duty to the very end.

FORTY-EIGHT

NEW PRESIDENT OF KAYANA

B oosted by a nationwide outcry by the people of Kayana, about the deliberate attempt to burn much of the capital city, and to assassinate Chief Onida Ana, the Kayana Peoples Movement won an astonishing landslide victory at the general elections. Chief Onida Ana was elected as the new President of Kayana.

She had made a full recovery from her injuries, and managed to attend the funeral of Peter Thomas who was laid to rest at the settlement's cemetery after a grand ceremony attended by thousands of fellow Indigenous Kayanese, and other supporters of the KPM.

A very emotional Chief Onida Ana spoke about Peter as her inspiration, guide, and mentor. She promised that when she became President, she would give him the highest honour of Kayana.

She said, "Today, as all of Kayana mourns the passing of our brave warrior Peter Thomas, we must continue to light up this land with his vision, and dedication to preserve our way of life in this beautiful environment. I know that he will never leave my side. He wanted me to live on, and to fulfil the promises and hopes of our ancestors. The Great Spirit, and those of all our ancestors are here to guide us. Let us all take advantage of this strength and determination, and make Kayana a safe, peaceful, and prosperous country for all of us. Farewell Peter. Thank you for saving my life. Thank you for giving me purpose. Thank you for being there. Thank you for being a true son of Kayana."

The President Chief Onida Ana spent the remaining months of 2035, establishing her new government, progressing the plans to rebuild the sea defences across the coastline, and encouraging the clearance of the areas affected by the fires in the capital city. Her trusted friend, Ruby Smith, was appointed to the crucial role of Minister of Finance, and the Headteacher of her old school, Jacob Holmes, was appointed as Minister of Education. Janet Gladstone was awarded the new role of Minister of Redevelopment.

The first debate on the President's budget for Kayana proved to be highly controversial to the small opposition minority. Ruby Smith proposed new investment in securing a substantial hydroelectric power station at a safe location further up the Great River, a rebuilding of the entire sea defence system, and most surprising of all, a task force to plan the move of the capital city to a new location further inland.

The President took full responsibility for the relocation of the capital city which she had proposed in her manifesto, and campaign. She knew exactly where that would be, and established an international team of archaeologists to investigate the "lost city". However, as soon as this was announced in parliament, the local Press and TV reporters splashed headlines which claimed that the new President was racist, and wanted to destroy the lives and prospects of the people of the capital city. This enraged the local population, and many of the people took to the streets in an angry protest. A large group, aided by supporters of the opposition parties, marched towards the parliament building.

The police were caught unawares by the hastily arranged protest march, and were left to look on with trepidation. The Chief of police tried to organise the nearby units of police personnel, and soon a cordon was set up to protect the area surrounding the parliament building. He then called for assistance from other units, and from the army. Their arrival helped to calm the situation. The President promised to speak to the nation after the end of the budget session.

Ruby Smith continued with her presentation of the budget, and proposed the set up and funding for a Kayana Institute of Technology (KIT) with direct links to the best of such institutions in the world. She wanted to encourage Kayanese both at home and abroad, to extend their interest and knowledge of new technologies, as a basis for the new economy of Kayana. All Kayana homes, schools, and businesses were to be given free access to the internet. The University of Kayana would be extended to house a new and substantial Indigenous Peoples' Research Centre, and an International Department for the Environment.

Janet Gladstone's Ministry of Redevelopment was to be responsible for all the agricultural, scientific, and industrial projects in a ten-year strategy for Kayana. Farmers across Kayana were to be given special subsidies to invest in more viable food crops, and higher yields of rice and sugar. A new, fully equipped and staffed Agricultural Centre was to be built for the benefit of farmers, students, and for scientific research to aid agriculture.

Kayana's population was forecast to be doubled by 2045 due to the country's economic success, return of expatriot Kayanese, and a rise in the birth rate across the country. There was a plan to encourage housebuilding on an unprecedented scale, along with reliable supplies of power and water for all.

President Chief Onida Ana and her ministers held their second cabinet meeting at the Presidential Palace in the capital city. Although she was expected to move into the Presidential Palace, she wanted to be able to travel to and from the benab in her settlement almost every weekend in order to keep in touch with the exploration of the old city, and to maintain her connection with local people. In view of the assassination attempt, the security service was increased for the Palace, and the visits to the settlement. The local warriors at the settlement also kept close watch around the perimeter as they had done since the attacks by criminal gangs.

The cabinet meeting was for the first time, opened with a short prayer in the Kayanese tribal language. The first item on the agenda was about the investigation regarding the murder of Peter Thomas, the arson attacks in the city, and the latest unauthorised protest march. The Chief of police presented an update on the investigations, and reminded the President and her colleagues, that such matters should be dealt with by the Home Office, and not by the cabinet.

The President said, "All I wanted to know is how well the investigation is progressing, and whether those responsible will be identified. On top of your work, I am calling for an Independent Inquiry about these three matters, and I trust that such deliberation will not compromise the criminal investigation."

The Chief of police said, "Your Excellency, we are very close to establishing what happened, and I will be making an announcement very soon."

Janet Gladstone said, "We all know that those events were perpetrated by political forces in opposition to the KPM. They chose the right moment to cause confusion and mayhem by setting fires to buildings not very far away from the mall, and then placing one or more gunmen to kill our President. Yesterday's protest march was another example of their involvement in attacking our President, and this government. I hope that the Police and the Independent Inquiry can get right to the core of those responsible simply because they are capable of doing something like this again. Of course, I want to see the full force of the law dealing with the guilty."

The President said, "Yes, I would like to see a quick resolution to this matter, and to know that justice will prevail. We must also strive to bring all Kayanese together as we move forward. Now that our first budget has been approved in parliament, let us put most of our energies towards implementing the things we promised to do. I wish to announce a proposal for a Kayana Peoples Day for all Kayanese to come together to celebrate the awards for outstanding achievements by citizens. I want to ensure that Peter Thomas is the first to receive such an honour, posthumously. I will make this announcement when I speak to the nation this evening."

President Chief Onida Ana and her government included many young, and relatively inexperienced Ministers and other professionals drawn mainly from the local population, and high achievers from abroad. They delivered rapid progress every year into the first five-year term of office. Kayana's economy began to change from a more traditional agrarian focus, to a more dynamic technology driven culture using the enormous intellectual capacity of the people.

The Transport Strategy was designed to use more modern inventions suitable for the country's geography. New superhighways were being built to complement the many waterways. The President aimed to have only electric powered motor vehicles and boats by the year 2040, and thus minimise reliance on other types of fuel. Air travel within Kayana was restricted to smaller, and more efficient eco-friendly aircraft. Likewise, tourism was only encouraged for the purpose of exploring, and learning about Kayana's pristine rainforests and waterways.

Health and Social Care Services were designed, and provided free at the point of use by the population, and in newly built hospitals, community clinics, and care homes for the most vulnerable. This was all funded out of a Health and Social Care Tax.

Education was provided free at all levels including pre-school, primary, secondary, university, and vocational institutions. Jobs for Kayanese graduates were guaranteed in every sector. The introduction of the learning, and use of the Kayanese native language, was made compulsory in all Indigenous villages and settlements, and a basic level was part of the curriculum elsewhere. Schools were encouraged to offer civic courses on Indigenous Peoples' history and culture alongside that of the African, Portuguese, East Indian, and Chinese Peoples of Kayana.

Sport and Leisure were initially invested in by the government, and the President encouraged the world's richest sports clubs to do likewise across Kayana, in Football, Cricket, Basketball, Athletics, Swimming, and so on.

All other aspects of Kayanese lives were similarly invested in by the government, and in partnership with the growing private sector. The President wanted Kayana to become a developed country that was almost entirely self-sufficient, by the year 2050.

FORTY-NINE

CHAMPION OF THE ENVIRONMENT

T he next five years to the eve of 2040, saw Kayana continue its fast-paced development, and expansion. Expatriots continued to return with their families, and financial wealth, with the intention of investing in all sectors of the economy. Most of the President's manifesto had been achieved, and the people enjoyed a much better standard of living than ever before.

President Chief Onida Ana's popularity grew to a level of hero worship amongst the Indigenous Peoples, and also the wider population of Kayanese, both at home and abroad. Her presence at international conferences was greeted with enormous respect by foreign leaders. Kayana was being viewed as a model economy which was successfully utilising its enormous wealth from oil and other natural resources, and at the same time, protecting its natural environment. The country was also being regarded as one of the happiest places to live. Amongst the many accolades that the President received, was that of "International Champion of the Environment".

The rediscovery of the ancient city that the President knew about, was also of international importance, and interest. A countrywide debate was conducted as to the possibility of locating the new capital city around the vast complex which was being extensively surveyed, documented, and restored.

The President and her team of local and international experts, proposed for the ancient city to become the central Hub of Kayana's new capital city. The design included eight large but interconnected Spokes for specific purposes. New housing and transport facilities were to be built between each Spoke for easy access. Every building would be self-sufficient and eco-friendly, using the most modern recycle systems for energy, and the production of clean water. All means of transport would be electric, and access routes were to be designed to encourage cycling, running, and walking. Every Spoke would have its own eco-friendly garden and leisure park to promote the diversity of the botany of Kayana. Special spaces for Indigenous villages were to be made available for the tribes that wished to move closer to their ancestral city.

Activities such as hunting and small-scale mining and logging, were strictly restricted and monitored by special units of Indigenous people. Sightseeing and other leisure pursuits were also limited, and had to be supervised and guided by trained personnel. All known endangered species of Kayana were given special status, including the jaguar, giant otter, tapir, giant anteater, anaconda, the Howler and other monkeys, sloth, the Harpy eagle, parrots and macaws, and many freshwater fish. The diverse trees, plants, and other unique botany were particularly subject to protection. No industrial waste was allowed into any of the rivers, lakes, creeks, and other waterways.

One of the most prestigious honours awarded to Kayanese citizens, was for Kayana's Champion of the Environment, which was announced on the annual Kayana Peoples Day. It was also on the first Kayana Peoples Day in 2036, that President Chief Onida Ana pardoned those who were implicated in the plot to burn the capital city, and assassinate her. Peter Thomas was posthumously awarded the first Kayana Champion of the Environment.

The main central Hub of the ancient city became the focus for local, and international interest. The temple complex was fully excavated, and a comprehensive programme of restoration was well underway. The dwellings around the temple, along with the walkways, were cleared with a view towards occupancy by people of Indigenous Kayanese ancestry. Visits to the complex were limited for academic purposes only. Other faiths were allowed to build Churches, Hindu Temples and Muslim Mosques for the multi-religious population of Kayana, at the perimeter of the ancient Indigenous Temple. The new city became an important meeting point for all major religious festivals of the Kayanese people.

President Chief Onida Ana, on the eve of her fortieth birthday, and towards the end of her first five-year term as President of Kayana, led a special ceremony to formally open the first of eight outer Spokes of the new city. It was built around the much extended harbour area of her settlement, and included several eco-friendly factories, warehouses, and other industrial operations for the manufacture and export of many old and new products. The Great River was dredged to ensure that ships could be towed to the deep water harbour. Most of the jobs created were taken by local Indigenous people who travelled from their villages. Other Kayanese people also moved to the Spoke to benefit from the development. The President was keen to ensure that all graduates and trained personnel across Kayana, were given job opportunities in the new city, and its Spokes.

The President who was flanked by an ageing Piaiman, and other members of her team, stepped forward onto a raised platform nearest to the original mooring. She looked around at the dramatically changed area, and smiled. The audience applauded her and the team.

She said, "My fellow Kayanese, this is truly inspirational for me. I pray that the Great Spirit, and those of my mentors Chief Koko and Peter Thomas, are smiling with great satisfaction. I also pray that this entire complex which we call Spoke One, linked to our secret ancient city, is what our ancestors of over five hundred years, wanted for all our peoples. I am very proud of my team, and all others who have worked so hard over the past five years, to transform our settlement, and this vast area into such a production base. I am also proud that everything here is energy-efficient, and pollution-free. We have managed to build this Spoke, and at the same time, secure all the rainforest and wildlife around us. My only regret is that my dear childhood friends, Onca, Kassi, and Kori are no longer with us. But their large extended families are still here living freely, and in close proximity to all of us. The new houses for all our peoples are modernised, but built in the same styles, and of the same materials we have always known. Our blend of ancient and modern is simple, beautiful, and efficient. We are now nearer to the general elections, and I hope that the Kayanese people will give us the chance to build the other seven Spokes over the next five to ten years. Long live Kayana!"

The Piaiman stood up, and leaned over his walking stick as the applause for the President ended.

He said, "President Chief Onida Ana, you are a most blessed leader. I have known you all of your life, and I have seen you grow up from a happy child who loved to play with your animal and bird friends. Then you became a serious scholar, and passed all of your tests with ease.

You stood up to abuse, and turned hate into love. You became our youngest Chief, and Chief of Chiefs, and then you fended off attacks to become our amazing President. I pray for you today, and for all of Kayana. Happy Birthday! May the Great Spirit always bless, and guide you!"

Everyone cheered, and began to sing "Happy Birthday to you!"

The President stood up, raised her hands, and said, "Thank you all. I now declare Spoke One open!"

The applause from the gathering had begun to die down when she turned to look across to the new, and extended harbour. A tall lonesome figure, with a neat white beard, walked with familiar strides towards the podium. He climbed up the few steps, and approached the President.

She embraced the visitor, and said, "Oh my God! How are you Mr Jennings? I have not seen you for years!"

John Jennings kissed the President on both cheeks, and said, "I am so sorry not to come to meet you, and to congratulate you for all you have done in Kayana."

The President asked, "Why did you leave Kayana so quietly, and quickly?"

John Jennings said, "I took early retirement, and wanted to spend more time with my growing family. So, I quit my job, and returned to Canada. But I have been following all of your progress in politics, and in what you are building here. Happy fortieth birthday!"

The President said, "Thank you very much. You and your family are always welcome here, and of course you can stay in our best facilities for free."

John Jennings smiled, and said, "Thank you. In fact, one of my sons would like to come and spend some time here to learn about your eco-revolution. I also wanted to say that I am so sorry for not attending Peter Thomas's funeral in those dark days that you had to endure. I shall visit his grave in the cemetery here."

The President said, "When your son comes, he could stay at the benab which has special guest rooms for visitors. In fact, this invitation is open to all of your peoples of Canada. Yes, Peter is a national hero, and martyr, who died to save my life."

John Jennings said, "Thank you. That is very kind of you. Peter's final act literally saved Kayana."

President Chief Onida Ana wiped some tears from her eyes and cheeks, and said, "Yes, I wish that he and Chief Koko were here in person, to see what their vision looks like. I miss them dearly."

John Jennings asked, "Could you kindly show me around this amazing complex of Spoke One and the incredible Temple Hub?"

The President said, "Of course my dear friend and brother. I shall also show you the plans for the other seven Spokes! Welcome to what I call our "SMART City"!"

FIFTY

HUB AND SPOKES

P resident Chief Onida Ana's fortieth birthday was celebrated in a grand way, commencing with a smoke ceremony at the ancient Indigenous Peoples' temple complex. All the Chiefs of Kayana, the leaders of various Christian sects, a Hindu Pandit, a Muslim Imam, a representative of the growing Baha'i faith, a Buddhist monk, members of the Government, members of the two main opposition parties, business leaders, ambassadors of foreign countries, and the growing population of the central Hub as well as Spoke One, were in attendance.

John Jennings stood beside the President who wore her customary Chief's headdress, Kayanese native clothing, and a pair of moccasins which he had gifted her. He was the representative of the Indigenous Peoples of Canada and the United States of America. Similar representatives from many South American countries and the Caribbean, performed native dances, played traditional music, sang ancient songs, and demonstrated fighting skills, to the delight of the appreciative audience.

The President turned to John Jennings, and said, "My friend, this must be how our ancestors would have assembled for important events in this city. I feel a great sense of satisfaction to see this vision come alive after hundreds of years. The Great Spirit and all of our ancestors' spirits must be smiling with immense pleasure."

John Jennings said, "I am really proud of you, and I am very happy to witness this today. I always knew that you were special ever since Chief Koko told me about you. That is why I always felt obliged to support you. This celebration is being broadcast across the world, and I hope that it provides a great sense of joy and happiness to billions of people far and wide, and of every race or creed."

The President smiled, and said, "Thank you for everything that you have done to help me realise this vision. Let us join in with the fun!"

John Jennings pointed to his knees, and said, "My legs may not be able to cope with the dancing anymore. But I will try."

She laughed, and said, "Don't worry. The drum beats will put new energy into your legs. Come on, lets join the dancers!"

The elders of the President's settlement, sat together on a wooden bench near to the dancing area, and looked on with great pride. Their well-worn, and aged faces were lit up by the highly energised drumming, singing, and dancing by the younger generation of Indigenous Peoples from tribes across Kayana, as well as the visiting performers. The elders sipped their piwari from neatly carved small wooden bowls which they held in their right hands. They gently hit their left knees with their left hands, and kept to perfect timing of the familiar rhythms.

The President reached out to one of the elders, took his hands, and gently supported him as he stood up. She kept a firm hold of his hands, and he responded to the tempo, and began shuffling his feet from side to side. His broad smile revealed large gaps in his front teeth, but his joy was immense. The other elders applauded the effort of their companion, and the President reached out to encourage all of them to get up, and join their small dancing group.

The sheer joy and happiness which engulfed the temple complex, lasted for at least another two hours before the President and her closest friends retired to her benab. John Jennings was eager to inspect the model plans for the seven other Spokes of the grand new capital city of Kayana.

The President and other members of her team lifted a light white cotton sheet covering the model of the grand plan which was placed on a large table in the centre of the main sitting area. She began to explain the entire system to John Jennings who looked on in awe.

The President pointed to the second Spoke, moving in a clockwise direction from Spoke One.

She said, "The whole system for this new capital city is based on our unique interpretation of what is known as "SMART Cities". The S is for a Self-sustainable system which is sensitive to our environment. The M is for the Management by the people who live here, and not by politicians or the government. The A is for Artificial Intelligence or AI, and is the main link across the entire city, and beyond. The R is for

Rainforest preservation. And, the T is for Technology, and most operations here will be technology-driven."

John Jennings said, "That is truly outstanding! Do tell me more!"

The President said, "After Spoke One which we officially opened today, the Spoke Two is dedicated to higher learning for all peoples of Kayana, and students from abroad. The central complex will be our Kayana Institute of Technology, and our Eco-University."

John Jennings said, "Wow! My son would be very happy to come here, and participate in that initiative. I shall try to support this development personally. My *Inuit* and *Cree* peoples should also be very interested in working with your peoples here."

The President smiled, and said, "Thank you. I think that will be wonderful. As I have said, you and your family, and your peoples, are always welcome here. The Spoke Three will be our main energy supply centre. It will have the recycling plant, and the water and sewerage systems which will utilise solar and hydro power. I hope that the outputs from this Spoke will serve not only the new city, but much further into the other regions of Kayana. The main mining companies, including your former corporation, have already committed their support to build the complex, and also use the power from this source. They will abandon their old, and almost obsolete power plants, and thus reduce pollution considerably. All citizens of the capital city will have subsidised power, water, and efficient sewerage systems. I also intend to improve sanitation in the surrounding Indigenous Kayanese villages and mining towns."

John Jennings paused, took out a small notepad, and began to enter details of the President's plans. He also took pictures of the model city's main Temple Hub and eight Spokes.

The President pointed to Spoke Four, and said, "My friend, Spoke Four will be a super complex of arenas suitable for major sports such as Cricket, Football, Basketball, Tennis, Golf, and Athletics. We will also build eco-friendly accommodation for players, visitors, and workers, to cover all year round sports and games events. Kayana could also become a site for a future Olympic Games."

John Jennings said, "Now that would be awesome for such a small country!"

The President continued, "Our government will obtain a share of any profits so that not only the Spoke will be properly maintained, but other such facilities around Kayana will be funded, and supported. Events will also include traditional Indigenous Peoples' sports and games, and we hope to host a kind of Olympics for Indigenous Peoples from all over the world."

John Jennings could not contain his excitement, and enthusiasm for the plans.

He said, "I am really very impressed by the boldness of your vision. This seems like an impossible dream. I am really bowled over by these plans. And, you have more to show to me. What is going to be at Spoke Five?"

President Chief Onida Ana took a sip from her water bottle, and said, "Thank you again. Well, we cannot have such a large and diverse city without the means to feed itself. So, I want Spoke Five to be the centre for the production of the healthiest foods, using the best and most up to date scientific methods of production on a large scale. There will be many acres of greenhouse structures powered by solar energy, and completely self-reliant. For example, all of our vegetables and fruits will be produced through air planting, and other methods. The food will be enough for the needs of the city, and also for distribution across Kayana. Here, we will turn around the idea of having to rely on millions of acres of land to produce such foods. Instead, the city will be producing the foods for itself, and for the rural populations!"

John Jennings asked, "But, what will happen to the existing agriculture sector?"

The President said, "We will continue to encourage the existing structure for agriculture wherever this is being undertaken, and try to support any struggling owners and farmers with subsidies, and the means to market their products both within Kayana, and abroad. Gradually, the whole agriculture sector will become more efficient, modernised, and reasonably diversified to support our competitiveness in this region, and further away in the international markets."

John Jennings nodded, and asked, "What about fishing and such like?"

The President said, "Well, I do not like the idea of fish farming. So, we will encourage the development of more localised fishing, and will support our traditional ways to grow and catch fish in the wild. This means that all rivers, tributaries, and creeks will be proactively monitored for pollution, and so on. The Eco-university will train people in such skills. We will also promote more use of our amazing variety of freshwater fish, and seek to reduce any reliance on frozen fish from the oceans. We prefer to invest more in protecting the habitat of the sea life, especially around our massive oilfields in the ocean."

John Jennings smiled at the other members of the President's team, and said, "Your plans are quite impressive. I just cannot believe that all of this is possible in one location. You must be very proud of yourselves. I see that Spoke Six is also interesting. Do tell me about it."

The President said, "My brother, you can see how the Hub and Spokes seem to be almost independent of each other. But, they are all linked and interrelated to ensure more efficiencies, and much greater strength. Whilst the Hub deals with the inner self, and the concept of a God or Great Spirit within each of us, the Spokes are designed to sustain both the physical body, and the mind. One cannot do without the other. Our health is very important alongside good food, diet, and exercise. So, Spoke Six will be our medical centre for both physical and mental illnesses. It will contain a large teaching hospital equipped and run to attract the best physicians, and medical scientists we can find. There will also be a medical school, alongside facilities for unconventional medicine embracing all the best of ancient treatments from Indigenous, African, Hindu, Muslim, Buddhist, and other cultures. We will encourage more integrated care to utilise the best cures available. Spoke Five will also provide the many herbs and spices locally, for consumption, and for cure. Our Piaiman is absolutely delighted with these centres, and he is busy advising on the plans."

John Jennings said, "This is truly amazing! It reminds me about the whole concept of the creation of the universe, and something which our Hindu brothers and sisters know, of the powers of Lord Shiva, and his cosmic dance. He is the creator, and destroyer at the same time. Both aspects of this existence sit side by side, and are so interlinked. This city can represent these forces, and show how they come together for our survival, and upliftment. This city is not just about economic strength, but for the advancement of its peoples."

The Piaiman took the opportunity to join in the conversation, and said, "Mr Jennings, that is indeed a good way to look at what we are trying to represent here in this wonderful city. The cycle of life is something of great importance to Indigenous Peoples. We believe that our existence is both physical and spiritual. So, this idea must be present in all aspects of our lives, and in where we live. This ancient city has been a secret for hundreds of years, and although it was abandoned, it has come to life again. But, as you can see, we are trying to link the old cultures with our new experiences. That is why I am so excited about this entire project. It is a realisation of our belief system, and linked to those of our peoples here in Kayana."

The President said, "Before we end our introduction to Spoke Six, it is important to mention that whilst all the facilities here will cater for our health and wellbeing, there will be spaces dedicated to burials and cremations. In this regard, there will be a specially designed hospice for all who reach towards the end of their lives. We come into this world with great expectation and joy, and we must leave with dignity."

John Jennings pointed to the next Spoke, and said, "I notice the grand scale of what appears to be a government building, and other structures nearby. Will that be the new parliament surrounded by several other establishments for the various ministries?"

The President nodded, and said, "Yes, Spoke Seven will be about government, and all aspects of running Kayana. But it will also house facilities for our love of the Arts, Music, and Dance. There will also be Museums, Libraries, Archives, and so on. Of course, there will be extensive conference and performance halls at Spoke Two."

John Jennings asked, "There is one thing that seems to be missing from these plans. Where will the most important lifeblood of any city be located? I mean, the shopping facilities."

The President said, "Due to each Spoke having a range of key activities, and of course, citizens and visitors present, there will be local small, medium, and large commercial and hotel outlets. It is important to note that there will be strict restrictions on building upwards. This will be the only modern city without skyscrapers."

John Jennings smiled, and said, "You seem to have answers for everything. What about an International Airport? Will there be one? If so, where will that be?"

The President said, "Now, this is a very good question. We thought long and hard about access into, and movement out of the city. I am very anxious about how the rest of the world is so dependent on air transport. There seems to be no end to this dreadful source of pollution. We have a saying that if the Great Spirit wanted us to fly, we would have been given wings."

Everyone laughed with the President.

John Jennings said, "But if there is no Air Transport, I would take a very long time to get here."

The President said, "I could speak with you without the need to fly. Besides, you could come and go by ship, and other river vessels. I will happily wait for your arrival."

John Jennings said, "There you go again. You always have an answer. So, if you do not wish to encourage Air Transport, how will you defend Kayana from aerial attack?"

The President said, "Aha! I did not say that there will be no flying into, and out of this city. So, Spoke Eight will have a Military Base with facilities for our air force. Alongside this, there will be an International Airport. But we want to test the possibility of having only fuel-efficient, and pollution-free aircraft. Now, this will be a challenge for all those who wish to secure a right to fly here. Meanwhile, we will continue to build up our river and sea transport, alongside roadways."

John Jennings asked, "And what about a Railway System?"

The President said, "Our country has functioned fairly well without a Railway System, and although it is vast, we prefer the roadways, canals, and use of the rivers. One efficient way to move around the new city, and the other towns in the country, will be new Cable Car Systems."

John Jennings smiled, and led enthusiastic applause for the President.

He said, "My dear friends, I have one more very important question for you. This wonderful new city of one Hub and eight Spokes will need the use of a huge amount of acreage, and which in turn, will require the clearing of a significant amount of the precious rainforest. This runs counter to your claims of protecting the rainforests and this environment."

The President said, "Well, first of all, we have a new strategy and action plan to protect, and sustain the entire rainforests and our environment across Kayana. All cleared forests will be reinstated not only with new saplings, but with their supporting community of other plants. There will also be a strict limitation on the amount of timber to be taken for commercial and private use. We will encourage a renewal of forestation everywhere there are abandoned farms or sugar and rice plantations. Owners and farmers will be compensated for any loss of land. We will continue to invest in the regrowth of the natural sea and river defences using mangroves. All future buildings, houses, and so on will be restricted in the use of timber, and owners will be offered alternative eco-friendly building materials. Every opportunity to sustain and rebuild our rainforests and environment will be explored, and implemented where necessary. This is only the start of a long term process of improvement, and development."

John Jennings smiled, and said, "That is truly remarkable. God bless you and Kayana!"

FIFTY-ONE

LONG LIVE KAYANA

The General Elections in 2040 resulted in a landslide victory for President Chief Onida Ana and the KPM. The Kayanese people were eager to allow her to push on with her plans through to 2045. She appealed to the people to limit their celebrations, and to spend more time in embracing those who opposed the KPM.

Although most of Kayana's national budget was earmarked for the new capital city, all other aspects of the economy were also being upgraded, and sustained. The traditional, but vastly reduced agricultural crops such as sugar and rice, were invested in to ensure that at the very least, they produced enough for local needs, whilst other crops suitable for the terrain, were introduced to complement those of Spoke Five.

Gradually, more residents began to uproot, and move away from the risk of living too close to the ocean front along the coastland. New towns and settlements further into higher terrain were also being developed by a partnership of government, business, and international enterprises. These areas were most attractive to the new Kayanese immigrants who were returning from abroad with considerable wealth.

Significantly, and as a direct result of the rapid growth of the Kayana economy, the population, along with good health and social care, and new jobs in all sectors, caused the local crime rate to fall drastically. However, criminal gangs from neighbouring countries, were still able to cross the borders unchecked, and new attacks on villages and the mining towns, except those nearest to the capital city, became an issue of grave concern for the President.

She ordered an expansion of the Kayanese army, navy, and air force, to patrol and cover the borders especially in the higher regions of the hinterland, and those rivers which were more easily accessible. The

President insisted on the formation of a special unit of mostly young Indigenous warriors who were best suited to the terrain, and were much more effective fighters. They were trained in the use of conventional weaponry, and also in their traditional blowpipes, and bows and arrows. The unit was also capable of paratrooping to enable them to move between locations very quickly. The navy was equipped with a fleet of swift gunships and speedboats, to move much more quickly in the rivers and tributaries. Most of the new recruits to the navy were Indigenous Kayanese living nearest to the waterways.

The air force was boosted by several new fighter helicopters most suitable for jungle activities, and warfare. The President was very proud to announce that the pilots were recruited from all sections of the population, including female Indigenous Kayanese.

No sooner had the defence units of the army, navy, and air force been in place, more arrests were being made of criminals trying to breach the borders. This success was well received by the President and all Kayanese, until news reached her of a massive build-up of armed criminals along the borders.

President Chief Onida Ana appeared on national TV, radio, and social media, to announce an invasion of Kayana.

She said solemnly, "My dear fellow citizens of Kayana. This morning, the first of May 2045, I received news of armed clashes between criminal gangs and our Armed Forces at almost every point of our borders. It appears that the criminal gang masters have collaborated to form one large army of marauding gunmen. Once again, I have alerted the leaders of our two neighbouring countries, and their responses have been very disappointing. This is not a conventional war as between countries, but a war on crime. I am declaring a state of emergency across the length and breadth of our glorious country, and I want you all to be alert at all times. Although the fighting is taking place in the hinterland, we must be prepared for any other type of attack. I am sending re-enforcements to the battlegrounds, and I hope that we will be triumphant, and rid our country of this problem once and for all."

The news of the war was a great shock for the Kayanese people, and thousands of citizens offered to volunteer to fight for their country. The President did not expect such a response, and asked the Chief of the Armed Forces to communicate with the volunteers.

They were not discouraged, and were allowed to join the backup units to support the troops in administration, catering, and vehicle maintenance.

The ensuing battles were vicious and bloody with several skirmishes of hand to hand fighting. Every time this occurred, the gangsters were brutally exterminated by the highly skilled specialist Indigenous warriors who moved amongst the bushy forest floors with great speed, and stealth. Many of the criminals were poisoned by the deadly blowpipes, and others were knifed with specially designed daggers. There were no casualties of Kayanese Indigenous fighters.

The fighting continued for several days until most of the invaders retreated, having abandoned their weapons, and fleeing to avoid capture by the Indigenous warriors. Those who were captured as prisoners, were taken to the central square at the capital city. They were made to stand up in long lines across the breadth of the open space, and inquisitive citizens strode up to the well-guarded barriers to see who they were, and what they looked like.

The President, wearing red and black war paint on her face, arms, and legs, strode purposefully to take up a central position on the temple stage facing the square. The Heads of the Armed Forces, and other members of the government stood silently behind her. She asked for a minute's silence in respect for those who were killed or injured in Kayana's first war.

The Piaiman led brief prayers on behalf of the peoples of Kayana. Then everyone, excepting the forces guarding the prisoners, took their seats. The crowd of onlookers grew into thousands as the news of the victory spread across the country.

The President stood up, looked around the temple complex, and said, "Today is a very sad and at the same time, a very happy one for me. I am particularly sad about the needless loss of life of those people who believed that the only way for them to acquire wealth, was to take it by force from our citizens. I am much sadder about the loss of, and injuries to, the small number of our Armed Forces who were so brave in defending our country and people. Our response to the brazen and deliberate attack had to be swift, strong, efficient, and decisive. We prevailed."

The crowds applauded, and many raised and waved their flags of Kayana.

The President continued, "I am happy that this conflict has ended, and I hope that we will never see such invasion again. We will strengthen our defences, and the numbers of Armed Forces around our country's borders as a way of ensuring that we have many more peaceful years ahead. I have spoken to the leaders of our border countries, and they have assured me that they will do everything in their power to hunt down, and stamp out the criminals who terrorise their citizens, and who tried to do the same to us. I am not a vindictive person, and I have the fate of these defeated men in front of me. I can easily order their trial, or, I can offer them one more chance to use their remaining years to care for their families. I am therefore ordering their release back to their countries. I hope that they will repent, and take full advantage of this chance to end this way of life."

The entire gathering cheered the President's action as the prisoners were escorted away from the square, placed on military trucks, and driven off towards the Spoke One harbour area.

The President took a sip of ice cold water from a glass, and raised her arms aloft to stop the applause.

She said, "My dear beloved people of Kayana. I have now come to the end of my second and final term as your President. I leave this position and responsibility to whomsoever you choose as your next President. I wish to thank everyone in this beautiful land, for all your support, understanding, and hard work to take a vision of over five hundred years, and bring it to reality. Even my ancestors could not have seen what we have created across Kayana today. The work must continue to protect our sacred environment, our clean air, our pure waters, and all of our exquisite creatures and forests. We are already seen as a country embracing ancient wisdom, and at the same time, using the best of modernity towards real happiness for all. I shall continue to be just the Chief of my group of amazing people, and someone else can take over the role of Chief of Chiefs. I want to use the rest of my life not to just sit back and watch how you will move Kayana even further up the ladder of success. I shall take up the many offers I have received from within and outside of Kayana, to speak to people about what we have achieved here. May the Great Spirit always be our guide, our protector, and our sustainer. God bless you, and God bless Kayana!"

The onlookers present at the Hub led a most passionate and sustained cheering, along with all of Kayana, watching the TV, or listening to the radio broadcasts. President Chief Onida Ana stood silently, and with great poise, allowing tears to stream down from her almond eyes, onto her red cheeks, and her quivering chin. She became once again, Onida Ana of Kayana, the Daughter of the Great River.

ALSO BY KHALIL RAHMAN ALI

IN PURSUIT OF BETTERMENT
Five Stories from the Indian Diaspora
Published in 2017

A collection of stories of families from
India, Guyana and the Caribbean, Mauritius,
East Africa and South Africa. The five
families share a compelling desire and drive
to achieve betterment through education,
work and business, against the backdrop of
the histories of the countries from which
they originate or leave.

The first story is set in India and London as the Shivwani family
grows from humble beginnings to international business success.

Little Guyana is the story of Inshan Khan who was sent to London
to study Law. His extended family also had to leave Guyana due to a
decline in the local economy, and became part of the emergence of
"Little Guyana" in New York.

Murali Dharam from Mauritius, arrived in London to study
psychiatric nursing. His romantic liaisons created family tensions both
in Mauritius and England.

Manubhai Patel and his family were forcibly expelled from Uganda
in 1972 and were faced with new challenges in Leicester, England,
including racial harassment.

In Durban, South Africa, where the largest population of Indians
have settled outside India, Professor Yusuf mentors two young PhD
students seeking answers about their country's emergence from
apartheid.

Paperback, 392 pages, ISBN: 978-1-910553-76-3
Price: £11.99 (UK only) / US $18.00

Ebook: £5.99
ISBN: 978-1-910553-80-0 (Epub)
ISBN: 978-1-910553-81-7 (Kindle)

ALSO BY KHALIL RAHMAN ALI

THE DOMINO MASTERS OF DEMERARA
Published in 2015

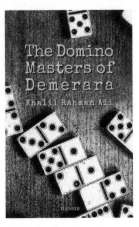

It is the 6th of August 1985, and the final and deciding game of dominoes between three rival teams from the sugar plantation villages of Anna Catherina, Leonora and Cornelia Ida, in Demerara, Guyana, is underway. Michael "Histry Maan" Brown, the selfappointed coach to the Anna Catherina ACES, reverts to new tactics to pass sublime tips to his captain, Vishnu "Double Six" Prashad.

The game is played out at a time when Guyana and its peoples were still emerging from a history of struggle through African slavery, Portuguese, Indian and Chinese indentured labour, political independence, racial unrest, mass migration and economic downturn.

Michael, Vishnu and their friends use every means available to continue to survive, and to build their lives in their multi-racial, multi-religious and multi-cultural society.

The game of dominoes provides them with the opportunity to demonstrate their competitiveness, their search for unity, and their resolve to face up to their challenges.

Can they succeed as One People, One Nation, with One Destiny?

Paperback, 188 pages
ISBN: 978-1-910553-07-7
Price: £11.99 (UK only) / US $18.00

ALSO BY KHALIL RAHMAN ALI

SUGAR'S SWEET ALLURE
Published in 2013

It is 1843, and Mustafa Ali, an eighteen year-old Muslim Indian labourer from a village near Kanpur, Uttar Pradesh, India, is forced to run away through the discovery of his forbidden love for Chandini Sharma, his Hindu childhood sweetheart. His dream was to find work, save his money and return to ask for his beloved's hand.

This dream took him further afield into the promise of good work, pay and conditions as an indentured labourer on one of the sugar plantations, thousands of miles away in the colony of British Guiana on the mainland of South America. His experiences on the Grand Trunk Road across Uttar Pradesh to Bengal, and on the treacherous sea voyage from Calcutta to Georgetown, tested his resolve to the limit. Then, when he and his companions were allocated to their sugar plantations, they had to endure and overcome more challenges of racial, religious and cultural differences, in addition to the unrelenting and punishing workloads in extremely harsh conditions.

This is a story that is shared by millions of the descendents of indentured Indian labourers who are spread across all parts of the world. Will Mustafa succeed in his quest?

Paperback, 312 pages
ISBN: 978-1-906190-66-8
Price: £11.99 (UK only) / US $15.00

Ebook: £7.79
ISBN: 978-1-906190-76-7 (Epub)
ISBN: 978-1-906190-75-0 (Kindle)